ONE NIGHT IN WINTER

Also by Allan Massie

Novels
CHANGE AND DECAY IN ALL AROUND I SEE
THE LAST PEACOCK
THE DEATH OF MEN

Non-Fiction
MURIEL SPARK
ILL MET BY GASLIGHT
THE CAESARS
EDINBURGH AND THE BORDERS:
AN ANTHOLOGY (Ed)

ALLAN MASSIE

One Night in Winter

Futura

First for Alison;
then, for David and Jenny Kenrick.

A Futura Book

Copyright © Allan Massie 1984

First published in Great Britain in 1984
by The Bodley Head Ltd

This edition published in 1985
by Futura Publications, a Division of
Macdonald & Co (Publishers) Ltd
London & Sydney

ISBN 0 7088 2747 0

Printed and bound in Great Britain by
Collins, Glasgow

Futura Publications
A Division of
Macdonald & Co (Publishers) Ltd
Maxwell House
74 Worship Street
London EC2A 2EN

A BPCC plc Company

PART ONE

1

A taxi woke me, the unmistakable throb of the engine waiting under my window; then the front door was firmly shut; the orange cat moved across the counterpane; the taxi departed; all was still but for that faint breathing which a house, recently emptied of motion, seems to give off. I looked at the French ormolu clock on the bedside table: Half-past nine, the boys in school the last half-hour; Ann would be lucky to catch her train at Paddington.

But of course she would do it. Ann doesn't miss trains. You can no more imagine Ann bursting past the ticket barrier as a train glides out to the west than you can imagine the Queen throwing down the scissors with which she is about to cut a tape in an opening ceremony and exclaiming that she has had enough of all this bloody nonsense. There is something a little queenly about Ann.

I felt no desire to get up—I rarely do—'Oblomov and I' is a favourite prefatory phrase of mine—and there was certainly nothing that demanded my attention. I scratched the cat under her chin for some time. Nobody serious comes to the shop before noon and, these days, not many after it either. 'You're losing your flair, Dallas,' old Solly Leibermann said to me the other week, 'or else you've less energy and interest than you used to have. It's no good telling me the stuff isn't about like it used to be. Other dealers find it O K.' I laughed it off, but I could have pled guilty on all counts. Ah well, the shop saw us through the boys' infancies and it has paid for a good many years' school fees. And now that Ann is a success, I'm quite happy to be a kept man.

I can't actually watch her programme. It embarrasses me. I would be inclined to convict myself of jealousy but for the fact that Gilesie can't watch it either; and he has really no reason to

7

resent his mother's success. It's not as if it was the kind of show that might lead to mockery at school. Apart from the fact that the parents of half his friends are media figures—some of them at least far far more yucky than Ann—her show is really enjoying the kind of vogue that might be thought to do him credit. The *Sunday Times* loves her; so does *New Society*. But on the other hand Gilesie's chums may not love the *Sunday Times*. I really know nothing of what my children think. They may be in full neo-Fascist revolt against their parents' liberal establishment. They may desire no better meal than the hand that reared them.

Who can tell?

Certainly not I. It has been borne in on me, at dinner parties, on holiday, even at the shop whenever the talk strays away from business (which it does often enough), even (God help me) watching television, that really I know nothing about anything, except Victorian furniture and china, both of which now bore me stiff, and county cricket, which is heading for extinction, and horse-racing and rugby. I still enjoy autumn Saturday afternoons watching London Scottish at Richmond, and trips to Newbury and Cheltenham to see good steeple-chasing. Perhaps my next (and surely final?) incarnation will be as a sports writer.

That would be a long way from youthful ambitions, and yet it would make my life a nice shape, wouldn't it? I blew the dust off my solitary novel (*This Strange Disease*, Bodley Head 1972) a couple of weeks ago, and what a faint tinkle sounded; like a thin electric bell in an empty house. Oh dear, oh dear. Ann was very nice about it, I remember, urging its merits at dinner parties, and insisting that I be treated with the consequence she considered due to a writer. It's ironic, isn't it, that it was one of those dinner parties to boost the book, to which she invited people we had vaguely met whom she thought might be of some importance, that launched her on her own career. I can't even recall the chap's name now—Sean something, bald, bearded, in jeans and cowboy boots. Anyway he was taken with Ann. They had a short affair. In the course of it he let her meet Michael Nawes, who was just on the way up and saw in Ann the very woman he needed to front the programmes he

8

was intending to make. And that shifted the balance in our marriage.

That novel title was, by the way, one of my few triumphs. 'Nobody,' I was assured at the publisher's, 'would buy a book with a title like *This Strange Disease*. It's a turn-off,'' they said.

I insisted, adamant, 'But it's Matthew Arnold, the school inspector himself. "This strange disease of modern life." Why it's the theme of the novel.' Well, I won, but they were dead right. Nobody did buy it, and nowadays I can see why.

I used to wonder what Ann really thought of it; if she didn't find it like lemon juice in the eye. But for a long time she played the loyal wife even in private. And still does in some respects, this being her way of expiating her own, not very deep or passionate, affairs. Among our friends, who are mostly these days hers, Ann is considered to put up with me 'wonderfully'. It was bad enough in the days when I was drinking; now that I'm sober, or fairly sober, I'm generally reckoned to be an empty vessel, a bore.

Meanwhile there was the morning post to descend to, and that encouraged me to stay in bed. September, my favourite month. Wispy and slightly liquid sunlight combing its way through the slatted blind; outside, the traffic's hum, argumentative shrieks from rich Arab children in the house opposite, and roller-skates on the pavement—the West Indian kids from the basement of No. 35 skipping school again.

I was forty last week. Some bloody fool at my birthday party unleashed a crack about the *mezzo del cammin di nostra vita* being a bit the far side of forty these days, what with increased life expectancy and all that. The observation set a tiny nerve working in Ann's cheek. I could see her visioning my long camel's ride to the tomb (to steal the title of my favourite novel, one that will bear reading and repeating time and again), and I guessed she was comparing the graphs of our two careers, and I thought a mere twitching nerve was actually a pretty restrained response. In reality, I suppose, when Francis, who is now fourteen, goes to university, that'll be about it. It will, in a boy-vacant house, be inescapably clear that our drift apart has taken us out of touching distance.

I got up and shaved. The one thing I am resolved on, is never to grow a beard; that way, sleeping wrapped up in newspapers lies. (A couple of days' growth is permissible.) Downstairs, I felt as if the house had really nothing to do with me—despite the fact that in my younger more eager days I had myself bought every piece of furniture in it. I used to think that with sobriety one would lose that morning feeling of being on sufferance, but now I still found myself moving carefully about the kitchen as if any noise might alert a reluctant host on whom I had parked myself the night before.

Perhaps that reluctant host is the Life-Force itself?

There was a letter from my bank on the kitchen table. I knew Ann no longer loved me, or cared about me, the day she stopped opening my letters. Well, I didn't care to open it myself. I knew very well what it would say, but the time is past when I'm prepared to trot round at bank managers' summonses. There was also a salacious card from Esmond, somewhere in the South of France—*voix d'outre-mer* that might as well have been *d'outre-tombe*, for all it signified. That realization gave me a momentary pang of something sharper than nostalgia: there was a time when nothing seemed more important than friendship, and I remember so clearly the misery occasioned by Proust's denial of its enduring value in I forget which volume of the great novel I shall certainly never read again.

Ann had left a note, saying she would be back late. Would I please give the boys their supper. 'Not spaghetti again,' though, in fact, pasta in one form or another is the only food we all three agree in liking.

The coffee bubbled. I pushed Ann's note and the letters aside, and sat down to drink it and study the race-card in the *Telegraph*. Actually my interest in racing is academic these days. I rarely bet. Even when I go to the races, what I enjoy is the cocoon of the racing world, its enviable self-absorption and freedom from doubt, not the gambling. And (actually again) I haven't been racing since I stopped drinking, and am not at all sure that I would care to get through an afternoon at the races without the comfort of brandy and ginger ale. It used to numb the impact of human contact.

Getting through the day has become, no use denying it, a

problem. Of course I do still go down to the shop most days, but it depresses me. There's one sideboard in particular, made not as I'd drunkenly judged by the fashionable Burges, but in some unremarkable Birmingham factory about the time of Queen Victoria's Golden Jubilee, that looks like being with me till her present Majesty's. The fact is, I was never cut out to be a shopkeeper, not even in a trade like the antique business capable, you would think (correctly) of accommodating any number of queer fish. Ann's family of course have always deplored it, not, to be fair to them, for snobbish reasons—I am anyway very much better-born than they (to use one of my dodo expressions). No, their objection has been firmly moral: the trade has no social value; one should be serious, of service. Scholarship is O K; so is Ann's present trade, propaganda.

Still, about one o'clock, I did make a move in that direction. And, to tell the truth, I felt pretty good. The sun was shining out of a Cambridge-blue sky with just a touch of gold braid at the edges; making a day like a Fats Waller record, with the same sparkle of affirmation against a background that accepted the sordid facts of our corrupted natures. I like passing the fruit-and-vegetable stalls with the fat Negro ladies cramming their shopping-bags. I like the pretty secretaries in their defiant lunch-breaks. I like the fat men scratching their bellies outside pubs. I like the little old lady, reputed to have fought in the Spanish War, who sits on the iron bench outside the Brick-layers' Arms in her hat decorated with pink and yellow wax flowers. I've seen her most weeks in the last fifteen years, and she has never acknowledged my greeting yet. I like London in fact; the drabber and dirtier it gets, the more I like its rhythm.

Amanda greeted me with the news that there was a sup-plementary rates demand.

'You really ought to go on a buying trip,' she said.

'The shop's full.'

'It's full of stuff no one is ever going to buy. You ought to clear it out and get some new stock in.'

I rubbed my hand along the non-Burges mahogany, and she didn't pursue the matter. Her suggestion had been purely formal. Instead she told me about the latest complication in her life. Amanda has a semi-detached marriage with a Negro drummer called Neville, who is usually stoned out of his mind, but quite good value in the intermediate stage. She has also a long-running affair with a Tory MP, whose presents supply the frequent mortgage deficiencies. He is a West Country Catholic, so that there is no question of marriage. Recently, however, Amanda took in a lodger, a thirtyish female barrister. One night when they were both feeling sorry for themselves—the barrister's career being a bit in the doldrums—and drinking hock, expressions of sympathy took them further than either had gone before with another girl, and they ended up in bed together.

'We both admitted at once it was more satisfying, more completely fulfilling, you understand, Dallas, more really us, than anything we had either experienced before.'

There was talk that they might formalize the situation, Amanda give up Ivor (her MP) and obtain a divorce from Neville.

'Now Charlotte's getting cold feet,' Amanda said, 'she thinks that coming out wouldn't do her any good at the Bar. After I've told Ivor, too.'

'What does he think about it?'

'Well, he's conventional and old-fashioned. Not to refine the matter, he's disgusted. He can't understand how he could have fancied a girl who can fancy a girl. He told me I should see an analyst. That from a Catholic.'

Ann made the same suggestion to me last month.

'There's a man I've heard of who might be just right for you,' she said. 'Samantha made Tatie go to him, and it did wonders.'

I shrank from the suggestion, and not just because of Tatie, an overweight publisher with a tendency towards satyriasis (if his wife is to be believed), just as for years I would have recoiled from the sort of discussion Amanda now regularly inflicted on me. In the end, though, you see that all your evasions are part of the web you have spun which, however odd it seems to outsiders (by which I mean everyone except yourself), is ultimately what sustains you.

'It all makes me feel such a fool,' Amanda said now.

If Ann was serious in her suggestion, it was pretty rum.

Why should she bother? Suppose I went to a trick-cyclist and was—to employ language loosely—cured of whatever is thought to afflict me, what then? Wouldn't she feel bound to try to make another go of our marriage? So I concluded that she was not serious at all, that she had spoken unreflecting, out of indifference; that it was just a glib off-the-cuff remark. But that wasn't Ann's style. Perhaps she had said it to rile me.

Then it struck me that she might have hoped that analysis (which it's quite obvious I can't anyway afford) would encourage me to break out, shift on to me the responsibility of bringing the marriage to an end. Or was she behaving like one of those women who insist on painting every room in a house before putting it on the market? Did she believe that after I'd been analysed I would be a more attractive proposition, that someone would take me off her hands? But then it mightn't be that at all. She might simply be making a programme on analysis, so that the subject was on her mind. Now, Amanda's report of Ivor's similar suggestion caused me to review the possibilities.

Whichever way, it was absurd. Nothing would persuade me to submit to analysis.

Oh no, shop-soiled, goods damaged in transit, that's rather the way I think about myself. And with reason. A piece designed for some sort of elegance, imitation Hepplewhite, now a bit knocked about. There's something, I admit, rather disgusting about narcissistic warbles like this; but then perhaps Narcissus himself experienced twinges of self-disgust even while he gazed rapt at his reflection. There's always a part of the mind that stands off and observes one's own behaviour.

All my life, since self-consciousness set in, I have kept random notes, jottings towards a *journal intime* (note how even in secret—?especially in secret—one dignifies one's behaviour with loaded vocabulary, froggy phrases to impress —whom? Narcissus again, I guess). I have half a dozen of these notebooks, thick hard-covered, dull-maroon volumes, bought from Heffers of Cambridge. I keep them in the deep right-hand drawer of my desk at the shop, under sheaves of dead invoices. What on earth would they reveal if I made my way through them? (Which I dare not.) A self that has always been the same, hence horribly embarrassing? Yet recurrently, I succumb to the temptation; a sort of solitary lust in action.

Story of Ariadne is one jotting I recall from ten years back or more: *story of Ariadne—? most profound mythological interpretation of married life.*

I suppose it meant something to me when I wrote it, yet I'm hanged if I make sense of it now.

Still, one comes back to that, married life; and it's astonishing how so many people who contrive to escape from it nevertheless do just that: come back.

Structure of life—la tour abolie?
Sense of a sort there.

Of course Amanda's problems don't really concern me; it's a long time since I installed double-glazing. Anyway, like most people who lead emotionally complicated lives, she enjoys troubles. She seeks them out. There are naturally exceptions to this general rule, unfortunates who unwittingly marry complications—the shadowy memory of Lorna Donnelly flickers across my mind as I write those words, a memory that before my reformation would have had my right hand reaching for the Gordon's—better not go into that. Not that I myself am one of those unfortunates. I married wittingly to avoid complication, and even now wouldn't describe my married life as complicated. Nor, I think, would Ann. Withered's the word.

I suppose people looking at us now, new friends, Ann's colleagues, wonder how on earth our marriage came about. Oh they can see, think they can see, why I married Ann. It's Ann's reason they can't understand. The joke is, this approach is all topsy-turvy. Ann, you see, now passes as the glamorous partner. She has style, swagger, what have you; and her opinions being a millimetre to the left of *Guardian* leaders, she is generally reckoned intelligent. What they don't realize is that Ann was madly in love with me, and I married her because of that. Well, the moth has extinguished the flame.

Ann would like me to have an affair with Amanda. I've no

doubt of that. But if, in the afternoon, I said to Amanda, Let's go to bed', she would tell me not be silly.

Instead of such an exchange, Neville called at the shop. He did so at a time when Amanda had gone round to collect an occasional table which my chum Joe was repairing, giving it new fake feet. There was nothing urgent about the collection: Amanda was simply fretting and action seemed preferable. I gave Neville a cup of coffee and he sat for a long time in complete silence, looking at his very large feet. He was wearing mauve baseball boots.

'Is she coming back?' he said at last.

'She won't be long.'

'I don't mean that, man. I mean, is she coming back to me? You know her, you know what she means to me, man.'

Actually, I had never considered that. I suppose I assumed that Neville regarded his relationship with his wife as something pretty free-and-easy; she was a good lay and she paid the rent. I would have put it like that. It has always been preferable not to try to imagine how people feel.

But there was pain in his voice.

Of course he might have been dramatizing it all; it is hard to take misery seriously when it is addressed towards mauve baseball boots.

'She's in love with that bitch. She crawls for her, man.'

Then he began to cry. He was very thin, with hollows in his cheeks, and an absurd goatee beard; the tears hesitated in the hollows, and found their way by a rivulet of a wrinkle down to damp the beard. His crying was unconscious of me; he cried as any of us might alone, in a November of feeling.

The back room of the shop had become very dark. It would have seemed tasteless to switch on a lamp. To comfort him, I made another cup of coffee.

Later of course it worked itself out. Amanda came back. Neville shouted at her. She calmed him down. She kissed the back of his neck, suggested they should go to a movie. I indicated the shop, undisturbed by customers, to express my approval. They consulted watches; decided they might go to a club Neville belonged to, for a drink, first. Amanda smiled (grateful, with the complicity of a conspirator) at me as they went through the door. The shop bell echoed behind them.

Not much of a scene in the end. Commonplace. Happens every day. Therapists might say Neville was right to cry, to shout, to kiss and make it up. We are all encouraged, aren't we, these days, to act out our emotions.

As for me, I settled to read a Dick Francis thriller.

Nobody came in, nobody telephoned. With a sense of evening I walked home. The light was just beginning to crinkle, a mist was seeping yellow-and-gold from the river. The boys were back. Francis was strumming his guitar. He didn't look up as I entered.

'Where's Mummy?' he asked, over plangent notes.

'Off somewhere. Back latish.'

'Oh.'

Neither of us mentioned that, if she was back late enough, we wouldn't have to watch her programme. Francis, more even than Gilesie and myself, can't bear it; he adores Ann.

'Do you have nothing to do, Dad?' he said.

'Maybe Mum's right, Dad,' said Gilesie coming into the room, 'maybe you should see a shrink. You never seem to want to do anything these days. Can't be healthy.'

He gave me a warm smile.

'We're really worried about you, man,' he said.

Francis lifted long-lidded eyes from his guitar.

'Sure,' he said. 'Can you let me have five pounds, Dad?'

Later we ate spaghetti. Francis made the sauce; he has long blond hair and sings as he works. Gilesie is slight, very thin, with tight black curls; he can eat spaghetti like a Neapolitan. He didn't resume the question of the shrink. Instead he said, 'What's Mum on about tonight? Racial discrimination in inner city comprehensive beehives or the disadvantaged condition of one-legged hospital porters?'

Francis frowned.

Gilesie said, 'Well, what good does it all do?'

I said, 'The bottom having fallen out of the antique business, it pays your school fees.'

'Oh sure, though I'd just as soon it didn't, but as an

investigation of society, sorry, as a social tool, it stinks. Period. I don't believe any of that guff. I'm not sure any investigation of society's possible. Certainly not Mum's way. I'm going to write a satirical novel about it when I find the right framework. I'd like to write it straight about the crazy notions of media publicists but everyone'd think (correctly) it was aimed at Mum's jugular. So I'll desist and stick the knife in someplace else. But someone ought to really send Mum up.'

Both my children split every infinitive they can; so does Ann since she became a celebrity. They speak in the canting London whine, the sub-voice of a sub-culture, self-apologetically pop, but Ann's voice remains obstinately educated. It floats and soars a bit.

Francis said, 'You'll never write a novel, Gilesie. You might write short stories but you'll never write a novel.'

That struck me as an intelligent remark for a boy of fourteen. Not necessarily true, but clever.

'None of us could write a novel,' Francis said. 'We're too partial.'

'Dad did.'

'Sure, once.' Francis smiled at me again. 'About that five pounds, Dad. I really need it.'

I am surprised to find myself recording this. The story I have to tell, the story with which I was confronted again later this evening, and on which I am reluctant to embark, standing on the narrative's brink like a nervous swimmer by the pool-side, is not the story of my marriage; it has, surely, nothing to do with the boys. Yet I feel urged to record their light and errant talk, in part perhaps because to do so is action of a sort, a pleasure too that delays what there will be no pleasure in recalling.

And it is not all irrelevant, any more than it is strictly true that my story is not also the story of my marriage, for if it is not directly that, I still can't disconnect the two. And the boys' prattle—that remark, that so perceptive and yet insensitive remark, of Francis's—'none of us could write a novel. We're too partial'—aimed as a squib to explode under Gilesie's feet,

17

nevertheless takes on for me, whichever meaning one attaches to the word partial (and I have no doubt Francis intended it to carry both possible significations at once), a daunting penetration. Partiality interferes with truth, and novels are true or they are nothing; they must carry an inward truth that goes much deeper than appearances, that can take wing beyond the particular; and yet their means of doing so are so absurdly limited.

I have to cast this story as a fiction, if only because I could not contemplate it as memoir. And not only because I dread the egotism of autobiography. I simply didn't know enough to cast it as memoir. Except for that one moment, atrocious in its sequel, that moment when I could still, in memory's new arrangement, have arrested the whole course of events, I was an outsider. My view was indeed partial, grotesquely limited by circumstance and character and class. The only way I can try to overcome that limitation is by casting my recital in the form of a novel, thus giving myself the freedom to imagine what the main actors thought and felt; and said when I wasn't there.

There is another reason too. It all happened so long ago, half a lifetime back, and I cannot recognize that juvenile Dallas as 'I'. To write 'I' in recounting his actions and states of mind is beyond me. I have to treat him as a character in the story, not a particularly attractive one, certainly no hero, a convenient point of view however.

I called it a recital, and of course it is that. Things happened; they are over and done with; lives were shaped or determined or ended; no fictional art can alter the facts. Why, you can check most of them in the newspapers of the day. 'A recital: fictionalization—if that—of a case, a theme, a pathology.' I found that thought, some Frog fellow's I fancy, noted down in a diary. It seems to fit the bill. Yet the key must be fictionalization. Without that, it's beyond me. And since the pathology seems to have made great nonsense of whole swathes of my life, the fictionalization may also be conceived as an act of justice. To fictionalize the past is an act of liberation.

Even so, it all risks coming close to apology; which I don't wish to write. Exemplary yes, but I retain the authorial right to intervene. The fact that it all happened more than twenty years ago can't deny me that. Things are never over and done with to that extent.

Yes, I am still confused; confused but not desperate.

Ann came back about half-past ten. The sound of taxi doors interrupted the silence. From the drawing-room I could fancy I heard the Yale turn, the swish of coats in the hall. I came out to the corner of the stair and saw that she was not alone. A thin woman with grey hair was standing with her back to me, under the hall light, divesting herself of a checked coat which, even at that distance, looked like something bought off the bargain rail of a chain store.

Ann sang out her return. She was filled with the virtuous fatigue of the traveller. She radiated money, health, responsibility, self-importance. She clasped Francis to her and made to ruffle Gilesie's curls. Then she thought of her companion.

'I'll show you your room,' she said, 'and then you can come down and eat something and have a glass of wine. Introductions later.'

She waved me aside, and the two of them made their way up the stairs, Ann talking, the other woman keeping her head lowered.

'A lame duck, one of Mumsie's lame ducks,' said Gilesie in his quoting voice as a bedroom door was shut.

I went to the kitchen to start cooking bacon and eggs; Ann regards this as the only proper dish after a train journey. She joined me there as the bacon was sizzling.

'How did it come across?' she said.

'Fine,' I replied. She wasn't seeking information for she would have seen a video recording of the programme yesterday. Her question was tactical.

An outsider might guess at more sympathy between Ann and myself than really exists. This is largely my wife's doing. She has a flow of articulacy, and she is one of those people, always more numerous than one imagines, who make a point of 'talking things out'. A problem explored is a problem on the way to solution; that sort of nonsense. The fact that I retain a reserve in the intercourse of our marriage is something that

(I flatter myself) few people spot. Ann herself has of course grown so accustomed to it that it probably never occurs to her that I might be keeping things back; she just assumes that I have nothing more to offer; what she may hope for, in her suggestion of psycho-analysis, is that it would encourage a new motivation.

There's the value of this sort of work; I hadn't thought of that explanation before.

She now, rightly sensing that my day would offer nothing of interest to her—she has long advanced beyond a response to the private miseries of a mere Neville, even though he is black—began to tell me of hers. She had been to (I think) Swindon.

'As you know it's always better to see potential clients' —this is how they refer to the unfortunates who are going to expose themselves on her programme—'in their habitual background. Otherwise what you get is a depersonalized fabricated image, misleading. You've got to know them on their own base . . .'—how often I have heard her say this, and wondered at the bland confidence. Doesn't she see that this assumption of knowledge remains something which she has imposed upon them? Do we ever know other people? It's true, certainly, must admit, that I have long concluded that Ann isn't going to be able to surprise me—she has never surprised me, not from our first evening when I realized that she wanted me—but, even so, I can't pretend that I know what she thinks, how she speaks when I am not with her.

'It's a fascinating problem,' she was saying, 'and she is clearly doing a first-rate job. The trouble from our angle, speaking purely professionally, you understand, is that she lacks personality. Actually that's not entirely fair. There is personality there, but it's very self-contained, boxed-up, repressed. I'm not at all sure that the camera will reveal it, bring it out. Of course, in one sense, that's how we want it. You know what Michael says, "the personality we want on the show is yours, Ann, that's what the punters ask for . . ."'

She flashed me a dazzling, personality-filled smile; I hadn't the faintest notion what the woman who constituted this fascinating problem was supposed to do.

I busied myself putting out knives and forks, filling the coffee pot; I gave Ann a campari-and-soda. She took it at arm's length, sitting back on a kitchen chair (French peasant applewood actually), the skirts of her café-au-lait corduroy jacket forming sharp Vs as they fell towards the floor. At such moments she has a look of Ingrid Bergman which is very impressive.

The woman who entered couldn't ever command the sort of attention that Ann extracted as her due. She was slight and grey, with a worn monkey face. Her hair was cut short, badly; she had applied lipstick and other make-up in her bedroom —her face had that renewed look that speaks of recent attention—but it made her seem calculating while it failed to do anything to dissipate an air of drabness and uncertainty that collected itself about her. She had, in her manner of entering the room, something of a dog skulking round dust-bins, at once furtive and intent. She was looking at Ann and I read suspicion in her eyes. I didn't immediately recognize her, and it wasn't till Ann began to effect introductions—which in my amazement I didn't hear—that she opened her washed-out grey eyes, looking directly towards me, and it came to us both simultaneously; and our amazed and incoherent silence filled the room.

There had been snow struggling out of a granite sky, early November snow, and I had been ashamed to be there, among a crowd come in hatred and anger and self-righteousness. She had been brought out alone, and that disappointed them, so that the women—they were mostly women, many well-dressed, most older than she—had been the more vicious. It was her confederate they had been hoping to shower with outraged insult, all the dung stored up in their virtuous souls, and they felt cheated. Cries of 'bitch' and 'whore' cut through the steely afternoon; one large woman in a fur coat near me cried 'filthy murdering dyke' and flung a handful of mud—I suppose from the language she must have spent time in the USA, 'dyke' is hardly a North-East term of abuse. One of the policewomen made to twitch a blanket they had hung round her shoulders back over her head—perhaps it had been there and had slipped off—but she would have none of it. She gave her head a little shake. The crowd read defiance in the gesture—it was indeed the most pitiful yet spirited defiance—and shrieked more obscenities. Then the police hustled her into a black van. My last image, as the engine roared into life, was of a pale-ash face, dried of tears which she must have shed, surely often, in the months before.

She couldn't not have shed tears.

How often that face had returned to me. In memory her eyes avoided mine, but perhaps she had not known I was there, been blind to any particular image. I had hoped that if she did see me she would take my presence there as a mute expression of solidarity, a witness. But she might have misinterpreted my being there. She couldn't, I supposed even then, have realized that I had come as an apology for all I had failed to do; that it was also a penance. And anyway such an apology couldn't have meant much to her. Her life, her free and choosing life, had been brought to a stop with a thud.

She came forward now and took my hand.

'I'm pleased to meet you,' she said.

We played the comedy throughout the evening. I wished —perhaps she did too—that Ann would leave us alone, but she didn't. She talked on and on, not about the programme on which she and Candida were presumably engaged, but more generally about her work and the problems with which it had confronted her. She told us, twice, about a cabinet minister who had said she was cut out for politics, and how another had said, that in that case he would quit. But I wasn't listening. I was watching Candy, trying to see the girl I had known in this abrupt and laconic woman who wore suspicion like bandages wound tightly round a suppurating sore. The moment she finished her bacon and eggs she lit a cigarette, apologizing to Ann for doing so, explaining that she couldn't bring herself to kick a habit that had for so long been 'the breath of life' to her.

'All of us ex-cons smoke like chimneys,' she said, and then

started because Gilesie had come into the kitchen and was hovering by the door.

Ann spoke to him sharply; in the last few months she has grown aware of his mockery.

'It's Dad I want to speak to,' he said.

'As if you hadn't had all evening.'

'I've just remembered it, haven't I,' he said, and I got up, and went through to the morning room with him, and listened to a confused story he had to tell. He had indeed had all evening, but what he had to say was something he hadn't till now been able to make up his mind about; whether he wanted to talk or not. It has nothing to do with my story, but it gave me a glow of confidence that Gilesie should after all choose to consult me about a question of conduct and emotional honesty. And this glow stayed with me when I had kissed him and sent him to bed, and returned to the kitchen to find that Candy had gone up in my absence and that Ann was now giving herself a glass of Remy Martin with her coffee.

It was on the strength of Gilesie's confidence that I now said, 'This is more embarrassing than you realize.'

'What on earth do you mean?'

'I knew Candida once. Long ago.'

'Then why didn't you say so? Really, I don't understand you . . .'

'Why? I suppose I couldn't think of a tactful way of handling it, and I imagine she felt the same.'

'Oh God,' she said, 'you and your reticence. Your ghastly old-fashioned Scotch reticence. To avoid complications you make things more complicated. Can't you see how bottling it up always makes it worse?'

She downed her brandy and stood up.

'You are tiresome, Dallas, you really are tiresome. Well, you'll have to sort it out in the morning. You'll have to get up and sort it out. It's essential that you do so. We have to be at the studio at eleven for a conference, and so you have to have it done by then. I'm not interested in the complications or in the past. None of that concerns me. It's the here and now I deal in. But you must clear up whatever is between you. Because if

23

you don't she'll be disturbed. I don't mind my clients being disturbed as long as they're creatively disturbed. But I know you and I can see there'll be nothing, but nothing, creative about what's between you. It'll just get in the way of what we have to do. And I won't be obstructed like that. She's doing interesting work, running a rehabilitation scheme for ex-prisoners staffed by ex-prisoners. It'll be a good programme, and I won't have you getting in the way. So sort it out, whatever is between you.'

She went upstairs with the swish of her Olympian demand. I was left at the table with my cooling coffee, aware that my boat had run on to a jagged and uncharted peak rising from the rock reef that ran like a spine under my life's voyage. I thought of Candida lying upstairs in our spare bedroom, under an apricot-coloured cover, and I wondered how, when she was alone, she confronted a life that had been distorted, wrenched wholly out of shape and context, by a few months' madness, a single action as dramatic and unquenchable in its effects as the fire lit by Macbeth's mounting of the stairs to Duncan's chamber.

But at least what Candy had undergone made it impossible for her to indulge in ignorance or self-deception. She had been given a limited choice. It wasn't open to her simply to patch up her life. It was all or nothing. And her sin had been an act of commission, an act of will. She was faced with having to live out its consequences. I had been able to dodge the implications of my own cowardice, my own ineptitude.

For years my evasion had seemed to be effective. I was ahead of the game. It is only in the last two or three years that intimations have come to me, like those first odours of autumn that a breeze brings up in early evening in August, of how that failure of nerve and decision has sapped my resolution throughout my life, has unmanned me. I am less than I should be because of it.

It would be vanity and perversion to say Candy is more fortunate than I. Look at her face now. Compare the candour that memory gives back to me. My hand, stretching out at the kitchen table for my coffee cup, shook, rattling the cup, like bones, against the saucer.

I can't, as I say, think of that young man as 'I'. I must write of that Dallas in the third person; objectify him if he is to be presented with any truth.

I despise him too much to do it any other way. My prose would grovel.

2

The owl swooped out of the elm-tree past the tower window and down to the obscure glen. The young man, Dallas, turned away from window and the summer night, towards the high-backed Victorian leather chair where he had spent most of the day by the empty nursery fireside, reading. He had not been waiting for the owl, but its passing marked a station of the night.

He picked up *Redgauntlet*, his third book of the day, which he had opened some twenty minutes before, and looked at it, and read again:

'"If he cannot amuse himself with the law," said my father snappishly, "it is the worse for him. If he needs not law to teach him to make a fortune, I am sure he needs it to teach him how to keep one; and it would better become him to be learning this, than to be scouring the country like a land-louper, going he knows not where, to see he knows not what . . ."'

That cut a bit near the bone for Dallas; his mother's brother, Hugh Buchanan, who was also the family lawyer and had been till last summer Dallas's guardian, had spoken to him, not of course in such ringing periods, but in a similar tone and to similar purpose, when Dallas had called at the dark-varnished chambers in Ainslie Place to see if the Trust could be persuaded to 'cough up a little more'. In London, in such circumstances, Dallas thought, a lawyer of Hugh's standing might have taken him out to lunch, probably in his club; Hugh, wearing his

Academical tie, sign of inflexible rectitude, had kept him sitting on a straight chair and lectured him, words in pinched accents falling deliberately as the first flakes of a heavy snow-fall might on the grey pavements.

Hugh had not been forthcoming. He was embarrassed by poverty, however genteel; embarrassed too by this nephew he neither liked nor understood, who had run away from Rugby where his own boys had flourished; and then, so his cousins reported, made a spectacle of himself at Cambridge.

Dallas hated it. The interview had been a joke of course, a joke to relate in letters to Michael and Esmond, Guy, James and Cornelian; most of all to the girls, Sarah and Judy. Yet the aroma of that stuffy room with its ranks of dead-leather tomes and the deed-boxes in the chipped cabinets clung about him.

He drank some claret and dipped into *Redgauntlet* again.

'"Latimer, I will tell you no lies. I wish my father would allow me a little more exercise of my free will, were it but that I might feel the pleasure of doing what might please him of my own accord . . ."'

Dallas shook his head. It wasn't in his case like that at all.

'Let me make it clear to you,' Hugh had said, with all the complacence of one to whom lucidity was a pleasurable exercise like punishment, 'the terms of the Trust are plain. We are obliged to maintain the house. It cannot be sold until you are twenty-five except with the unanimous agreement of your three trustees. That consent I for one have no intention of giving. Canaan may be of dubious value. It is nevertheless the Trust's only substantial capital asset. So it must be maintained. Repairs must be effected, rates and electricity and Dod's wages paid, and so forth. Such expenses consume most of the income from a capital already reduced by the necessity of providing for your education. No need to dwell on that. A painful subject. With the residue we make you a modest allowance which cannot, in any way, at any time, be supplemented. We have just sold shares to settle your Cambridge debts. You are a poor man, Dallas, whatever you may imagine. What are you going to do with yourself?'

Dallas made a vague fanning gesture, lost in the hostility of the lawyer's office, which was cold and stuffy at the same time.

'Your cousins have all embarked on careers, though I don't mind telling you that they will each eventually come into a lot more than you will ever inherit.'

A faint pink dawned in Hugh's grey cheeks. His fingers closed on a paper-weight that stood on the desk, knuckle bones standing out white.

Dallas's long upper lip trembled. He flicked at a bit of dust that had settled on his suede jerkin—a garment that he knew to irritate Hugh.

'I used to think that the law was the thing for you. I thought you would make an advocate. That was when you were younger, much younger. Now,' Hugh sniffed twice as though aware of the gin on Dallas's breath, 'there's no chance of that. It's a question of steadiness. The law would give you steadiness, but it requires a basis of the quality in the first place. I don't suppose it's any use asking you whether you have any notion yourself.'

He sucked in his cheeks and looked straight at Dallas.

Dallas said nothing, only anxious to get out . . .

Now, in the recesses of the house, a telephone rang. Dallas didn't move. He had been thinking, most of the time, of his friends in the weeks he had been at Canaan, and probably it was one of them calling—who else could it be? But he didn't move. Presently the ringing stopped and he picked up *Redgauntlet* again. He read for a long time without reflection. Outside the pines grew blacker, the monkey puzzles (no longer symmetrically grouped since two had crashed in last January's gales) sharpened themselves against the purpling sky, and then grew fuzzy and at last merged in a pall of darkness. It was night and there was no moon. The owl cried down in the glen. Once more the telephone sounded. Dallas still didn't move. He read on, his imagination alive on the Solway sands, with the dark menace of *Redgauntlet*, and Greenmantle's promise of Romance that would never be attained, alive in the stinking closes around St Giles and the windy hopelessness of Parliament House, alive in a world made good by friendship, youth and the aching pain of a loyalty that was doomed to failure. He read on, into and through the night, till the bottle was empty and pink touched the sky like an awakening rose. Then at last he made his way by a long corridor and down two steps to the room where he had slept as a child.

September sun woke Dallas, and, after lazing long time in half-dream of girls, he slid sticky from his bed, showered and dressed himself in pink shirt and blue jeans. Treetops sparkled with dew or light early morning rain below the nursery window. The sun caught a chestnut and threw it down the sky with a glitter of red-gold. Dallas made coffee. The position of the sun suggested it was about ten o'clock. The day stretched serpent-length before him.

Below on the terrace he could see Dod, the gardener and handyman, who kept the grounds more or less under control and patched the roof and, in Hugh's phrase, 'must be held responsible for general maintenance'. He had come there, long ago, before the War, in Dallas's grandfather's time as 'orra loon', and stayed ever since, as the other staff dwindled and then vanished. He walked under the windows, along the terrace, carrying an oil-can, his shoulders, seen from above, more bent than ever. Dod lived in a cottage up the glen. Last summer he had put in a bathroom there. Dallas remembered he must sometime mention the leak he had discovered in the ceiling of what had once been his mother's bedroom; he had gone there in a vague, restless, wandering fashion a couple of days back and found a wet patch on the lilac carpet, and a great yellow-red stain, like an unattended wound, spreading across the plaster.

There was nothing to be done with the house. It wasn't worth thinking of. Even his plans for pleasure there had crinkled at the edges, gathered mildew in a damp August, died with the first frosts. He had planned, or rather sketched out, the fancy of a house-party, a re-union of chums, at the end of summer. But he had done nothing about it. Michael and Esmond sent love from Mykonos, Sarah from Florence where she had started a course of art history. James wrote a long, funny letter from Rome, Guy a sharp satirical one from New York where there was a branch of the family merchant bank that demanded his urgent attention. Cornelian sent a card of Harlow New Town where he had started his publishing career humping packages in a warehouse. Only from Judy had he heard nothing.

As for himself he had written to nobody.

But he had Canaan. It was his. Looking at himself now, in his pink shirt and twenty-second year, he seemed to have nothing else, no aptitude, no bedrock of conviction, no sense that a certain way was how he was going to live. Even his ambition, poor lukewarm thing that it was, unmentionable to all but his closest friends, could hardly breathe. And, back in his own country, he felt half a foreigner.

He looked out of the nursery window. The grounds, despite Dod's attentions, were overgrown; paths, which in his grand-father's time had provided walks through the policies, were now lost beneath the tangle of rhododendrons; they were swallowed up, the rhodies advancing like democracy. A couple of old ponies still cropped the grass in the two meadows through which the burn wandered; huge clumps of thistles, reeds and rushes, choked the young grass; the iron railings of Edwardian elegance were joined in many places by strands of sagging wire. Even the chapel which his great-great-grandfather had built in the 1870s, to the design of a pupil of either Street or Butterfield, had been abandoned, its roof removed.

The house was a bit of a joke, though it had given him a touch of glamour at Trinity—'I have this baronial barracks in Scotland' wasn't a bad cocktail party line. But his friends, whose tastes ran to the Rococo, could see no merit in it. The word 'baronial', though technically accurate, drew attention to the family's disappointment, for Mr Gladstone, though some-times a neighbour at Fasque, had denied Dallas's great-great-grandfather the peerage he had coveted and intrigued for; why, he hadn't even been consoled with a baronetcy. Partly in consequence he had become a Liberal Unionist; but that hadn't done him much good either. Still that ancestor, whose self-consciously righteous portrait still hung in the hall, had been the last man of action on that side of the family. Since his time they had merely existed, a bit in decline each generation; and getting poorer.

He took his coffee downstairs and through the cold, high-arched hall and out on to the terrace. Honeysuckle twined over the railings. He sat on a teak bench made from a battleship that had been engaged at Jutland. Dod had disappeared. The air was still. A blue silence prevailed. Dallas sat there, waggling his foot, thinking of this and that, and of Judy.

Thinking of Judy hurt a bit. It meant seeing her perched on a table in a short skirt, or stretched out in a punt in jeans and a striped T-shirt, or lying back naked on her divan in Girton or in his bed. It meant hearing her clear, contemptuous, refusing-to-understand-anything-that-didn't-appeal-to-her voice, a voice that wasn't quite the voice of a little girl—it wasn't one of those dolly-bird voices that would soon be fashionable —but it did retain a clever, little-girl quality; and indeed, though the term hadn't yet been coined, she was a dolly-bird, but one who refused to be a doll. It meant wondering who she was laughing at, now, in London; and altogether imagining too much. Dallas experienced a rush of warmth and weakness; in a spasm of desire he spilt his coffee over his jeans.

The sound of a car coming up the drive interrupted him. He rose, thinking it would be the postman, but instead of the little red mail-van, a pale-blue Mini came round the corner, driven too fast, scattering the gravel chips. It came to a stop, with a skid of tyres. Dallas was dismayed to see his cousin Grant Buchanan bounce out of the car. He himself waited on the grass, coffee mug dangling from his right hand, jeans clinging damp to his thigh.

'The old man said you were camping in the ruins,' Grant said. 'Thought I'd come and give you a look-up. I'm on my way to Aberdeen to do an audit.'

He held out his hand. Dallas gestured with the coffee-mug. He took in the three-piece striped suit, the stiff white collar, the Old Rugbeian tie. In the Buchanan Cousins Dislike Stakes, Grant won by a neck. He and Dallas were the same age, to within a couple of months.

'Glad to see it hasn't fallen down yet.' Grant put a laugh in his voice. 'You know,' he said, 'I don't absolutely agree with the old man about it. I think it could still be developed. I'm not a hundred per cent sure it's absolutely too late. The Old Man's a bit old-fashioned at times. He's not always absolutely alive to what can be done.'

Grant sat down on the bench.

'Must say it's good to get out of the city, breathe decent air. And what have you been doing with yourself?'

For Dallas, Grant breathed something different, less welcome: prosperity and a drive to success. Dallas knew himself to be more intelligent, more sensitive. Grant was a figure of fun. Guy, who also believed in success, in making a lot more money, had found him ludicrous—'a dim provincial pseudo-Midas'. And at Cambridge Dallas, with a pink carnation in the buttonhole of a luscious cream linen suit, for the first time made his superiority manifest, except for one thing: Grant never noticed.

Grant, as the tie suggested, had loved school. Except that 'loved' was not a word you could apply to him. He simply belonged there. For Dallas on the other hand all it offered were weeks of denial, interspersed with fear and odd spurts of intensity fearful in themselves. He knew from the moment he entered the long corridors of school that they weren't going to trust him there. Not even on the rugby field. He was fast and had been a star at prep school, but they looked at him and knew that a hard tackle in the first ten minutes would disrupt his game and that, faced with the difficult tackle himself, the blood in his veins would turn to water. He could always hear them talking about it, Grant's voice loud among them. And he'd run.

First year at Cambridge wasn't much better. He was leggy and nervous, and didn't know what to say. His hands floated out of control at cocktail parties. But that summer he had suddenly put on six or seven pounds, and when he went back up in the autumn, everything was changed. He soared, cherished, in demand, while Grant still plodded the streets wrapped in an Emma scarf.

Grant said, 'What are your plans? What gives?'

There was a glisten of sweat on his temple and upper lip. Dallas lit a cigarette.

'Nothing much. I have to go down to the village for my car. They've been fixing something at the garage. Maybe you could give me a lift.'

'Oh, I didn't mean for today. I meant something a bit more long-term. You're surely not staying on here, are you?'

'Why not?'

'I don't mind telling you,' Grant said, rolling that deeply-satisfying phrase round his mouth, 'I don't mind telling you that you're giving cause for concern. The Old Man's just a shade worried. I mean, you must do something.'

'We could go to the pub,' Dallas said, 'I could do with a beer.'

In making the suggestion he hoped to discomfit his cousin. Family encircled him, like hosts of Midian. His recent encounter with his Uncle Hugh had thrown him back to sullen adolescence. The Buchanans refused to accept him as he was able to present himself to the rest of the world. They persisted in seeing him as a problem; very well, then, they should have a problem. The fact that all Dallas's friends would regard them as utterly tedious, gloomily middle-class, couldn't protect Dallas from feelings of inadequacy in their presence.

So; to the pub.

The bar of the Royal Hotel was on the mean side. Dallas, who hadn't been there for a couple of years before his return in July, had been depressed by the changes he had found. The stone flags had been covered by brown linoleum, the recess behind the door removed, and a new, longer, pine-planked bar installed. The modernization was designed to make it 'more functional', open things up a bit, make it less of a drinking-shop; unsuccessfully. The poverty of imagination revealed in the enterprise was characteristic of something that went beyond the personality of the new proprietor, Dougie; it was evidence of a denatured and broken culture.

Now Dallas looked at Dougie across the bar and smiled and ordered beer.

'This is my cousin, Grant,' he said.

Grant hardly acknowledged the introduction; instead he

turned his back to the bar and lifted his chin and looked round, like an art critic at an amateur exhibition.

'Are you paying cash for this, Dallas?' Dougie said.

'No,' Dallas said, 'put it down to me, please. I'll let you have a cheque in a day or two.'

'Well,' Grant said, 'cheers. You must get a bit bored here though, don't you?'

'Bored?' Dallas said. 'The whole tide of human life is to be found here. Isn't that right. Dougie?'

'I couldna say, Dallas.'

Grant began to tell him about the accountants' office where he had started working. What he had to say scarcely riveted attention. Instead Dallas drank his beer and watched sunbeams lighting up the dust in the air. The beams shone through the top half of a window, which was now plain glass, into which Dougie had inserted a device to expel air. The lower smoked glass half of the window still bore the outmoded legend, 'Maclay's Alloa Ales'. Dallas was for the moment happy. A morning pub, with enough beer to cloud the future . . . The sound of laughter and a tiny affected scream came from the little sitting-room across the passage at the foot of the stairs. Laughter boomed again, like someone insisting that the company keep time, no defaulters permitted.

'That's Fraser ben there,' Dougie said. 'He came in an hour back wi' a couple of quines from the toon. Div ye ken fit he said? He's said they'd a' come frae a political meeting. Did ye ever ken sic a man? It was easy seen they'd been boozing a' night. The whisky was coming aff their breaths like morning mist.'

He looked in the direction of the laughter with an expression half-apprehensive, half-envious.

'Will you take something yourself?' Dallas said.

'I'll take a nip. I've been bringing in beer from the cellar.'

'Fraser who?' Dallas asked.

'Div ye no' ken Fraser? He's an awfy man. Fraser Donnelly the contractor. Bides the other side o' the hill. I'd have thought ye'd have kent Fraser. A'body else does.'

A shout summoned him to the other room.

'I don't like this sort of thing,' Grant said. 'Take it from me,

Dallas, it's not a good idea to drink in the morning. I don't mean the occasional beer, but all that . . .' he gestured towards the laughter, 'that's bad. Haven't you got any real plans yet? It's a bit of a shock I admit starting into work after Cambridge, let's you see how lucky we've been. I'm absolutely shattered at the end of the day, I don't mind telling you. Do you know, I've even decided not to play any rugby this year, not till I'm properly established at the office. Seems a wise move. I remember discussing it with your friend Guy Marburg, and he absolutely agreed with me that you've got to get stuck into your business straight away. That's what it's all about when you come down to it. Squash keeps me fit. After all we've had our fun. Not that business isn't jolly fascinating. This audit I'm on my way to do . . . you'd never believe what a balance sheet can tell you about a company.'

'Wouldn't I? I'd have thought that was what it was bound to do, tell you about a company.'

Grant ignored the frivolity, Buchanans always did. He explored the ramifications of balance sheets for some time. Dallas half-listened; more eagerly he attended the hilarity that sounded from the other room.

Grant said, 'It's risky what you are doing here. The wrong kind of risk. Life's not a game, it's something you've got to plan. For instance, I don't mind telling you I've no intention of getting married for at least five years. Can you say as much?'

Dallas disregarded the question. Marriage was not something he had thought of. Equally he hadn't marked it as a stage to be reached at a given point. There were no given points in life; absurd to think there might be. He was spared from any follow-up by a little cough behind him; a small man, like a modest, bearded rat, had entered the bar.

'Why, it's Dallas,' he said. 'Is there no sign of our good Douglas?'

'He's through there taking an order. There's some sort of party going on.'

'Some sort of party?' The little man fingered his tartan tie. 'And who would be having a party? It sounds a lively affair.'

'Lively enough,' Dallas said. 'Oh, this is my cousin, Grant Buchanan. Grant's an accountant in Edinburgh. He's been bullying me about my future. Grant, this is Gavin Gregory, the Reverend Gavin Gregory. Mr Gregory's the minister here.'

'For my sins, for my scarlet sins,' Gavin Gregory said. 'An uphill job, a stey, stey brae.'

He cocked his head sideways, like a sparrow. The clergy have really become awful flirts; he twinkled from Grant back to Dallas, and flicked a sharp little tongue across his lips. Gavin Gregory had called at Canaan a few days before and drunk a lot of claret and giggled as he spoke of the role of the Church in the modern world.

'You mustn't think this is one of my haunts, Grant,' he said. 'Not like young Dallas here'—he laid a light finger on Dallas's sleeve—'but we're out of sherry at the manse, you see, so I've come to replenish my stock. Mr Macintosh at the shop only keeps Cyprus. Well, that's not exactly true. I believe he has South African also. But I won't drink South African for political reasons, or Cyprus for gastronomic.' He giggled again. 'Sherry's respectable, you know. Not even my strait-laced elders frown on sherry. I have some strait-laced ones, you know, Dallas, they're not all to be found boozing here every night. So you're from Edinburgh, are you?'

'That's right.'

'That's very interesting. A lovely city. My wife hails from Auld Reekie herself.'

'Ah.'

'Yes, indeed, her folks live there to this day. Up in Brunts-field.'

'Ah yes,' Grant drew back, declining commitment. He swirled the last beer around in his glass. 'Look, Dallas,' he said, 'grand seeing you, but I should be moving on.' He turned to Gavin Gregory. 'I've an audit to do in Aberdeen.'

'Right,' said Dallas, 'see you sometime.' He climbed on to a bar stool.

'My father will be glad to hear that I called in,' Grant said.

'Well, young Dallas,' Gavin Gregory said, 'and have you been ruminating on our conversation the other day?'

He had a habit of moving towards you as he spoke, making a little pecking gesture with the head: 'Have you been—peck

—ruminating—peck—on our conversation—peck—the other day, question-mark—peck.'

'I told you,' Dallas said, 'politics don't interest me below the level of gossip.'

Gavin Gregory waggled a finger at him.

'That's because you are anglicized. You can afford your detachment.'

'I'm amused at the notion that I can afford anything. Do you think Dougie would object if I went round the bar and pulled myself a pint?'

'You'd surely never do that . . .'

'Why not?'

'So you really liked Cambridge?' The minister was evidently a man who couldn't let a conversation go, even when it was several days cold. 'Did I tell you I could have gone there myself? But I'd spent four years in the Navy before I decided to pursue further education, and I felt I had been too long out of Scotland as it was, so I plumped for Edinburgh. And I've never regretted it. Never. It gave me a firm basis, just as my subsequent two years in Malawi—Nyasaland it was then —gave me political perspective. And do you know what I learned? English imperialism's the same everywhere. The Navy, the Uni, Africa—that's the triad that formed my mind. Now,' he touched Dallas's arm again, 'I expect you're wondering why, in this day and age, an experienced and travelled man, who's seen a bit of the world and that includes the worst and seamiest as well as the best, should go in for an old-fogeyish thing like the ministry. I'll tell you, young Dallas, I sometimes wonder myself'—giggle, peck—'but you know, it's not so strange. What other profession gives you so good an opportunity of taking a stand on the really important fundamental issues?'

'When I was a boy,' Dallas said, 'staying here with my grandmother, your predecessor once asked me if I had never thought of going into the ministry myself. His reasons were a bit different. "There's not a house in the parish," he said to me, "that I can't go into and get given a cup of tea . . ."'

'They all say he was an awful man for the tea. That's the old-fogeyish side of the ministry right enough. And it's not helped

36

by this business of the parish, which between you and me, is a
bit out of date. You've got to encourage folks to lift their gaze
from the parochial and consider the broader issues. The parish
is no longer an organism . . .'

He might be right, even Gavin Gregory, whom Dallas already
dismissed as of no account, a curiosity. But it was a recent
development. Dallas's family, being Episcopalians, had always stood a bit outside the parish. It was one reason why they
didn't fully belong. They had, questions of class aside, been
outside the general run of things since they had bought the
estate and the recently built house back in the 1860s. 'Out of
Crimean War profiteering,' Dallas used to like to say; without
evidence.

For two generations they made a point of looking for
Episcopalian families as tenants when a farm became vacant.
Then before the Great War, most of the farms were sold, and
the then laird, now bereft of all land except the Home Farm
and the house policies, had married as his second wife Dallas's
still surviving grandmother whose family was Presbyterian.
But she, educated mostly in Paris, was anti-clerical, something very unusual in the pious, church-going North-East.
No they had never really belonged. If the parish was an
organism, they had acted on it from without.

It was a big parish, starting on the fringes of the high moors
where a few sheep farms and crofts were dotted at the neck of
the glen. The glen proper was deserted, but for a couple of
cottages, and was now mostly given over to forestry. It didn't
even boast a ruined croft, though there had once been a clachan
at the bottom of the pass across the Mounth. The glen opened
out to sour, hard-won, big-bouldered fields divided by stone
dykes: elemental land, calling, in a sketch for a novel the
seventeen-year-old Dallas had begun, for strained affected
prose, full of muscular verbs and jagged adjectives. (That
sketch had surfaced among some papers on his desk at Trinity,
causing considerable amusement to James and Cornelian;
James had written a parody which made Dallas laugh through
his blushes.)

Then the ground fell away to the village of Monreath where

Dallas was now drinking in the Royal Bar with the minister, none of whose predecessors for more than a hundred years would have set foot in a public bar. The 1841 statistical record of the County, which Dallas had found in his grandfather's library, informed him that Monreath had then possessed five alehouses and another two in the Kirkton across the water. That record had been written by the parish minister but of course there was no means of knowing whether his acquaintance with the alehouses had led him across their thresholds. Dallas thought not.

It was, as his affected prose had striven to say, indeed hard country, breeding narrow, self-certain men, with little taste for grace or frippery. Only when the corn was yellow did the glen lose its hard, sour look. Canaan was different, for the policies had been planted with many trees, chestnuts, sycamores, elms, limes, fine beeches, and in early summer (which Dallas hadn't seen there since he was a child) the grounds were turned pink, red, and purple as Kashmir by the rhododendrons in bloom.

'Of course,' Gavin Gregory said, 'I can't deny there's an awful lack of awareness of the broader issues. They've a narrow view of society here. What I say is they're marooned in their own concerns: beasts and neeps, that's what they care for. But I try to open windows.'

Shouts came from the other room, and, again, a girl's scream.

'Heavens, that is a noisy party. Who would it be, I wonder?'

'Dougie told me. Some contractor, can't remember his name.'

'A contractor? Oh if it's Fraser Donnelly, that explains everything. But surely you've met Fraser, haven't you?'

'You forget I'm almost a stranger here.'

'He's a great Nationalist, Fraser, that's how I come to know him. He's by way of being a coming man, and a great one in his way, and generous as the day is long. Oh you'll have to meet Fraser. We'll go on through.'

'All right,' Dallas said, 'but we'd better get ourselves a drink first. What'll you have?'

He went round behind the bar and drew himself a pint. The Reverend Gavin Gregory giggled a bit, shifted his shoulders in a curious twisting motion, and settled for a whisky.

'Fraser drinks deep, you'd better give me a double,' he said. 'He won't just have a head start, it'll be head and shoulders and half-way down to his middle.'

Dallas noted the drinks on the pad across which his account already stretched.

3

The room they passed through to was small and square as a child's block, lined half-way up the wall with pale chipboard, distempered above that, smudgy and streaked. A yellowing cicatrice of nicotine stained the ceiling round the light. It was a room not often used these days, now that girls would come into the Public Bar without embarrassment, but it was still sometimes occupied on Friday and Saturday nights when some of the older villagers would bring their wives in for a drink. Dallas hadn't found himself there since his prep school days when he would sometimes call at the hotel for bacon and eggs while his pony was being shod at the smiddy.

There were four people in the room besides Douglas who was standing by the table round which the others were seated; he had the air of a man who had been waiting longer than he liked for instruction. The big man, waving a half-smoked cigar, was clearly in the middle of a long story: 'And so I says,' he said, 'never mind that . . .' He had, Dallas could see straightaway, the look of a man who would not easily be brought to mind anything he didn't choose to. His face was flushed and his tousy hair, with just a touch of grey in it, had a dead look; needing a wash; but the little eyes were sharp as a pig's. They darted towards the minister and Dallas, as they stood in the doorway, and then the cigar, imperiously, even imperially, waved, gestured them to a seat, and the audience they would be granted when the anecdote had been brought to its thunderous conclusion.

Dallas, not listening, looked at the others. The red-haired girl with green, slanting eyes and the translucent, freckled skin of her type, was instantly sluttishly desirable. Those eyes didn't leave the narrator. Her cigarette-browned finger rubbed itself along the lower lip of her big, open mouth. She hadn't looked round when Dallas and Gavin Gregory entered.

'She sleeps with that lout,' Dallas thought.

There was a big, too-blonde woman in too tight a sweater of a bright green colour that did nothing for her heavily powdered face; it was too old and solid and knowing, and red was starting to force its way through the powder. She took up a very small lighter in her ham of a hand and lit a very small cigarette which she had taken from an emerald-coloured case. When she took the cigarette away from her lips after a single puff, its tip was already touched dark-red.

Only the boy seated on the bench that ran along against the wall welcomed their arrival. He gave them a quick impudent smile, the smile of a cabin-boy anxious to please, and moved up the settle to make space. Gavin Gregory tripped forward and sat beside him, and whispered in his ear. The boy giggled, lifting his shoulder and lowering long eyelashes.

Dallas was left standing by the door while the story swirled on, ending on a burst of laughter, after which the narrator leant over the table, seized the whisky bottle by its middle and poured drinks into all glasses. He waved the still unfinished bottle in Douglas's direction.

'We'll need another of thon. Well, minister, we missed you last night. We'd a grand meeting. You should have heard my speech. It fair made the auld fogeys on the platform squirm.'

Gavin Gregory smirked, 'I was sorry not to be there . . .'

He introduced Dallas. 'So you're the young laird?' the big man said. His tone was genial, the irony heavy but not offensive. He expected Dallas to share the joke. Reverse introductions were effected. As usual Dallas didn't catch all the names. The big man, of course, was Fraser Donnelly. The red-haired girl was called Kate; the boy, Jimmy.

He pulled up a chair from beside one of the other tables and sat at the angle between Kate and the too-blonde woman. The girl's profile interrupted his view of Fraser Donnelly. He drank deeply of his beer, looking at her; she was the first girl he had seen since July that he wanted.

For Dallas the afternoon was swallowed up in a muzz of beer and sexual desire. When he thought about it long afterwards it was hard not to read an atmosphere of desperation into the party in the little room; but that was romantic, an example of memory imposing anticipation on itself.

The man Fraser was a tease, a sign – Dallas remembered reading somewhere – of inner unhappiness. His first target was Gavin Gregory.

'What would your elders say if they saw you now? Does your Maggie ken you're oot? What for do you keep Maggie frae me these days? Are you ashamed of her or of me? Or are you feart? Maybe you're feart.'

Gavin Gregory responded to each sally with a little giggle and a twitch and eased closer to the boy Jimmy. Dallas noticed too that Fraser's voice ran up and down a scale of accent. It was rougher, coarser when he teased the minister, as he played the old role of rustic Lothario. He turned to Dallas and the accent became consciously correct. Once he addressed Kate in the broadest Doric, so broad that Dallas, who prided himself on his ability to understand even Dod (and that when he hadn't got his teeth in) was quite lost. The girl herself didn't reply above a breathy whisper. Dallas couldn't catch what she said. She hardly took her eyes off Fraser. There was tension between her and the too-blonde; Dallas caught the scent of antagonism, strong, pervasive, and disagreeable as the dried-blood smell of sage.

Fraser pushed the whisky in his direction, and a fresh glass from a number grouped in the middle of the table in a manner that suggested that Fraser had been ready for his party to be augmented.

'I like a loon that can take a dram,' he said. 'Tak your hand aff Jimmy, minister, he's no ane o' your auld shipmates. Jimmy loon, awa through and fetch us thon other bottle. I doubt Dougie has gone to sleep.'

The blonde woman said, 'You'll get yourself in trouble, Gavin Gregory. And fuck me if I help you when you do.'

For Dallas the day, moving into afternoon, supplied something he had been missing since the summer. Dissipation moved with the measured steps of a formal dance; he heard old music in his memory; saw sunlight streaking into a finer room; heard a wind-up gramophone play a loved refrain:

> How you gonna keep them down on the farm
> After they've seen Paree . . .

How indeed?

He tried, while Fraser and the minister and the too-blonde, their little scuffle seemingly forgotten, were all suddenly talking in animated and friendly manner about the political meeting of the night before, to engage Kate in conversation. He asked her all the usual questions, where she came from, what she did. She answered, without suggestion of interest, hardly bothering to look at him, that she lived in Aberdeen and didn't do anything.

'I'm out of a job just now,' she said, 'I can't be bothered with one, to tell the truth.'

'But you have something you used to do, or would do, have you?'

'Oh, I was trained as a hairdresser,' she said. 'But I ask you, what's the point?'

She watched Fraser reach across the table and catch the too-blonde's wrist and press the back of her hand against his mouth.

'Jimmy's an awful time getting the whisky,' Kate said.

She edged her chair closer to Fraser and took a cigarette from the packet that was lying on the table, and then guided his hand that was holding the cigar towards her lips in order to light her cigarette. When she had done so she kept hold of his wrist. He transferred the cigar to the other hand and put his arm round her. With her free hand she removed the cigarette

42

from her mouth and Fraser leant over and kissed her on the lips.

'My, but you're bonnie,' he said. 'You see, minister, the truth of the matter is that a national movement requires a revolution. It makes nae sense without it. Chiels like Provost Barclay want independence so that a'thing else can stay the same. They want to keep their puking wee municipal corruptions and their Sunday greeting faces and a' their fusty notions. Oh them and their Sunday faces and their wee sma'toon *Sunday Post* morality. An' then there are others, who are just auld-fashioned Romantics, with their blethers about Scotland as their wee white rose that smells sharp and sweet and breaks the heart. You've inklings that road yourself, Gavin. But me, I've no patience wi' the lot o' that. No bloody patience at all. It's over and done with. For me, Scotland's worth a revolution, and ripe for one. No' your old-fashioned, wave the red flag revolution. I'm no' thinking of that, it's a load of blethers too. No, what I'm interested in is a real revolution, a revolution of consciousness, a revolution of morals. The hell wi' the auld Scotland of kirk and kailyard. I want a new Scotland that's free and rich too. There's no harm in bringing a bit of Texas to Scotland, as lang as we take our new morality from California. That's where the new age is being born. Kate here kens that,' he hugged the girl again, 'she's what they ca' the counter-culture . . .'

He turned to the girl and lowered his voice.

'Are you no' my wee counter-culture quine?'

'Oh,' Gavin Gregory said, his voice on the thick side, 'I'm with you there, Fraser, never fear. A new morality . . .' he poised on the words, savouring them, holding them up for admiration as you might point to a stained-glass window; it was as if this abstract term represented for him the New Jerusalem, shining with golden harps, decorated with lissom seraphs, that his predecessors had preached. 'But, Fraser, there is a but,' he said, putting aside the vision, 'when you say you're no Romantic, I can't altogether agree. You're a practical man, and like many such, you're impractical when it comes to something that you really believe in, outside your usual line of country. You see visions then yourself. And that's where the

43

man without special qualities like me has the advantage of you. We can take the broad view. And the broad view, politically speaking, demands that we follow a more cautious course, one which is, paradoxically, narrower. You mustn't frighten folk off, by publishing your beliefs in the market place. The Party needs the Provost Barclays of this imperfect world. We do indeed. Pro tem, at least. Later of course it'll be a different business.'

The blonde woman sniffed, loudly.

'Knickers,' she said.

The boy Jimmy came back with the whisky.

'It's not my fault I'm so long,' he said. 'Dougie had forgotten all about it, on purpose like if you ask me. He's gone upstairs and to bed, would you credit it, locking the bar behind him. I'd to fish the key from the pocket of his breeks.'

He poured whisky into all the glasses and pulled up a three-legged stool, and sat down beside Dallas.

'Have you known Dougie long then, Dallas?'

'No. I've not been here much in recent years.'

'You've come back home then like?'

'You could say that. For the moment anyway.'

'And you've just finished at university, have you?'

'Yes, that's right.'

'Cambridge, was it? What took you there?'

'Oh I don't know, just seemed the place to go at the time.'

'But you're a Scot, aren't you?'

'Don't see what that's got to do with it.'

The boy smiled. He had a soft ingratiating smile.

'Some would say it had. Fraser for one.'

'Oh yes?'

'I went to the uni myself. Aberdeen of course. But I dropped out last year.'

'What do you do now then?'

'Most of the time I drive Fraser around. He lost his licence, you see. I'll lose mine soon enough if I go on drinking whisky like this. So you don't really know Dougie then? Now there's a man that's in trouble, his wife walked out on him, you ken, so he gets fleeing every night. You won't have much experi-

44

ence of a pub where the customers take the keys to the bar from the landlord's breeks?'

Dallas looked at Jimmy, liking him; took in the spaniel eyes and the curving lips, and thought he'd have fancied him two years back, as the Reverend Gavin Gregory fairly obviously did now, and good luck to him.

'And are you a Nationalist too?' he said.

'Oh aye, a bit of one. I'd have to be in this show. But I'm not really political. You could call me lukewarm, politically.'

'And what about the girl?'

'Kate? She's my half-sister, you ken. Oh aye, she's into it.'

'Your half-sister? She's not very like you, is she? I'd never have guessed it.'

'Och we've only our dad's word for it, and he's an awfu' line-shooter. A real bullshitter, our dad. But Kate's red-hot.'

'Red-hot?' Dallas thought, glancing at the girl whose eyes were still fixed on Fraser Donnelly. Not just politically; he was sure of that.

Jimmy said, 'And are you planning to stay in Scotland, Dallas?'

'Who can tell?' Dallas said, not ready to say how much he hated that word 'planning', not wanting to answer 'my girl's in London, my heart's not in the Highlands', unwilling also to talk of his ache for Mediterranean skies, for geraniums tumbling over high villa walls, for the shifting feel of metal café chairs on cobblestones, for the warm aroma of melons and open drains; it would have sounded like boasting, somehow.

'I expect I'll do what I feel like doing,' he said. 'That's my only rule of life.'

'Fraser'll like to hear that. It's his too.'

'And is it yours?'

Jimmy smiled again, like a blithe confiding cherub: you looked to see wings sprout.

'Och I'm easygoing. I take things as they easy come, easy go. I'm no' one of those folks that have to make them happen their way. It's my sunshine nature.'

Dallas, despite the nostalgia he had engendered by thinking of Mediterranean idylls, felt warmed by the intimacy of the afternoon, something he had been without since he had found himself for the last time on that bare platform of the Cambridge railway station, with the future stretching out under the pearly East Anglian sky, and him feeling like a man who has been decanted from the cinema and finds twilight in the streets.

Fraser interrupted.

'Losh,' he said, 'the wee minister's passed out. Did you ever? Just like a wee light. That last nip was the switch. This'll never do,' he laughed, 'we canna leave him here. Folks would hae a gala day wi' that story. There'd be a fair stour. Jimmy loon, ye'll hiv to run him back to the manse. Will you do that, son? And then when you're back we'll maybe see about making a move wirsels.'

The blonde woman said, 'You should just tip the wee bugger into the gutter. That's what I'd do.'

'I bet you would,' Fraser said, 'but we're no' a' sic teuch folk as you, hen.'

Jimmy said to Dallas, 'Will you give me a hand with him?'

The little minister was light as his faith. He hardly made a whimper as they got him up from behind the table and hitched his arms round their necks, and marched him, wavering like a Dashing White Sergeant set that was out of control, towards the door. Kate held it open for them, and they got him into the yard, and propped him against Fraser's Jaguar while Jimmy fumbled with the locks. Then they heaved him into the back seat and climbed into the front of the car themselves. For a minute or two they sat there laughing foolishly.

Jimmy said, 'It's a grand life if you dinna weaken.'

'Gavin Gregory's weakened all right. What'll we do with him at the manse?'

'Och we'll tuck him up for the night.'

'Hand him over to his ever-loving?'

'If she's there. She might no' be so willing to receive him.'

'Maybe we shouldn't take him to the manse. Why don't we take him to his church, stick him up in the pulpit?'

'It's a grand idea,' Jimmy said, 'but the kirk'll be locked.'

'Maybe he's got the keys on him?'

'I doubt that. They'd no trust wee Gavin wi' the keys o' his kirk. He's no' exactly persona grata wi' the Session. They're feared he'd sell the plate to buy himself booze.'

The manse door, painted dark green a long time ago, now scuffed and peeling, was opened by a small red-headed boy of seven or eight. He took one look at the three of them and turned back into the dark hall shouting,

'Candy, it's Dad wi' Jimmy Cullas and another loon. Dad's awfu' drunk again.'

Dallas found his hilarity wiped out, though, even as he was conscious of embarrassment that almost, but not quite, amounted to shame (and really there was this time no call for shame; he was being a sort of Samaritan, even if not the best kind, the original of the story not having presumably been reeking of whisky and creased with laughter as he handed his charge over to the innkeeper), he still knew what a good story this could be; could even now relish the anecdote he would construct from it; and knew also that sharing this moment established a link with Jimmy.

The steps of the approaching girl were slow, sullen and reluctant rather than angry. She came to them wearing dirty jeans and a thick sweater and sandals, and she hadn't combed her hair. She had dark smudged eyes. Wisps of cobweb clung to her shoulder.

She said, 'Would you mind putting him on the couch through there?'

She had opened the door and shown them into what was presumably the minister's study. The air smelled as if it had been there a long time, used far too often. They dropped Gavin Gregory on the couch, and he gave a little snocher. He almost rolled off, but then steadied himself. Jimmy took an overcoat from a peg on the back of the door and placed it quite gently over the minister, and tucked it between the body and the back of the couch so that it wouldn't slide off.

The girl said, 'I don't suppose it's any good offering you some tea. Or coffee.'

Dallas said, 'As a matter of fact I'd like some coffee very much indeed.'

The words surprised him.

'Me too, Candy,' Jimmy said, 'I'll have to drive Fraser later. Lord knows where he'll want to go next. We were on the way home, but I dinna ken.'

'You'd be better out of that, Jimmy,' the girl said.

They followed her through to the kitchen. It was a big room with a linoleum-covered floor. The window looked out on a yard, but a bush had been allowed to grow half across the glass, and the room was dark, and lit only by one naked bulb in the middle of the ceiling. An old range stood dusty and unused in the chimney-piece. The girl plugged in an electric kettle.

'Where's it going to end?' she said, not speaking as if she expected an answer. The red-haired boy had disappeared. Dallas could hear his voice raised in altercation with another child; somewhere upstairs, a long way off.

'I was feared it would be Maggie let us in,' Jimmy said. 'Is she no' here then?'

Dallas realized that his first puzzlement had been cleared up; this girl, who seemed to be about his own age, wasn't the minister's wife.

'Well, you're in luck,' she said, 'aren't you?'

She spooned coffee powder into three mugs, filled them from the kettle and brought them all to the table. A bottle of milk and a bag of sugar were already standing there. She indicated them and a dirty aluminium teaspoon.

'Who are you then?'

'I'm called Dallas.'

'Dallas something? Or something Dallas?'

'Dallas Graham.'

'He's the young laird, you ken,' Jimmy said.

The irony, not unfriendly, might have been a means of lightening the atmosphere; only neither Dallas nor the girl found a response to it beyond Dallas's half-embarrassed smile which she didn't anyway see.

'And are you in with Fraser Donnelly also?' she said, keeping her eyes fixed on the little whirlpool she was stirring in her Nescafé.

'Oh, I hadn't met him before today.'

He liked her pale face and cool accentless voice, and the dark hair cut short like a schoolboy's but thicker at the back.

'What do you mean "in with him", anyway?'

She looked at Jimmy instead of answering, as if his question was foolishness.

'It can't go on, you know. In fact it's stopped going on already. Maggie's had enough. She's gone.'

'Without the kids?' Jimmy said. 'I don't believe it. She'd never have gone without the kids.'

'That's just it,' she said. 'It's not definite yet. She's gone away to think about it. I said I'd look after the kids for a day or two. Give her a chance to get things straight. But when they are straight it's obvious what the answer will be. It's obvious.'

'Oh I don't know,' Jimmy said. 'Things often look different. Besides, old Gavin's not so bad really. I'm sure she can handle old Gavin.'

'It's not just Gavin, you know it's not.'

She spoke in a way that suggested an accumulation of weariness, though without any of the sharpness of feeling, the disgust, anger or reproach that, Dallas thought, the business might have been expected to evoke; not of course that he was quite clear about the business; the whole thing was like coming into the cinema in the middle of a film. It was astonishing though how quickly you always picked up who the characters were, and even the thread of the plot. And he had no reason to think life didn't fall into patterns, like the movies.

But if her voice revealed little of her feelings, when she screwed up her face, and said to Jimmy, 'I don't know why I'm speaking to you like this, you're on Fraser's side,' she looked about twelve and lost; it pained and attracted him.

'Can I help?' he said.

'I shouldn't think so. I mean what could you do? You don't know anything.'

Then she blushed.

'I'm sorry,' she said, 'that was rude. It was kind of you to offer.'

'Don't mention it. All part of the Dallas service.'

She smiled. When she smiled she looked a bit like Judy but without the arrogance.

'It's OK,' she said, 'I'll manage. The children are fine, and Gavin's no trouble to me. I don't care for him, you see.'

'We'll have to go, Candy,' Jimmy said. 'Fraser gets in an awful state if he thinks he's been deserted.'

'Oh yes,' she said, meaning, Dallas thought, fuck Fraser.

Yet maybe even then Dallas was wrong; there's no way of telling. Certainly Candy would have liked to think that way, to dismiss Fraser from her consciousness and other peoples' lives with that easy expletive. But you can't delete people like words from a tape. And even in those first hours in the pub Dallas had felt Fraser's power.

Who was he, he wanted to know. A contractor; he knew nothing of contractors. A politician? Only of sorts. Dallas had met a few politicians; he had sat beside a Cabinet Minister at a club dinner a few weeks before coming down from Cambridge; and he couldn't regard protestations of Nationalism as real politics. Himself by sympathy and temperament a Jacobite—he had made a mark in his scholarship exam for Trinity with an essay written on the theme of Rosebery's observation that 'the Scots are all Jacobite at heart'—this very emotional attachment (which he was able to recognize as an expression of nostalgia, a statement of his dislike of the Modern Age) disqualified him from seeing anything more than Jacobitism in Scottish Nationalism.

Yet, he had to confess, it hardly fitted. That club in Cambridge had met once a term for a lavish dinner; they wore eighteenth-century dress, wigs and velvet breeches and lacy shirts and ruffles, and buckled shoes, and wide-skirted velvet coats—Dallas even acquired a swordstick. They drank oceans of claret, and the Scots among them, who were then a majority, toasted 'the little gentleman in black velvet' and 'the King over the water', even though the present Stuart monarch was an ex-Panzer officer. The Cabinet Minister had drained a bumper to 'the memory of Charles Edward', and passed out. Even Dallas could see that Fraser's nationalism was a bit different. He could hardly picture him in velvet.

As for his talk of sexual revolution, that disgusted and excited Dallas simultaneously. In the manner of his youth and generation he was ashamed of the disgust, not the excitement.

Part of the disgust was caused by Fraser's age; sex was a matter for the young; he couldn't quite yet imagine fancying someone older than himself. But it was also aroused by class-consciousness; it was unseemly and a bit off for the middle classes to talk like this. They lacked the style to carry it off.

He tried, very soon after that first meeting, to analyse the matter in a notebook.

I couldn't use Fraser Donnelly as a character in a novel. He wouldn't fit. And, besides, he's something completely new to me. I would have—I can see this—to make him as dominating as Charlus. And a rustic Charlus . . . is that possible?

And yet . . . it's a matter, isn't it, of will. He imposes himself on the company. They all have to think the way he does. And yet (again . . . you see my whole attitude is hopelessly full of qualifications) he's gross, intolerably vulgar. So are most people, you may say—Guy for instance certainly would—but obviously I can't include myself in that category, and yet he diminishes me, even while he defers, or pretends to defer, to me in conversation.

Is he laughing up his sleeve at me as he does so?

What do I know about him . . . admitting I don't know enough to use him fictionally.

He's forty-ish. Comes out of the West, that mysterious land of Glasgow Rangers and overalled armies marching from factory gates with spanners sticking out of their pockets, and huge cranes swinging erections across the sky-line, and bare crowded pubs where all cigarettes are Woodbines, and razor-slashings and crumbling tenements with Greek stucco lintels and art nouveau tiles in passages that stink of urine. Comes from there to our bleak, sure-of-its-different-and-wholly-individual-self North-East where rhetoric withers in the east wind. (Transport him in a novel a bit further up still, to Buchan, to a village like those near where Uncle Edward used to live, where the colours are all grey and brown; have a passage comparing vegetation in Buchan and on the Firth of Clyde; would that get closer to making him live?)

Contracting and haulage business. Mobility, no overheads but your rolling stock. Appeals to natural pirates, encourages contempt for those whose existence is circumscribed by office walls and regulations. Made his money, I suppose, in the restrictive post-war days

Company promoter too? Black market? NB what was his war record? Find out.

Connection must exist between natural authority and standing at an angle to the law and to convention; again, cf Charlus; even more perhaps Redgauntlet himself, with his contempt for the comfortable, for 'the common cant of the day'. That's it, must be it: contempt for the common cant of the day.

Of course Dallas was young, easily impressed, without adequate basis for any judgement. He couldn't see who spoke the common cant of the day. And which day? They all have their cant—yesterday, today, tomorrow—which has this in common: that it substitutes for the discrimination of true feeling a surefire response. Anyone in tune brings out the jargon with the click-clack of a speak-your-weight machine.

I find it macabre, you know, to read these notebooks; and it is very hard not to patronize the boy as he fumbles towards the realization that his imagination simply wasn't up to the task he wanted to set himself; as he looked for patterns in life's Turkey carpet.

I read late into the night and smoked cheroots and drank Vichy water, and so came down in the morning fuzzy, twitchy and jangly. Ann and Candida were at the kitchen table and I wouldn't have been there at all if Ann hadn't come through to the room I sleep in (originally a dressing-room) and insisted I get up. 'You must talk before we set off to the studio. I'll leave you together to do it, if you like. But it's got to be done. You bloody well can't shirk it.'

'It didn't seem to be worrying Candy last night. You don't think it would be better to leave things as they are?'

She didn't.

And now she made an excuse—notes to be written up—and left us, as she had threatened, alone.

'You don't have to,' Candy said when the door was shut.

'Don't have to what?'

'Talk it out. It was none of it much to do with you. We would do better to leave things as they were last night; with formal non-recognition.'

'I can't imagine you like looking back.'

'Of course not. It's there, its effects survive, but that's it. My life's my work now. This work that your wife is very fortunately going to publicize. I've paid what they call my debt to society, and don't think by the way this work is intended to discharge that any further. On the contrary, it's my debt to myself I'm paying now. And there's nowhere, obviously, that you come in.'

'You look very well,' I said, 'and very secure.'

'Oh, I am.'

'But it must have been hell.'

With impertinent, importunate tongue I flicked at a decayed tooth, seeking the twitch of pain that assures the guilty and neurotic of their being.

'Hell? I don't know. One gets out of the way of using big words like hell. I'm sorry to be snappy. It's pre-telly nerves. And I don't really like your wife I'm afraid. It's not her fault. The thing is, she offends my way of thinking which—if you'll forgive me one big word at breakfast—I have to call "existential".'

'You mean, with her, it's all theory?'

'Oh she tries to be imaginative. Imagination leading to empathy, that sort of thing. But imagination is not enough. I've never, as you may remember, had much imagination myself. But it wouldn't have helped if I had, any more than the principles, the code I tried to live by, did. I can see that now. You can only know by experience. Only what happens can really teach. After all, Lorna'—there was no tremor as she said the name, which I had been waiting for her to pronounce —'wasn't short on imagination. It didn't help at all. You could even say it contributed to the muck-up. No. Tell me about yourself. Do you still have Canaan?'

'No, it went.'

'I'm sorry. I liked thinking of you in Canaan. It was a beautifully fanciful house, even fantastic. I used to think of you there quite often.'

'Oh,' I said, 'it was completely impossible. I took a scunner at the place. It reminded me of too much. You see I could never think of staying on in the North-East. So I sold it. No real buyers of course. It went for almost nothing. It was the sort of house that even Historic Buildings people sneered at in those days. Now I'm just an antique dealer, an increasingly unsuccessful one I'm afraid.'

'But you've a wife and family,' she said. 'Two sons, is it?'

'Yes, two sons. That's what I have.'

'Might have been worse, mightn't it? At least you didn't end up with that frightful woman . . . the one you brought to that party in the cottage.'

'No,' I said, 'I avoided that. Even Dallas had that much sense.'

She looked at me with that grey look that had always expressed appraisal that fell short of understanding.

'You were a bit green,' she said.

'I didn't know you knew about her. You never met her, did you?'

'Not to speak to. But I saw her clinging to you, and I saw you watch her out of the room. And then there were kind friends—Jimmy Cullas for instance—to tell me all about it. He said you were really crawling for her.'

'It was part of the infection,' I said. 'And I didn't crawl far.'

'It put me off you,' she said. 'Even when I thought you were specially nice it put me off you. I kept seeing you with her. And so did Lorna. As you say though, it was part of the infection, part of the plague.' She gave me, at last, that half-mouthed smile that I so often had pictured on her face, and said, in that always surprisingly deep voice, 'Sometimes I wish it was really another life. I try to think of it as another life, but you never really shake off foolishness. That's what I tell my clients, what they've got to face up to. You can ignore what happened—up to a point . . . that was always a favourite expression of yours, wasn't it?—but you can't pretend it didn't happen. Or that it wasn't your own doing. We do make our lives.'

'It's hard to learn that,' I said.

4

Dallas woke, in his clothes, sun slanting through a tear in the curtain. Body shifted on sofa across room, got to feet; door closed, steps moved down corridor into silence. Dallas lay, not thinking, not remembering, clouds shrouding inquest on time past. Head stabbed. Eased self on to belly, out of sun-shaft. Dozed.

Pressure on shoulder. Hand, fingers pressing.

'Brought you a cup of coffee.'

Dallas groaned. Hand didn't leave shoulder. Squeezed.

With a shudder Dallas rolled over, to remove it, groaned, heaved half-upright. Jimmy was sitting on bedside, in T-shirt and dark blue knickers.

'C-Coffee,' he said again. 'How goes it?'

'Don't know. Say not the struggle naught availeth . . .'

'You don't mind that I stayed.'

'Nuh-huh.'

'I couldn't risk driving more, not after that brandy.'

'Brandy? We drank some brandy, did we . . . no wonder.' Did I make a pass? No, it wouldn't . . . Dallas glanced at Jimmy whose fingers now played a little tune on naked thigh . . . have been resisted. Could have but didn't revert.

'Coffee,' Dallas said, 'thanks. Be a lamb and improve it, would you?'

'Improve it?'

'Yes, a modest insertion of brandy, no end of an improvement.'

Jimmy picked up the brandy bottle which, Dallas now saw, had been brought (prudently) through to the bedroom and was now standing on the floor by his bed, and poured some into the cup.

'OK?'

'Fine.'

Silence, while the brandy restored life to shattered frame. Something a bit creepy about the boy's willingness to oblige.

'What's Fraser's wife like?' Dallas asked.

'All right. A good-looker. Why?'

'Often wonder what wives of men like that get out of life, that's all.'

'She doesn't do too badly. She's got her kids. And she's not short of money.'

'How many kids?'

'Three of them. They're all right. Keep her busy. Fraser thinks she's a bit strict with them. He's crazy about them himself, spoils them. But the money's important to Lorna. She was brought up without it, you know. Like me. It's maybe hard for you to understand, Dallas, with all this, what it means to a girl like Lorna, who's been raised in a wee back close in Aberdeen to have a big farmhouse and a fitted kitchen and a charge account at the best dress shops in town. She's a lot to be grateful for . . .'

And to put up with?

'All the same,' Dallas said, 'how does she feel about your sister? And that big blonde. I could see she's been Fraser's mistress, even if she's not now. How does Lorna feel about Fraser running round with other women? Especially one that looks like your sister.'

'Kate's not a whore, you know.'

'I didn't say she was.'

'No, I know you didn't. She's a serious girl, Kate. She really feels. Tell you the truth, Dallas, I don't understand her even if she is my sister, well half-sister. I'm no' sure I'm not a bit feared of her.'

'She's in love with Fraser, is she?'

'In love? I don't know anything about being in love.' Jimmy giggled. 'She likes fucking him, I suppose. But the point is Fraser's fun to be with, there's always something happening. You saw that yesterday yourself. He took to you too, I can always tell. He really wants you to come to that party of his.'

'Will his wife be there?'

'You're really curious about her, aren't you. It's not likely. She doesn't often go up to the cottage.'

Dallas turned to lean on the point of his elbow, thinking of the strangeness of marriage, something none of his friends had yet quite committed.

'How serious is this Nationalist business?'

'You're full of questions this morning. It was all jokes last night.'

'Oh well,' Dallas said, 'grey, grim, morning light, you know. Keen morning shafts of intellect. I'm curious, that's all. Most of my friends find politicians jokes . . .'

'Oh aye,' Jimmy said, 'wankers.'

It was a word he was trying on, just as there had been a hesitancy about his suggestion that his sister liked fucking Fraser Donnelly. It wasn't language quite natural to him. The gap between words and thoughts perceptibly existed. He was working to close it. The words still offended an innate delicacy that he found inappropriate to his role. To cover his recognition, and the embarrassment it caused him, he leant over to take a couple of cigarettes from the packet on the bedside table. He lit both and gave one to Dallas.

'Well,' he said, 'Nationalism's important to Fraser, but, like he said, he sees it as part of a bigger revolution. And that's what he's really after. It wasn't just the whisky talking. And he's got a point. I believe it fine when I'm with him.' He looked down at his bare legs, crossed, with his left foot dangling. 'How can I no'? The old morality tells people like me that we're wicked, damned a' to hell. And, even if you discard that Calvinist hell-fire nonsense, there's no place for me that I can see in conventional secular morality either. And so, aye, I'm with Fraser, you see. I think I'll join you in attacking that brandy. There wouldn't be any lemonade, would there?'

'Ginger ale, through in the nursery, where we were last night.'

Jimmy offered him more brandy.

'Thanks,' said Dallas. 'By the way,' he said, remembering, 'I'm sorry about last night.'

'Doesn't matter,' Jimmy said, smiling. 'You can aye hope, can't you? Would you like me to run you a bath?'

*

Dallas lay in the water to which he had added a dash of Dettol. The heat and the antiseptic smell steamed away the notion that he had made some sort of fool of himself. Instead the feeling revived that life was on the move again. His boat had been caught in the doldrums; now a wind had freshened; he could feel the sails billow. 'Merrily danced the Quaker's wife, and merrily danced the Quaker,' he sang. He twiddled his toes. 'If you don't like the whelks, don't muck 'em about. If you don't like 'em, other people may.' His friend Guy had once said, 'The really ghastly thing about you, Dallas, is your ability to come up bouncing. After a night's debauchery that would have sunk and astonished a Nineties' decadent, you come up fresh as a dozen of Overtons' oysters.' Yes, indeed, so, 'How you gonna keep 'em down on the farm, after they've seen Paree . . .' 'Hideous Caledonian barbarity,' Guy had shuddered, 'you are a purblind optimist.'

It had been the purest affectation coming from Guy, himself a sunshine boy of unusual energy. But Dallas felt the memory like a tribute. 'There is nothing like the Life-Force, nothing in the world.'

Moreover, he could smell bacon frying.

A few minutes later, dressed and clean and pretty, with only the occasional flash of aetherial disembodiment to recall yesterday's excesses, the sensation being anyway itself enlivening and capable of making the world seem an odder and funnier place, better too, he sat down at the nursery table before the plate of bacon and eggs that Jimmy, himself now dressed to the extent that he had pulled on a pair of jeans, but still bare-footed, had set before him.

'How odd,' Dallas said. 'I feel unaccountably well, your authentic breakfast-eating Brooks Brothers type.'

'Do you plan to stay here long then?'

'Who can tell?'

'You were talking last night of a novel.'

'Was I? I'm always inclined to talk of a novel when I'm plastered. It's a purely platonic relationship, mine and the art of fiction. You, it suddenly comes to me, were talking of philosophy.'

'It was the only thing I did at the uni that made sense.'

'Very good bacon this, made from happy and contented pigs.'

'Mind you, it was the philosphers I didn't have to study who made most sense. Kierkegaard and Nietzsche and Sartre. I got a lot out of Sartre. I think I'm really an Existentialist.'

'Aren't we all?' Dallas said. 'It's all in Dostoevsky of course. But his prose style was shocking.'

'What you feel, is,' Jimmy said. 'I like that. You've read Camus, I suppose. I really go for Camus.'

'Grand stuff,' Dallas said. 'You're a very good cook too.'

'Oh aye, it comes from my mum being on the drink. Gave me a horror of women and a love of cooking. Curiously it didna turn me against the booze.'

'Ah yes, the Remy Martin syndrome, child psychologists call it. Quite the worst sort of children, child psychologists, Jimmy. The best psychologists, of course, must grant that, but the very worst children.'

Jimmy smiled, 'I'm talking about myself too much.'

'It's the effect I have on people. It's the result of my curiously sympathetic personality. When the Reverend Gavin Gregory (whom God preserve) came up here the other day, he talked about himself all the time. They call it the novelist's touch. But there's a man with problems now. Ours evaporate beside his. Lead us not into Thames Station, as the choir boys are said to pray.'

'I was never in the choir,' Jimmy said.

A mood of shared September silliness; fragrant wisps of remembered summer hung round the windows.

'What shall we do today?'

'I'll have to see what's Fraser's plans. I've got his Jag, mind, and I'm sort of his driver.'

'We could go to Aberdeen, have lunch and take in a movie. Take the day off, resume the having of the fun, as Hemingstein puts it. Champagne would be nice. Don't you think?'

The truest natural-lords and natural-commons division of life lay between those for whom champagne was the natural response to happiness and levity, and those for whom it was a wine only to be consumed on ritual occasions. Dallas and chums subscribed absolutely, paid-up life members, to the

Cavendish-Rosa Lewis school of things; a bottle of wine was more likely to mean champagne than anything else. His friend Esmond had had lodgings above their wine-merchant, to whom Dallas had declared his intention of dedicating his first novel; they had often drunk Mumm at the hour when other undergraduates returned from the river or football field to tea and crumpets.

So: 'Make the day a slice out of life,' Dallas said, 'you deserve it.'

'I might, but I'd have to call him first. I'm a bit worried too about how things might stand at the manse. If Maggie's really gone. Well, I don't know how wee Gavin'll take it. He's awful high-strung.'

'That seemed a competent girl, that Candy.'

'She doesn't like him though. Gavin's no good when he's not liked, he can't take disapproval.'

'I'd have thought he would have had plenty of practice.'

'In Gavin's case, no amount of practice'll make perfect.'

There was a little tremble to his voice, and to his fingers; not caused by drink, not in the first instance anyway.

'The thing about Candy is,' he said, 'that she's awful direct. Because she sees things simply, she thinks they're simple.'

Dallas nodded. It fitted. She wasn't the sort of girl who would pass the champagne test.

'All right,' he said. 'I rather liked her though.'

'Oh aye, there's nothing wrong with her. She's just limited. Maybe I should give Fraser a ring.'

Fraser was ebullient, expansive. Take the day off, take the Jag, take what you please. Let licence be unrestrained. As for him, he'd a dreich day ahead of him with accounts and papers. He wouldn't be needing Jimmy. But he'd expect him the next morn, bright and brisk, and he was to remind Dallas of the party at the cottage. No excuses would be accepted.

'You know something,' Jimmy said, 'I feel sort of free.'

'We could take my car,' Dallas said, 'if it's been mended, that is. I never got round to asking at the garage yesterday.'

Jimmy shook his head; he liked being in charge of the Jaguar.

60

They passed down the empty steep street of the village and across the river and up the hill to the manse.

'We should go in, you know,' Jimmy said. He lifted his foot from the accelerator.

The sun hadn't got round to the front of the manse yet, and you could see dark stains on the harled wall where water had run down from a leaking gutter. The gate was open. Curtains were still drawn in the front room where they had deposited Gavin Gregory the afternoon before.

Jimmy got out of the car and rang the bell and then hammered on the door. Dallas sat in the passenger seat watching him. He lit a cigarette and rolled down the window. Jimmy looked at him over his shoulder, banged the door again. Dallas sensed the sound booming through the barely furnished hall.

'That's odd,' Jimmy said, coming over to the car.

'Everyone out?'

'I suppose so. It feels wrong.'

'Maybe Candy's taking the children for a walk, and the minister's . . . oh there are a hundred things he could be doing, aren't there? Perhaps he's visiting the sick.'

'I suppose so.'

Jimmy drove some time without speaking. Dallas smoked with his feet up on the shelf in front of him.

'You don't like Gavin much, do you?'

'Hardly know him.'

'He's got troubles and he's irritating in lots of ways, but he's been a good friend to me.

Dallas set store by friendship, but he couldn't think of any way in which Gavin Gregory could qualify as a good friend. You could hardly take him seriously, and he was a bore. Dallas knew from reading that the anguish and fears of the poor and ugly are as urgent as the miseries of anyone else; he didn't feel it. Grotesquerie banished sympathy; and there was no denying that Gavin Gregory was, in his small way, grotesque.

Grotesque or not—and there were (I fancy) moments when he might have felt himself to be so—the little minister had to wake up; and he must have done so joylessly.

The girl Candy heard a shifting and groaning from the sitting-room or study where he had been deposited. It was cold there—the manse was a damp house—and she remembered that, going through in the evening, unwillingly, to see that the little beast was still alive, she had been so disgusted by the fumes of beer and whisky that she had thrown the side window open. It faced north too, and there was a wind from that quarter, a grey North Sea wind with no kindness in it.

When she heard the minister wake, she began banging pans in the kitchen so that he would be aware of her presence. Then came a retching from the cloakroom; and then silence for a long time again. About twelve o'clock the bell sounded—that was Jimmy—but she didn't heed it. Nor of course did the minister. There could have been nobody he much wanted to see, or, if there was, he lacked the nerve to chance answering, and he stayed, virtually a prisoner in his own room till early in the afternoon when Candy, sitting smoking and drinking coffee in the kitchen, heard the front door close. Only when she was quite sure that he had gone out did she go through to tidy up in the room where he had slept.

On days like that he used to walk the byways of the parish, but, though he tried to avoid members of his flock—there were stories told of how he had been seen to disappear into a ditch when he observed others approaching—there were plenty of accounts given later of how he would skulk for miles, muttering to himself and sometimes laughing. Exaggerations possibly; the word had gone round that he was half-mad. Dallas had underestimated his condition.

There was no doubt he had enough to confuse him. His marriage was in ruins, and, even if his marriage had meant less to him than it should to a man (and who am I to blame him for that?), its disintegration was painful. Even the relief it afforded him—for the emotions were mixed—frightened him. Cast loose from the anchor of marriage, he was at the mercy of his dreams; they might now demand to be made flesh. Then he knew that a report on his condition and conduct had already been submitted to the Presbytery. And he was wading through debts like a man who has stumbled in a quagmire.

It was because of his debts that he directed his uncertain

steps to Fraser's house. He had walked six or seven miles in his roundabout fugitive's fashion by the time he got there, and he was worn out. In fact Fraser wasn't there when he arrived, and he found himself alone with Lorna. She was shocked by his appearance, and her first instinct was to get in touch with his wife. So, making some excuse, she telephoned from the kitchen. She got of course Candy, whom she hardly knew. She explained that Maggie had gone away for a few days 'to think things over', and that she, Candy, would just as soon the minister stayed where he was.

'To tell the truth,' she said, 'I find it all utterly disgusting.'

That was so exactly Lorna's own feeling that she warmed to Candy, despite the fact that her reply landed Lorna with the minister; so their first real contact was firmly moral. They were united in disapproval. Lorna agreed that she would keep the minister there till Fraser returned. He wasn't after all fit to leave on his own; and Fraser shouldn't be long.

So she gave Gavin Gregory tea, ignoring his request for whisky.

And it revived him—that was the extraordinary thing. Within half an hour he was chaffing Lorna, and within the hour reproving her. But he was still highly nervous when Fraser arrived and they went through to his office.

They talked, apparently, about money. The upshot was that Fraser handed the minister a huge fat wad of greasy notes, and he did it in front of Lorna. He could easily have given the minister the cash while they were closeted in the office; but he waited till they were back in Lorna's lounge and he had ordered her to give them both some whisky, before producing the money. That was like him. He relished the chance to make his patronage public.

'Of course he enjoyed doing it that way,' Lorna said. 'He's always enjoyed doing favours in a way that humiliates the other person. And then he started talking. It was one of those teasing talkings. You know how Fraser loves teasing . . .'

'It's a sign of unhappiness, some people say.'

'Not in Fraser. He teases to find things out; it's a sort of test. He teases to find out what hurts folk, what they are afraid of. He gets really excited, you know, if he finds out something they're ashamed of. And then he twists it to fit his philosophy, his filthy philosophy. Do you know what he said that day; he told Gavin Gregory he'd sent Jimmy off to Aberdeen with Dallas. "I could see the way Jimmy was looking at him," he said, "that it would be a right kindness. After all if some folk havena the nerve, the poor loon must look elsewhere." '

The minister tried to giggle at that, but he was so white in the face, and holding his fingers so tense they were like sticks on a frosty morning, that he couldn't even giggle.

'Freedom,' Fraser said, 'is fulfilment. You'll never be free, minister, while you're feart to fulfil.'

'He wasn't just teasing the minister,' Lorna said. 'He really hoped Jimmy and Dallas would hit it off together. It excited him to think they might. Even then I was advanced enough to wonder about him and Jimmy too, but it wasn't just a gossipy excitement. It was the thought of power.'

Lorna told all that to Candida, more than once; it was a scene that surged to her lips, like nausea. And Candy told Dallas, when she was, as she thought, trying to open his eyes to Fraser's true nature. And the words have lain buried in me, like inscriptions and papyri hidden for centuries under the lava of Pompeii.

I've never pretended there was a miscarriage of justice; yet, if everything had been known, everything connected, who could really say justice had been done?

5

The holiday mood was corrupted by Jimmy's concern for the little minister; it would take a certain amount of champagne to remedy matters. That sympathy was a bit rum; it was like the expressions of grief which an air crash or any other publicly-labelled 'disaster' will call forth from people who know no one involved, a splurge of emotion in the sincerity of which Dallas had not found himself able to believe.

Duck and Bollinger came like sun after overnight rain; roses blossomed. They went on to a gangster movie where the sheer rightness of every cliché, the clockwork response to each situation, the self-containment of an America that found its optimism hardly impaired by the syndicates and that had not yet begun to indulge its guilt at the expense of the rest of the world, saw them spirit-dancing through the afternoon.

They settled over pints in the tartan-lined back bar of a hotel conveniently placed across the lane from the cinema.

'Now that's what I call neighbourhood planning,' Dallas said.

The bar was early and empty, they its first customers.

Jimmy said, 'Don't you find it strange living up there all by yourself?'

'Sure,' Dallas said, 'it makes me feel just like Garbo. I'm not likely to be there much longer though. Expect I'll go to London in the fall.'

'What'll you do there?'

'Who can tell?'

'We're both a bit in the same boat, aren't we?'

'The good ship Limbo, as distinct from Lollipop.'

'I mean, I canna go on working for Fraser either.'

'Money is rather a problem though, don't you find.'

'Where'll it lead you, my mother says. When she's sober enough to articulate, that is.'

'Something'll turn up,' Dallas said. 'I expect anyway. Meanwhile, as I said, the good ship Limbo. And all who sail in her.'

He looked approvingly around the bar. In one sense of course all bars were in the kingdom of limbo, the never-never land of those lost girls and boys who had been caught half-way out of their prams. Yet they constituted also a world of double time. On the one hand, time was arrested, drinkers lived in a time capsule; on the other the clock marched inexorably towards the appointed hour when the wire-meshed grill (now framing the gates that beckoned to the Promised Land) would descend with dull finality, and the worshippers would be driven out of the temple, like mere money-changers, to resume their diurnal tasks. Meanwhile round succeeded to round, and so forth.

'It's a sort of game to you still, isn't it?' Jimmy said.

'A game, a Sphinxian riddle, a toy, a bauble . . .'

'And I can easy see the attraction of treating life as a game. Only what happens when . . .'

'The great referee in the sky blows his final whistle?'

'I wasn't thinking that far ahead.' Jimmy trailed his fingers through a little pool of beer. 'No, just when someone dings you on the shins?'

'Hurts like hell, dear boy. But if I laugh at anything, 'tis that I may not weep. Byron, as I'm sure I don't need to tell you. One of the great games-players of all time. Out, hunchback. I was born so, mother. You can't beat that for a dramatic opening. The Deformed Transformed, what a title too.'

'Oh aye. Some folks might say Fraser treats life like a game too. All that fooling around and drinking and whoring and shouting his mouth off and the rest of it. It looks like play, but it's no' really. Underneath, you see, he's in dead earnest. And maybe a cold despair. I can never believe he hopes for anything more than the fun he's having that minute. Maybe I sound confused.'

'Maybe you've been reading too much Monsieur Sartre, a joker of course, but not the jokiest of jokers.'

'Maybe.'

'Laugh-a-week Sartre they call him, not laugh a *deuxieme* Pernod Jean-Paul.'

A half-drunk glass, lined by foam turned to scum, interrupted the spell that the Spectre of the Left Bank had cast upon them. A hand descended on Jimmy's shoulder. He looked up; quickly apprehensive.

'It's no' the law, boy, relax.'

'I never thought it was.'

'Did you no', stranger.' A red-haired, freckle-faced young man in a shiny, too-blue suit sat down without waiting to be asked. His sharply striped tie hung loose, half-mast from unbuttoned collar. He asked Jimmy where he had been a' these weeks. Jimmy introduced him as Alick. He looked at Dallas in hard silence then, surprisingly, thrust out a hand.

'Pleased to meet you.'

'Alick here's a reporter. Is that what you call yourself, Alick?'

'It'll do.'

He looked fixedly at Dallas; hard blue eyes, winter morning eyes, daring him to take questioning further, to invade his secrecy. Dallas smiled; he couldn't think of other response.

'Where did you meet in with this wee bugger?'

Dallas let the question go, glancing at Jimmy who didn't however seem disturbed by the contempt Dallas identified in the tone of voice.

'Saw a friend of yours the other day,' Alick said.

Jimmy coloured, didn't reply.

'That blonde bitch I met you with once.' Alick twisted the corner of his mouth upwards; it might have been a smile. 'It was in the Kirkgate. They wouldn't serve her, told her to get the hell out.'

'She made a scene, did she? She's no friend of mine by the way.'

'I hadn't thought she was just your sort. Aye, she made a scene. They near fetched the polis. But she went. Screaming curses like any ordinary fishwife.' He looked back at Dallas. 'Jimmy aye makes some gey queer friends,' he said. 'You never ken who you'll see him wi' next.'

There was something curiously offensive in his tone, and in the way in which, taking a Woodbine from a crumpled packet, he struck a match on his thumb-nail. Little sharp lines ran down from the corners of his eyes, and sandy-red hair was going back from his forehead, but he still couldn't have been more than twenty-five, and the offensiveness surprised Dallas.

Who said, 'Oh don't we all?' He coloured the words with his most languid drawl. Alick gave him a hard-man's smile that refused to be impressed by English poofters.

'So how's things, Jimmy? Are you still in wi' the Tartan Tories? That muckle friend of yours, he's heading for trouble, you ken. No' all the connections he boasts about'll save him. They've got their eye on him. I'm warning you for your own good. They've been asking questions, and they dinna like the answers that're coming in.'

'Oh aye,' Jimmy said, 'Special Branch too, I shouldna wonder. What would they want with Fraser? They're more like to be concerned with you, Alick. Alick's a Trotskyist, Dallas. He's a real Red mole in the capitalist press.'

They talked what might pass for politics for a few minutes. Dallas hardly listened. There was no need to. He knew all the phrases: national revival, socialist transformation of society, industrial regeneration, lackeys of imperial British state. No. He looked across the room. An oldish man with liverish complexion and saddish eyes, bloodhound jowls and trembling hands, was spilling pound notes over the bar counter. The barmaid put out her hand to collect them and he seized her wrist, and spoke with what looked like urgency. Sweat stood out like raindrops on his forehead. Then, losing interest, he dropped her hand, took a red-spotted handkerchief from his pocket and dabbed it at his brow. The girl picked up his glass, held it under the whisky bottle suspended on the gantry, and released a double. He put water into it, and drank half at one swallow.

'And are you a Nat too?' Alick asked.

'Me? Heavens no.'

'I see. No' a Tartan Tory. Just an old-fashioned tweed yin. What's wrong with your crowd, your friend Fraser, Jimmy, is the daft attempt to harness a new morality to an auld politics.'

'Does either ever change really?' Dallas asked; the old man was now giving a snuffling laugh under his straggly moustache.

'It's convenient for the likes of you to pretend they don't.'

'Here, you've no call to speak to Dallas that way.'

'Have I no'?'

The winter eyes froze on Dallas.

'Couldn't say, I'm sure.' Dallas tried for airiness. 'Don't know, you see, just what you imply by that phrase "the likes of you". What likes? What me?'

He swept up the pint glasses and headed for the bar. The old man lifted his head.

'You young people are all the same,' he said.

68

'Three pints of heavy.'

The barmaid took the glasses.

'Don't mind him. When he's had a few he aye thinks he's back in the army.'

'I said, you young men are all the same.'

'Well then, that makes things easy for you, doesn't it? I mean, if we were all different, you might get confused.'

He got a watery-eyed look. The old man resumed contemplation of his whisky.

'One thing I will grant you is you don't seem to believe in marriage.'

'If you want to debate marriage, I'm the last person to talk to. I've no experience, hardly even any theories.'

The old boy—surely a major, he looked like one of nature's majors—fished in his wallet. He spilled three much fingered photographs on the bar.

'My wives,' he said, 'Go on, look at them. Examine the bitches.'

They could have passed for photographs of the same woman. All had hair drawn back from their brow and a beaky nose. One of them had a deep indentation running from the corner of her mouth in a diagonal to her jaw-bone; it could have been the disfiguring consequence of a motor accident or of a moral discontent that cut her face like the Firth of Forth. They were all faces of strong character. 'You like to pick 'em tough,' Dallas was about to say when the likely-major said,

'I was faithful to all of them. *Fides ardebat nec consumebatur.* They all left me. Women. It's the brute in man they look for.'

His gaze flickered to the barmaid. She stood polishing glasses and paid no attention. No doubt none of it was new to her. Barmaids are like priests, confessions part of the daily round; surprise is beyond them, often even interest. Dallas nodded and carried the beer back to the table.

'Sorry to be so long. I was nobbled. The old boy there was telling me about marriage.'

'Well,' Alick said, 'he's an expert on the subject.'

'You know him then.'

'A'body kens Councillor Mickle. He's a friend of your boss, Jimmy, too. Another big haulage man, no' to mention haein' a nieve in every business pie in town. You don't want to be taken in by that way he has of carrying on. He's fly, is the councillor, right fly.'

'I'd marked him down as a major.'

'He ca's himself Colonel.'

There was resentment in his voice. Dallas recognized what he had never directly encountered, only read about: the destroying rage of the *Untermensch*, denied, thwarted, put upon. There was energy there too; it was men like this Alick who made revolutions. Not afraid of disorder, welcoming it indeed, fomenting it even, they could rise over it, using others' destructive passions for their own creative ends. He was quite different from the parlour marxists and nuclear disarmers Dallas had known at Cambridge, boys and girls moved by pity or funk or jealousy of Daddy or—there was irony here —by family tradition. He compared Alick with Dick Bradshaw who had had a room on his staircase at Trinity and who was so intensely politically active, and a great bore too. Dick was a gentle, heavily spectacled chap. His leadership of left-leftie movements was merely what was expected of him—his father had written tracts for the Left Book Club; Gollancz was Dick's godfather; his mother had been one of Cyril Joad's pupil-mistresses. There was no anger in Dick, nothing raw. Instead you found concern, the belief that a chap ought to take a decent line, was morally obliged to, and also a Puritan distaste for the rich that was ultimately an aesthetic judgement as much as a moral or social one. What had happened was that the English Establishment, of which Dallas already recognized himself as a privileged and fascinated spectator, had simply divided. Establishments were like atoms; you could split them. The old atomic theory had been exploded just up the road in the Cavendish Laboratory, and in similar fashion, Cambridge had dealt with the traditional Establishment. So now you had an Opposition Establishment, which was permitted to take over the Government in name anyway from time to time, even though it was temperamentally happier in opposition. It existed as a safety valve for Revolution. The great thing for the country, the oh-so-terribly English thing, was to have your Dick Bradshaws on tap, to siphon off discontent. They acted as moral governesses for the more virile and insensitive real Establishment. And it was astonishing how well it worked.

Dallas formulated the theme while the others gossiped. He was only half-perceptive. Certainly Dick is some sort of Treasury minister now; I saw him on television the other day. But Dallas underestimated the Establishment's absorbent abilities. In his young romanticism he couldn't see how Alick Duguid's keen edge could be blunted, but it was Alick, his career advancing through political journalism, Parliament, then a lost election and television, who hosted the political chat-show on which Dick was appearing. And yet what happened now might have alerted Dallas.

The councillor-colonel lurched to their table and sat down. Neither Alick nor Jimmy showed surprise. On the other hand they made no immediate attempt to include him in their conversation, now dealing with names unknown to Dallas. Their indifference didn't faze the councillor. He let his loose-fitting hound's-tooth tweed coat fall away from him so that its skirts folded themselves on the carpet dusty with cigarette ash. The whisky had calmed his hand's tremble; he looked about ten years younger after it.

'Closing in a minute,' he said. 'Drive me to my place and I'll give you a good malt. There'll be some people coming in. Girls among them, I shouldn't wonder.'

Jimmy looked at Dallas.

'What do you think? Should we be getting back?'

The councillor-colonel didn't speak. He had made his offer. Now he left persuasion to the silent exercise of his will.

Alick said, 'You drive us up, Jimmy. It's no' out of your way. You can aye go straight on if you feel like it.'

'I suppose we could do that,' Jimmy said.

The councillor-colonel inclined his head, generously acknowledging submission as a judge might assent to a good point made by a junior counsel. Dallas himself was happy to let things take their course, on the whole more inclined than otherwise to fall in with the invitation. It was less the promise of the malt, less even the prospect of girls, for after all a man like the councillor-colonel might apply that term to any female not yet eligible for the geriatric ward; rather Dallas responded to the promise of continued exploration after weeks of his own company.

So, when they had all got into the Jaguar and Jimmy had driven them perhaps a mile from the city centre and up a shortish drive with overhanging branches and stopped before a mini-Balmoral made of granite that gleamed silvery in the moonlight, Dallas said, 'Let's go in for a bit, Jimmy.'

They mounted broad steps and entered a large hall. It was lit by a huge centre contraption shaded in stained glass; stags' heads decorated the walls. In a room off to the left a gramophone was playing *South Pacific*. The councillor-colonel dropped his coat on a big oak chest, stained chocolate-brown, and led the way into the room from which the music was coming.

Four or five people were sitting in deep chintz-covered chairs; all had glasses in their hands. A few more were playing poker at a table in a recess. Someone gave a half-hearted cheer as they entered.

'Ah, party-time,' the councillor-colonel said. His voice had taken on new vigour, fruity, not without a note of salacity. Alick made straight for the drinks tray and armed himself with a tumbler of very brown whisky. He sat on the sofa beside a big-nosed woman, dressed in purple, who could have been the original of any of the snapshots Dallas had been shown in the hotel.

Dallas took stock. This was a raffish provincial society he hadn't known to exist; not admittedly that he had many patterns. His experience was of the orderly and seemly, such as he associated with his grandmother, or the boring and stuffy to be found chez Uncle Hugh. But here, in a room to be designated (unmistakably) 'a lounge', he found an assortment that didn't fit in either category. There was a range of class he wasn't accustomed to, a lack of homogeneity. Provincial businessmen in a small way and their wives, that was obvious; but Alick Duguid and the too-blonde from yesterday's pub certainly weren't petit bourgeois. As for the councillor-colonel, there was something fishy about him; you caught even on the briefest acquaintance a whiff of financial dishonesty, municipal graft and corruption; yet he was, equally undeniably, old school tie. Harrow? Fettes more likely? Possibly even Rugby itself? And one of the women sitting at the poker table with a green cigarette holder stuck out of the corner of her mouth had, when she opened that mouth to call for another whisky-and-soda, (which, he noticed, she was promptly supplied with), one of those voices that were made to bray across open fields and wide lawns. It was a horror of a voice.

A girl in a short and unbecoming yellow dress came up to Dallas. And she had the same floating, plummy voice.

'I don't know you,' she said. 'I hardly ever know anyone at Daddy's dos. I'm not often here actually. It's all rather a surprise when I am.'

'Well, I've never been here before myself. My name's Dallas Graham.'

'Oh. Rosemary Mickle. That's what I call myself anyway. How do you come to be here then?'

'I was brought.'

'Daddy's so indiscriminate. He picks people up in pubs. He'll get himself filled in one day, the people he picks up. Look at that awful young man, the one with his tie at half-mast' —she gestured towards Alick. 'He's been here before, you know. Daddy met him in a pub. He said he was interesting. I ask you. He turned out to be a Communist. What's more, he works on the local paper. When I found that out I don't mind telling you I wrote to the editor and asked him what the hell he meant by employing Reds. He hadn't even the good manners to reply. But I remember noticing you came in with him.'

'That's right. I expect your father found him an interesting chap. I don't know him well myself.'

'Oh no he didn't. Daddy doesn't find people interesting. But that's what he'd like us to think. He'll do anything to stir things up. It's boredom really. Come and sit down. I hate standing around.'

She took Dallas by the wrist, lest he escape, and led him to a small hard-backed settee, and sat down, only then releasing

73

his wrist. She crossed her legs, revealing a long line of rather thin but muscular thigh. She took a cigarette from a packet in a little jewelled bag she had been carrying and waited for Dallas to light it. She looked straight into his eyes; he couldn't help responding.

'You may guess I can't take it here for long. But I mean, what is one to do? One must have some sense of responsibility.' She looked at him again, with devouring eyes. Her words didn't make any sense. Maybe she too was a little drunk, but Dallas didn't think so.

A shortish man in heavily checked plus-fours came and stood over them. 'Gather you're Bobo Graham's boy,' he barked. 'What I want to know is what you mean by coming here with that bloody awful nancy-boy who drives that equally bloody contractor chum of Norman's about. Bobo would turn in his grave. You jolly well answer me that, young man.'

'Oh go to hell Brian,' Rosemary said, 'just go to hell and don't make a scene about it. It's so boring.'

'They're all over the shop,' the little man said. He seemed in a state of high excitement, elated by his little fusillade perhaps, but still ready to accept Rosemary's rebuke. He nodded abruptly three times, and turned towards the drinks table.

'What was all that about?'

'Oh Brian, don't mind Brian, nobody does. He used to be a racing-driver. He's never made much sense since he was shot out of a car at Silverstone. He's a bit pathetic. Daddy's an old chum. He's a motor-racing fan. Besides, they were in the army together. Brian's only a major though. It's all terribly boring.'

She stopped talking. Dallas couldn't think of anything to say. Silence increased the tension her discontent bred. Dallas didn't know what she expected of him. That was always the problem when you moved into a different sort of society. You lost your bearings. And there were, he realized, no hard-and-fast conventions that now told you whether you continued polite conversation or were expected to invite a girl to bed. Not that he wanted to do that. She wasn't pretty enough; he had never been able to fancy anyone who wasn't. There was something unhealthy about her rather sallow skin. He didn't like the way her mouth twisted down at the left corner. The pale (dyed?) hair needed a wash, the gamin cut ought to be appealing but didn't strike him that way. It should have gone with an innocence of expression he couldn't find. She picked at the hem of her dress with long nicotine-stained, nail-bitten fingers, drawing his attention to the point where her legs crossed.

He looked round the room. No one new had arrived for some time, and the party had taken shape. The Major was now lecturing Jimmy. He had him pinned between the wall and a mahogany, glass-fronted Victorian bookcase. Without great decision, probably requiring direct action, there was no way out. A cloud of cigar smoke hung over a corner of the room where the colonel-councillor had settled with a couple of heavy-jowled red-faced types with close-cropped hair, both wearing business suits. No doubt a deal was being struck.

Dallas said, 'Who are those chaps with your father?'

She drew her tongue over her lips.

'I hate flirtation,' she said. 'I'll show you the house.'

'She laid you, didn't she?' Jimmy said.

Dawn was breaking over the sea to their left, the sun rising far off, light creeping in from the Baltic. The Jaguar's heater worked well. Dallas was sleepy. What had happened in that pale chintzy bedroom had been brisker than anything of the sort he had previously experienced. It wasn't only flirtation Rosemary hated; sentiment too was out. 'Don't,' she said, as Dallas tried to kiss her lips, 'I don't like it.' That hadn't prevented it from being exciting, not exactly satisfying, disturbing even—Dallas had never been in control—but undeniably exciting. New. Afterwards Rosemary had said, 'That's it. You go downstairs. I've had enough of those creeps. I'm going to sleep'; and when, after dressing he had bent to give her the good-bye kiss he thought the occasion called for, she had actually been asleep; or feigning it. She had moved in a small gesture of dissent as he brushed his lips on the back of her neck.

It was certainly true what Jimmy had said; she had laid him, no question of it.

'You'll maybe see her at Fraser's party. The councillor'll sure be there. They say she's a nymphomaniac.'

He brought the word out doubtfully, perhaps solicitous of what he might imagine Dallas's feelings to be though considering he ought to be warned; perhaps sceptical of whether any meaning could really be attached to such a word, given the sort of folk who were likely to use it.

'She's had two husbands, neither took, and now she calls herself Mickle again.'

'It's not a name I'd choose.'

'The first one was a lad from the fish market. They ran off when she was seventeen, on holiday from boarding school. The councillor had to buy him off but they were married right enough. I canna mind who the second was. She was a flame of Fraser's for a bit too. She's a' kinds of snob, they say, but no' a sexual one. Now she goes to South Africa every winter. Christ kens what she gets up to there.'

They drove through the milking morning. Lights came from farm buildings. They passed an early tractor, the occasional car, a fish lorry thundering south.

Jimmy said, 'Thought you'd better know in case you were thinking of getting involved. They do say she's a right hoor.' He hummed a little tune, a Scots air that Dallas recognized but couldn't name. 'Did you see that comic turn that was talking to me?'

'The chap in the plus-fours, got up for pink gins at Sunningdale?'

'Aye. Major Brian Campbell-Vallins, CBE, DSO I don't think. You never saw the like. Bent as a fish-hook and thinks naebody kens. They say he's had six wives. They say one of them ended on his honeymoon. The wife spotted him making up to the Italian waiters and walked out. Pathetic, isn't it? When you see a man like that, you can see the point of Fraser. Whatever else, he doesna live a lee. My, but I'm tired.'

Dallas had left Rosemary and come downstairs in some

trepidation lest their absence had been noted and embarrassing questions were now asked or comments made. However, a flood of new arrivals distracted any attention from him. He was surprised to find his cousin Grant among them.

'What on earth are you doing here, Dallas?'

'Oh, pissing around, just pissing around. And you?'

'I was invited. It's one of Colonel Mickle's companies I've been auditing. I tell you Dallas, it's good to realize we still have such keen business brains in Scotland. It just shows you what a load of bloody nonsense this Nationalist business is.'

'Oh yes?'

6

Dallas itched; the irritated flesh prevented return to the torpor of the past weeks. It was partly hangover of course. He put himself on a regime of coffee, and soda-water, and bread, and cheese, and eggs, and he took a couple of long walks, up through the rhododendrons by paths that often threatened to disappear under new growth, into the pine-forest and, climbing all the time, on to the open moors, still purple with ling heather. One afternoon, having at last collected his old Light-Fifteen Citroen ('Gabin') from the garage, he took his fishing-rod and drove up Forestry Commission roads to where a path led to three lochans in a high coarse-grassed valley. He fished them all afternoon and caught a couple of brown trout, with mud-coloured flesh from the black peaty water. He sprinkled them with oatmeal and cooked them then and there in a skillet over a little fire made from twigs, bracken and heather. They tasted good. He lay back on heather, in harmony, smoking a cigar, feeling himself a Buchan character, and listened to what he supposed were larks, or perhaps meadow pipits (he liked the name), and what he recognized as peesies and a curlew; lay

77

there, content, till the evening mists of September swallowed the sun before it sank behind the hills, and crept chilling up the burn; he grew cold and had to walk briskly back to the car. The next day it rained: a steady, penetrating, cold, misty rain; chill dankness seeping through the fissures of the house. He drove to the coast, and walked for half an hour by a slate-coloured sea till that was almost lost in fog, and he retreated to a hotel where, adhering to his abstinent diet, he ate a large high tea of finnan haddie and poached egg, followed by sliced bread, baker's scones and grocer's cherry cake.

But back in Canaan silence and indecision weighed on him like a promise made but never performed. His eyes strayed to the telephone; it was a magnet, an imperative. In bed, despite himself, despite the lists he tried to compose, he thought of Rosemary, and repeated in imagination what they had done. Once he tried to write to Judy, but everything he said came out flippant, silly, contemptible; on serious matters his mind was a dried-up fountain-pen, a typewriter with an exhausted ribbon. It would have taken more than a Plato to see his words as the shadows of ideas he wanted to express. He found himself near tears; everyone had forgotten him. There was no light in the sky, just that grey insistent mist brooding over the glen, swallowing the occasional bird, crow or pigeon, that broke momentarily into view. He descended the three flights of stairs, imagining a car's approach, but there was no one there; just a stretch of gravel and the drip of the rain from a broken gutter. Back in the nursery he sank again into *Redgauntlet*.

In this mood of mixed depression and self-conscious decorum he started writing, and in two days scribbled several thousand words of his own Jacobite novel. His hero was a middle-aged sceptic, unimpressed by the demands of either side, yet drawn involuntarily by old loyalties and self-respect to the Prince, whom, when they met, he found himself both liking and despising. The concept delighted Dallas. He spent happy hours describing meals and costumes and fabricating dialogue in a lukewarm dialect. He wasn't even alarmed when he realized he had given his hero a leopard in his coat-of-arms, and that his reflections on Scotland had more than an echo of Lampedusa's Sicily. On the contrary, he thought it a nice conceit, not recognizing how such nice conceits can be the kiss of Judas to a literary work. But he was pleased too by the way that he had, as he thought, subtracted his own personality from what he was writing; it didn't occur to him that his personality was hardly strong enough to impress itself on anything.

Meanwhile for two or three days he pursued his hero, elaborating antithetical arguments on action until, suddenly, he was checked. He didn't know what to do with him next, couldn't get him to move.

He had scarcely thought of Fraser Donnelly; when he did so he felt a rare shame. Not caring to analyse such unpleasantness, he skipped his immediate problem of action, and wrote a long jewelled description of the Prince's court at Holyrood.

He glowed, wrote an absurd letter about the work to Esmond, an elegant young man with something of the same old-fashioned, dandy-aesthetic Romanticism which Dallas's novel breathed, and set off to post it. The air was soft, the mist had cleared, the afternoon was free even of the lightest wind, and the leaves glittered in red and gold. He walked to the village, aware of a strong disinclination to go to Fraser Donnelly's party the next evening. Why should he? He was living the way God (if he existed) intended. A red squirrel darted across the road and raced up a pine tree, pausing on the first transversal branch to appraise him; it looked like a friendly critic. Dallas gave it a casual Yankee salute. Hi there. Rooks pecked their way across stubble fields. Across the glen on a broad south-facing slope a combine harvester moved with monstrous deliberation.

Coming into the village by the back road he saw the manse gate was open and a girl's small backside perched above straight, jeaned legs stuck in a flower bed. He paused, and the girl, sensing she was observed, lifted her trunk from her weeding and turned round.

'It was a nice picture,' Dallas said.

'This garden's a hell of a mess. I don't know why I'm bothering to weed it. After all, it's not really my concern.'

As at their first meeting, when he had brought the little

minister home, he was struck by the clear lines of Candy's personality, even if he couldn't define just what its nature was, and wasn't sure either that he would find it wholly sympathetic when revealed. But he liked the lack of complication he saw there, something which didn't exclude a certain fragility. It would be easy to hurt her. And she was, in a Quakerish way, sexy.

She still didn't smile but came and sat on the wall beside him. Despite her weeding which, judging from the pile of discarded weeds on the path, she had been at for some time, she was pale and unheated.

'You're still here then,' he said—not a very bright observation.

'If you're looking for Gavin,' she said, 'I can't help you.'

'I wasn't,' he said. 'I was just walking by, and then I saw you. Or rather I saw your bottom.'

And a very nice bottom, he didn't add.

'Like some coffee?'

'That would be nice, if you can be bothered.'

She was probably lonely. It was obvious she didn't care for the minister—and who could blame her for that? He imagined her existing in the gloomy and tawdry manse in a pall of silence broken only by Gavin Gregory's discordant chatter to which she didn't listen.

Certainly the kitchen was silent enough. You could hear the cheap alarm-clock tick, tick.

'The kids are playing with friends.'

Dallas watched her neat movements. His affair with Judy seemed these last days memory only, fragrant but insubstantial; he couldn't believe she wasn't sleeping with someone else, and, to his surprise was unmoved by the picture; she belonged to another life. And what had happened with Rosemary Mickle made him all the readier to fall for someone else. (Yet he couldn't think of Rosemary without excitement. In a dream she had said, 'I'd like you to beat me.' He had woken alert and appalled.)

But Candy would respond to any caresses with a brusque, 'Don't be silly. Stop bothering me. What do you think you're up to'; the bitten lip, the averted head. Dallas in his immaturity divided girls into the breathing-sexy, who were approachable, and the chaste; it didn't yet occur to him that here, as in other areas of life, appearance might lie, reservation conceal strength of feeling, hostility to boarding in the case of a girl like Candida not necessarily representing absence of passion.

So, now, he sat, ignorant, shy, unable to think of anything at all, polite, innocuous, to say.

She made the coffee and sat down. The sharp rectangle of the table, covered with a stained oil-cloth, came between them.

Perhaps, having met him with Jimmy and the minister, she thought he was queer. Or perhaps she didn't realize about that. Most likely she didn't.

She said, 'Maggie's coming back for the kids tomorrow.'

He stirred some sugar into his coffee.

'I've been busy turning out drawers. End of chapter. Then I went into the garden for some fresh air, and found myself weeding. I don't know why. It'll be a wilderness before long. Do you often find yourself doing things you can't find a reason for?'

'All the time.'

'It feels a bit like the end of term here. I thought I was through with that sort of thing. Only there's no great holiday feeling of release.'

'Oh?'

'There should be. I don't know why there isn't. But I didn't even think about why I was weeding. I just did it. It didn't even puzzle me while I was at it.'

'You should always yield to the irrational. A couple of years back I was all for Reason. My eighteenth-century phase. Not now. Comes from reading Proust, I think.'

It didn't embarrass him to mention Proust to this girl, though he had nothing to lead him to suppose that she was sympathetic to that strange shorthand and unreliable practice of learning about life from literature; not that Dallas classed it as that yet.

She said, 'There's precious little reason attached to human relations, that I can see anyway.'

'Almost none in my experience.'

81

'I'm sure though a clean break's the right thing for Maggie. She's been in a frightful state. There was a time I thought she was ripe for murder, the way she looked at him when he came in drunk. But then she got beyond that. It all turned to contempt and disgust. You wouldn't kill someone simply because he disgusted you, would you? It sounds crazy, doesn't it, but these are the sort of thoughts I've been having.'

She lit a cigarette, the last from a crushed packet of Cadets. A couple of saucers were full of stubs and ash, all the cigarettes smoked right down to the filter. The sink brimmed with dirty dishes. Plates with scraps of bacon and smears of egg still sat on the table.

'How well do you know Fraser Donnelly?' she said.

'Didn't I tell you? The other day was the first time I met him. I hadn't even heard of him before. I hardly know anyone here. All the same, in one sense anyway, he's the sort you get to know pretty quickly. He rather forces his character on your acquaintance. Not many depths either.'

'He's a devil,' she said. 'I really mean that,' she said. 'Literally.'

The clock on the church tower collected itself and struck, five times. There was a whirr and a choke before each chime rang out.

'Have you heard the way he speaks?' she said. 'It's the kind of dirt that gets under your skin. He's filled Gavin, who's a fair sort of idiot, and feeble, no doubt about that, but still the sort of feeble creature who mightn't have made out too badly, left to himself and his family, with all sorts of really disgusting notions. Fraser Donnelly gives Maggie the creeps. He does me too. If half her stories are right, he really is the devil I said he was.'

Her voice, still low, took on a note of unexpected madness; she picked at the seam of her jeans.

'This sexual liberation stuff he talks,' she said, 'sexual revolution, it's horrid, dirty, just an excuse to ignore everything decent, go against it.'

'The day I was with him, he said there's no indecency like the indecency of family life.'

'There you are.'

82

'I don't know much about family life. The idea's hardly new though.'

'I'm not interested in whether it's new. I believe in the family,' she said, her eyes grey as the North Sea.

'That doesn't mean anything though. It's like saying you believe in sheep or the trees. How can you fail to? They're there. But you don't have to approve of them.'

'That's just clever,' she said. 'It doesn't mean anything.'

The conversation wasn't a turn-off. He liked her less for it; the Quakerish austerity might represent a refusal to encounter experience; it didn't make her less desirable. Her frigidity, expressed as little-girl assurance, even attracted him. Liking can come after sex, if at all. And liking, he reflected, can even inhibit desire, so the converse . . . the image of Rosemary's thin thighs disturbed him. He caught himself blushing. And gazed at the shallow valley between Candida's chaste breasts.

'You haven't met his wife, have you?'

'No.'

'What that brute's done to that girl doesn't bear thinking of. She's a super girl, really super. I tell you, it's all horrible.'

'How does she feel? Is she still in love with him?'

'How can you ask that? She hates him. She couldn't fail to.'

The verb 'hate' excited Dallas. But, concerned with his own feelings, alert to the way in which as she pronounced the word, Candy's fingers, delicate and trembling, touched the corner of her mouth in an action quite at variance with the meaning of what she was saying, he caught no whiff of enlightenment. It was months before things assumed any order in his mind, and longer still before he realized how incomplete our subjective judgements of other people are bound to be. It took living in Italy to teach him how partial our appreciation is of the life that swirls about us; how these Romans whom he relished (in one case slept with) nevertheless lived a life that was not just foreign to him, but concealed, almost absolutely unknown. He sensed that feelings and thoughts, even when they rise to the surface and find expression in expansive gestures or verbal articulation, are still never more than shadowy and incompetent renderings of the feelings which stimulate that expression. It took living with foreigners to reveal to Dallas that we are always surrounded by foreigners; that everyone is foreign. (Even the fact that I seem to have come to the end of any feeling for Ann, that I have run through the whole labyrinth of marriage and find myself facing the opening marked 'Exit', doesn't mean that I understand my wife, even though in my accumulated dislike I label her 'shallow'.) 'The past is another country; they do things differently there,' wrote one of Dallas's then favourite novelists. 'Not just the past, my dear,' he scribbled in one of his Heffers notebooks; 'so also is the present.' And then, looking out of his attic window over the Campo dei Fiori towards the glimpsed roof-tops of the incomparable Palazzo Farnese and the tip of St Peter's dome, he noted 'And after all, in the end, there are so many moments when one is a foreigner even to oneself, conducting a lifelong discourse in a language one so imperfectly understands.'

Now, in the darkening kitchen, half-conscious of other undercurrents of feeling, he knew Candy's otherness, yet wanted to have her; not exactly to possess her, for he didn't think of the sexual act as a deed of possession, but rather as something which simultaneously denied and intensified that state of otherness. He also knew that if he couldn't have her—and the whole tenor of her conversation and the almost visible virgin armour she wore suggested she certainly wasn't up for grabs—he wanted a drink instead; a desire absent the last few days.

'Is that clock right?'

'A bit slow, I think.'

'What about a drink? They open at five. If the kids are out it would be a break for you.'

To his surprise she agreed. In the pub she asked for a half-pint of beer.

'Light or heavy?'

'Oh, light. I don't much like alcohol, but I don't mind beer, and I rather like white wine so long as it's dry. I like hock. Daddy drinks a lot of hock.'

'What does your father do?'

He welcomed the chance to broaden the conversation, divert it to channels less given to choking.

'He's a university lecturer. At St Andrews. Mediaeval English literature. Vague and civilized.'

'How do you come to be up here then?'

'Oh, didn't you know? I thought I had told you. Maggie's a cousin of mine. I spent a lot of time with her after my mother died—that was when I was twelve—Daddy not being frightfully well equipped to bring up a daughter. So it was natural to spend holidays here. Now it seems right to help with the kids. I don't know what she's going to do, she's got no money of her own, and her parents aren't what you'd call sympathetic. Her father's a bank manager.'

She was still vulnerable out of the manse, but less defensive. The pub was nearly empty. Dallas nodded and exchanged greetings with a couple of foresters he had met before who were the only other drinkers, and then he and Candy took their drinks to a little table by the dead fireplace.

'It's hell,' she said, 'for women in Maggie's position. Actually life's pretty fair hell for most women anyway. *Droit de seigneur* may have been abolished. You wouldn't think so to look at the way men behave. They think of us as chattels. Actually Fraser Donnelly's a hypocrite the way he talks, and it makes it worse, but not really any different that Lorna's such a super girl.'

'You're a feminist, are you?' Dallas said, using a word not then in fashion; he had come across it perhaps in Virginia Woolf.

'I believe it's a man's world, and women are treated rottenly.'

She didn't accompany the words with any light smile that might have made them acceptable.

Dallas said, 'Most of the girls I know get along all right.'

Then she smiled, briefly, as one who has been granted the argument.

'They're lucky then, but the fact is you probably haven't looked at them very hard. Also I imagine most of them are students. And Cambridge. And single. That all helps. It's when you get married that a woman has really had it. Look at

Maggie, look at Lorna Donnelly. They've nothing to call their own. They're kept slaves really, kept in their place by drudgery or drugs in the shape of household possessions. Hoovers are the opium of the housewife, new curtains too.'

They talked like this for some time, generalizing from a narrow experience that denied them any exact knowledge of how it is. And they grew apart without however feeling angry with the other. It was just that the different points of view acted as magnetic poles which they couldn't resist; the drift dissipated the febrile tension that had held them together. For Dallas Candy lost with each assured sentence that air of remoteness which, giving her mystery, had heightened her sexuality. Just as day dispels morning mist which, lingering round the branches of cherry trees, has given even a municipal park a strangely Romantic air, so this conversation brought Candy into full view: a narrow little girl, a bit of a prig. Dallas wasn't even sure that he didn't actually dislike her. She recalled one of his sharpest moments of sexual disillusion: he had travelled two bus-stops extra enraptured by the profile of a quattrocento Madonna; who had then opened her mouth and spoken in the flat, ugly accent of a Birmingham shopgirl.

And he could feel Candy's interest in him ebb. It wasn't any longer enough that she might have liked the way the hair fell over his left eye.

She made an excuse about the children's supper, and left, declining his half-hearted offer to see her back to the manse.

But then he found the picture she had presented to him as he looked through the manse gate sharper in his mind than her conversation, and saw her again, like Cinderella smoking Cadets in that shadowy kitchen, and remembered also how she had first appeared in the hall when he and Jimmy had carried the little minister in.

Who himself at that moment entered, cock-sparrow trim with a dancing light in his eye and the false confidence of a music-hall comic facing the Monday-night first house of a provincial tour. He was, he said, on his way to meet Fraser. 'But a wee fortification first.' They were off to a political meeting, a rally. Why didn't young Dallas come? Sparks would fly. He would learn something of the new Scotland.

'I'm still finding out about the old.'

'It's dying. Let it go. There's a new spirit abroad. There has to be. The old Scotland of the Kirk and the Edinburgh Establishment's stifled by cobwebs. Come with me and greet the new.'

It didn't appeal. Dallas was sure it was all nonsense. He'd read de Tocqueville after all. He knew the durability of a country's institutional fabric. 'What will you do about the Scottish Office?' he asked, only half joking. Gavin Gregory looked blank a moment. The question had no meaning for him. He moved on, and was supported by, the foam of ideas. He had no sense of the solid flesh of the Grant Buchanans; he had never met Uncle Hugh. And if you hadn't confronted that Scotland, then you were throwing your speeches into an east wind. And yet the minister's own father-in-law was a bank manager. What would the new Scotland do with bank managers?

'Of course we'll have to nationalize the banks.'

'That'll hardly affect the *fonctionnaires*.'

And what, he thought as he walked home, having declined the invitation to the meeting, but, as a gesture of good-will, having promised to be at Fraser's party, and what about people like me? What of the remnants of the landed gentry? A ridiculous question; just as well he hadn't asked it, even of a clown like wee Gavin. He had no land; the word gentleman was a social joke. And yet, and yet, for Dallas and a few others, it was still there. He felt himself to be different. He didn't, however he might pretend to Cambridge chums, belong to the aristocracy; yet even that wasn't quite absurd. His position wasn't so dissimilar. Noblesse, however petite, did oblige. Loyalties were confused. He was certainly Scottish. Apart from a French great-grandmother he had no ancestor who was anything else. The family didn't even have much tradition of Empire service to confuse matters by substituting a primary loyalty to the idea of Britain. Did it all come down to education and class awareness? For the fact was that, while he would have insisted to anyone that Scotland was an entity, yes a nation, he wasn't terribly impressed by the concept of nationality; and he couldn't take the idea of a Scottish state seriously. That was an old song, long ended, sold down the river. This detachment gave him the sense anyway to recognize that the solid element, the Uncle Hughs, wasn't and weren't going that way. It would take a revolution to displace Uncle Hugh, and not just Fraser's California-style import either.

Though undoubtedly Fraser was this far right: California would put some skates under the New Town of Edinburgh.

Would that leave anything behind?

Muzzy beer thoughts. He stumbled over a loose stone at the entrance to the avenue that led to Canaan. It was dark under the beeches and chestnut trees. At one point on the steep part of the hill the rhododendrons which grew all along the banks met over his head to form an archway. For some forty yards it was like walking through a cavern.

7

A slight figure extricated itself from the bucket seat of a small sports car. Rosemary Mickle advanced in leopard-skin coat.

'I was out driving. I often go driving when I'm fed up. Then I remembered this was where you said you lived.'

He didn't believe her. He knew why she had come. And though it flattered him and excited him, he trembled as one who had been marked down, deprived of choice.

He led her, not touching, over to the terrace. The silence didn't disturb her. But what could he say? Absurdly he thought of the two Russians on the Trans-Siberian. 'I come from Smolensk.' Steppes pass. 'I come from Vladivostock,' says the girl. Long Russian silence: 'I go to Omsk,' says the girl, forcing the pace. Towards evening he admits 'I go to Tomsk. Enough of this loff-making, take off your clothes.' Perhaps it wasn't the right moment; Rosemary didn't strike him as a girl to see a joke.

He gestured to the house, 'Rather a wreck, I'm afraid.'

Her fingers twisted the dead honeysuckle that wound itself on the terrace railing.

'Would you like a drink?' he said.

She shook her head, little white teeth pressed hard on her lip. Her hand groped under his shirt and played him, like a salmon to the shore. Fingers felt under his jeans, opened the button. His own unintended hands found their way under the fur. The two stumbled towards the house like drunken sailors home to their ship.

'It's a long way upstairs.'

Instead she drew him into the drawing-room, chill Edwardian necropolis, as if she had been there before—and yes, of course, she must have cased the joint. Let the leopard fall, stepped out of black dress, stretched out on bearskin rug before the marble chimney-piece and gilt mirror.

Later, panting and sweaty, 'Let's move upstairs.'

'All right,' she said, 'now,' and bit his shoulder.

'We could do with a drink,' he said, 'I'll get a bottle.'

'Don't get sentimental,' she said, when recovering they lay naked in his bed drinking brandy and ginger ale. 'It's too wet for words. I can't stand people who get sentimental. Did your wet pansy chum tell you I'm a whore? I bet he did. Queers always think a girl who likes sex is a whore.'

Jimmy had given him chapter and verse to substantiate the charge, but he let it pass. Instead he sipped brandy and fondled her breast.

'Why don't you come to the South of France with me?' she said.

'No money.'

'You don't need to worry about that.'

Curious thing was she didn't enjoy it. It was a grind. She was tense all the time. Going like the clappers but never giving, never really taking. That made it quite something fucking her, like nothing he had known before. It was something she had to have, but he didn't understand how she felt about it. And she hardly, once they were started, touched him willingly; she was absolutely on the take.

'I'm off this next week,' she said. 'Why don't you come? I

can't imagine you're not like me, bored to hell with this fucking country.'

Be my stud. It was an invitation he had never received before.

She shifted away from under his hand's grip. But the thin legs twined themselves again round his. The high floating commanding voice contrived a whine of appeal. Around them the huge empty house crouched. There was no sound but the occasional creak of timber. Dallas could see her on the terrace of a smart bar, a smartish bar, in tight white trousers and unbuttoned shirt, scanning the street below with her china eyes that never stayed still.

'It's difficult,' he said, 'I don't know. I'm in the middle of doing something. I've all sorts of arrangements to make.'

'Don't be wet,' she said. 'There's nothing keeping you. I'm sure there isn't.'

She moved her knee against his thigh.

'Don't be wet,' she said again, and he hadn't the sense not to tell her about the 'novel'.

'Oh Christ. Another fucking phoney. How wet can you get? Don't you see all that stuff's dead? It's nothing but conceit, like Fraser Donnelly's politics. It's an ego-trip. Daddy's politics I can live with, they're just graft and the necessary organization, but this sort of muck, this Romantic nonsense of spouting things that don't matter a whore's curse to anyone, that makes me sick. You know nothing about fucking nothing. You're a baby.'

She turned away, and buried her face in her crossed forearms. In a little she was asleep. Not a calm sleep. She stayed tense; occasionally muttered; once swore loudly; all the time Dallas felt the anger in the sleeping figure. He himself remained wakeful, thinking of the strangeness of his situation, in bed, not sleeping, with a woman he didn't care for, who had annexed him. A wind got up, blowing branches against a window. The owl called, faint in the distance, its cry borne seawards by the breeze. Once he laid his hand on Rosemary's shoulder, but she twitched, dislodging the light touch. At last he drifted into sleep heavy with dreams.

They woke to a grey world. Wind scudded clouds past the

bedroom window. Gouts of rain splashed it. Trees creaked. Rosemary had woken first. Dallas came to in an empty bed. For a moment what had happened refused to disengage itself from dreams. Then he heard footsteps and got up, putting on a dressing-gown. Rosemary was standing by the nursery window, smoking a cigarette. She was wearing jeans and a sweater which she must have fetched from her car. Had she made arrangements for a prolonged stay?

'Tea or coffee?' he said.

'I made tea.'

They remarked on the weather, politely, like guests unknown to each other meeting in the breakfast room of a small country hotel. Things were changing between them. That first encounter in the suburban mansion had been of the flesh alone. True, the dislike Dallas had felt before they went to bed had complicated things a bit; she was from the first something more than an anonymous bottle-party lay. Then, what Jimmy had told him had quickened his interest, against his will. She had come, unbidden, in dreams, taking monstrous shapes not very different from those she had assumed last night. Now—was it the mere fact of having had her sleeping beside him, so giving him some notion of the garrisoned ramparts she held about her?—something of responsibility corrupted his dislike. He might call her a whore; he couldn't think of her like that. What did she feel about him?

But it was of herself she talked. She let slip, unprompted, snatches of autobiography, of what—to use the term loosely —he had to call philosophy. It wasn't attractive what she said. She picked with her thumbnail at the tip of her left index finger where the skin was red, raw and torn away, as if by rats.

'I don't know what lies you've been told about me,' she said. 'People here love to tell lies.'

It was her refrain. The absurd voice still floated in plummy assurance, but it could not deceive. No lies could be as brutal as the truth she lived with. She was a woman who could not answer the question: 'What am I for?'

'You're bound to have heard about my first marriage. They can't forget that, it was the juiciest piece of scandal they'd had for years. It decided them all I was really awful. Derek worked in the fish market you see and I was just turned sixteen. It would have had a chance if they had been ready to give us one. I really loved Derek . . .'

She held a cold tea-cup against her cheek, rehearsing the weary line, 'I really loved Derek'; a Forties line, Hollywood, a Lana Turner movie; it carried with it, on great wafts of perfumed sincerity, all the desperate conviction of Lana Turner.

'I really loved Derek. But he was an innocent. We were both innocents. He couldn't take the complications. They gave him a glimpse of a world he had never imagined existing. I couldn't really blame him when in the end he behaved like a rat and not like a man. Or maybe most men are rats. In my experience they are.'

Her speech had the rhythm of a tired monologue; a running complaint articulated, like a gramophone playing a torch ballad in an empty house. She told him of the school she had been sent to.

'They couldn't stand me there. They looked down on me. They were frightfully county and though Daddy calls himself a colonel they soon found out it was just a wartime commission, in the RASC too, and that he was really just an Aberdeen businessman. His cars were always too flashy, that's what gave it away. It was hell. I nearly ran away, often, but I wasn't going to do that. I wasn't going to let them beat me. That's why I have this absurd voice.'

It gave Dallas a little stab of renewed desire, that she recognized the absurdity of her voice.

'That's where I learned it's eat or be eaten. I set myself to make a meal of them. And I did. Do you know I go to South Africa every winter? You could come on from the South of France with me. I feel at home there. Here it's all make-believe and hypocrisy.'

8

'It's grand you've come. And you've come thegither.' Fraser
Donnelly's piggy eyes glinted. He enveloped Rosemary in a
bear-hug, clapped Dallas too hard on the back. 'This is Liberty
Hall. Booze on the sideboard. I'd say to you,' he dug Dallas in
the ribs, 'birds in the hay, but you're well armed already.' He
brought his mouth to Rosemary's ear and nuzzled her. She
drew back, like a startled pony, but he held to her elbow and
whispered.

The cottage was really a farmhouse, of a style common in
the North-East: L-shaped, two-storeyed with bow windows
jutting out from a sloping roof. A long single-track road approached it, running up a side glen from the junction where
the main valley diverged towards the Mounth. A mile up the
road, which was unfenced, with passing places every few
hundred yards, the farm-track, pitted with wide, sometimes
deep, puddle-holes, and made awkward where rains had
swept away protective soil to reveal jutting stones, ran by a
burnside. The house stood half-way up a hill facing north.
Rowan trees grew in the garden. The dykes were broken
down by time, neglect, straying sheep. The garden itself had
reverted to couch grass and weeds. A few ragged persistent
gooseberry bushes survived among the nettles, thistles and
briars. At the back of the house the pigsty's roof had fallen in.

Rain still fell on a drenching diagonal as they approached.
Rosemary's will had prevailed. They were together in her red
T R 3. Dallas's suggestion that it might be better, 'more convenient' if each took their own car had produced a sniff and
'of course, if you're ashamed to arrive with me . . .'

Wind arched silver birches that straggled by the burnside.
Stream gurgled, brimfull, with sand-coloured speed. Wind
swirled rainy mist across the braeside. The yard formed by

93

three sides of the abandoned steading incongruously housed Fraser's Jaguar, an old Bentley, an Austin-Healey Sprite, assorted family saloons as well as the two Land-Rovers that alone seemed to belong. Dallas almost stepped in a wide yellow puddle as he disengaged himself from the little car. Faint residual whiffs of dung hung round the abandoned midden. Light and music summoned them to the house.

Fraser said, 'Well, Rosie, what do you think of it?'

Dallas was glad he hadn't been asked. It was got up as a Hollywood set. But the trouble was you could walk round it. Elvis Presley thudded through, soared over, the sound of the party breaking ice.

Rosemary didn't answer.

Fraser said, 'Your dad's no' here yet. He's bringing the gang wi' him. And, you'll never credit it, the Tory candidate for the county, an advocate loon from Edinburgh. We'll hae to see that we compromise him, eh? Maybe Dallas here'll ken him, wi' his smart Embro connections that the wee minister was telling me of. Mansie Niven's the name. They say he's a bright chiel, for a Tory. So maybe we'll no' bother compromising him, just convert him, eh? But you must be dry as stookies. Jimmy loon, we could a' do wi' a drink here.'

Dallas indeed knew Mansie Niven, though Mansie was five years the older. They had been at prep school together, Mansir for one term—memorable for its whimsical mixture of petting and persecution—his dormitory captain. For a few of those childhood weeks that so easily challenge notions of eternity, he was the most important person in Dallas's life. They met again more recently in Edinburgh, at the Buchanans. Mansie, reading for the Bar, had been taken up by Dallas's great-aunt Isobel, relict of a Senator of the College of Justice. Dallas responded again to Mansie's style: flash, impudent, self-consciously superior to his surroundings. But that was before Cambridge.

'I've a surprise for you too, Rosie,' Fraser said. 'Just you wait and see what it is.'

Dallas felt Rosemary stiffen.

'You know surprises bore me,' she said. 'I don't like them. You might remember that.'

She held on to Dallas, daring him to deny they were a couple. When Jimmy, who had been busy tending others, at last armed them with drinks, Rosemary looked straight through him, but kept hold of Dallas. Jimmy smiled, tentative, half-shy; commiseration and amusement in the concealed half of his expression. 'She laid you, didn't she?' he had said. Well, he was right; Dallas was well and truly laid, laid out in fact.

'We'll have a chat later,' Jimmy said, 'I'm rushed off my feet. Fraser should have hired bar staff. He likes to say he likes to keep it in the family. Grand, it leaves me the domestic drudge. See you by-and-by.'

'Christ, what a creep,' Rosemary said, 'I can't stand these creeping Jesus queers. Here's a sparrow for your cat, can I polish your arse, please sir.'

Her jaw hung slack with discontent. Dallas saw no reason to defend Jimmy. He said, 'Do you want to dance?'

'Christ no.'

She didn't want to sit down either, nor to drink, for she stood there, silent, islanded, clawed on to Dallas as if her arm was a causeway that alone linked her to the mainland where other people lived; and she didn't touch what was in her glass. She looked on the coming and going around them with a resentment that chastened Dallas; it was perhaps the expression of a corrupted Puritanism. The big too-blonde woman came up to them, opening the red gash of her decorated smile to reveal big horsy teeth.

'Aye, aye, Rosie, cradle-snatching now, is it?'

Rosemary looked over the woman's right shoulder, not offering any reply. A man's arm crept round the woman's waist and drew her away.

Rosemary said, in that awful carrying voice, 'You may think I'm a bitch but I'm a saint compared to that cow.'

'Don't be silly,' Dallas said, 'why should I think that?'

She pulled her lower lip back with her tooth.

'I told you, most people do,' she said.

'Anyway,' he said, 'I've met her before and I know she's ghastly.'

'You don't know much though, do you?' she said.

The lip, gnawed by the tooth, turned white. Her eyes flickered over the throng that swirled round them. Why on earth had she insisted on coming? It wasn't as if he had had to persuade her.

He now found himself pushed back with his shoulders touching the wall. There was nothing to say to Rosemary, here, at a party. Was she waiting for something particular to happen? Her brooding sulkiness had a more than usually explosive quality. Was it the threat of Fraser's surprise? Then Dallas saw Candy across the room, and waved; but she hadn't spotted him. He was amazed that she was there; she would hardly have come with Gavin Gregory surely.

Rosemary went even more rigid; he wouldn't have thought it possible. She wasn't about to have a fit of some kind, was she?

'Christ, no,' she said, 'oh the bastard.'

Fraser was pushing his way through the crowd, more easily than most would have managed. Indeed as he got into the middle of the room the crowd parted, like the Red Sea letting the children of Israel cross out of Egypt. He was leading a man who might have been his younger brother, with the same heavy frame, the same reddish sandy hair going grey at the sides and a bit thin at the front, the same flushed face with the big, slack, greedy mouth and the squashed too-small nose. Only the eyes were different. Where Fraser's were small, darting, alive and piggy, this man's were glazed pale blue, empty, uncomprehending.

'Here's the surprise I promised, Rosie. What do you think of it?'

'Hi Rosie. Longtime.' The man lurched forward to kiss her. She bent her head back and away so that the kiss, aimed for the mouth, landed awkwardly on the line of her uptilted jaw.

'What ditch did you dredge this up from?' Her voice floated more absurdly than ever. 'I thought we had an agreement. I thought you were well paid to keep out of my life . . .'

'Oh Rosie, it was a hell of a long time ago.'

American overlaid the indigenous accent. He put out a hand, which drew attention to its size by the uncertainty of the gesture. He didn't look good and he was sweating heavily.

'Och there's been a lot of water under the bridge,' Fraser said. 'You ought to let bygones be bygones, Rosie. It's no right to keep up grudges. You're a free girl, you ken. Accept it and be grateful. I met Derek here in a hotel I'd stopped in the other day. I thought there was something familiar about his face and then we got talking. You ken what a friendly soul I aye am. And then of course we got acquaint and he asked if I ever saw you. Och you don't need to fash yoursel', Rosie, he's been married and divorced since your time. He's got five bairns. Show her the photie of your bairns, Derek loon.'

She turned to Dallas, 'I told you about this creep. He ran out on me. It's perfect cheek bringing the creature here, Fraser. You know that jolly well. You know Daddy paid him and paid him well to keep out of my life. He hurt me and ran. Get him the fucking hell away from me, understand.'

Her voice shrilled on the last instruction. Dallas was relieved to see that nobody appeared to notice. Fraser just smiled, like a man who has backed the winner, brought off a happy effect. As for the oaf Derek, he stood bemused, like a steer suddenly finding itself in the middle of the bull-ring with the sun's light blinding and the crowd screaming.

'Och Rosie,' Fraser said. 'It's time you stopped playing this money game. You canna hide behind a fortification of pound notes. You and Derek werena to blame, either of you, face up to it. The pair of you was fucked up by bourgeois convention and bourgeois morality. You were baith victims. Christ, Rosie, you ken that fine yoursel'.'

Dallas, embarrassed, felt for the man Derek. Perhaps he had come here hoping for a sentimental reunion. If so, either he could never have known his ex-wife very well, or she had changed. Which was of course probable. It must have been a dozen years ago, or more. Now, as attention was distracted from him, while Fraser and Rosemary argued, he was acting on Fraser's suggestion and had pulled a wallet from his breast pocket. His big fingers, thick and awkward as Corona cigars, fumbled the job of extracting a photograph. At last he got it out, pushed it towards Dallas.

'My kids. There's five of them like. Marty and Jason, they're the twins. Abe and Marilyn. The wee girl's Rosie.

Bonnie, that's their mother, doesn't know my first wife was called Rosie, see. I forced the name on her, what do you think of that?'

He spoke like a man imparting a bar-stool confidence, who didn't look for an answer. Then he withdrew the snapshot, which had shown a bunch of what Dallas took to be pretty standard American kids, complete with baseball caps and T-shirts, and stood holding it limply in his paw, his lips moving soundlessly.

Meanwhile Fraser had somehow carried his point. Rosemary was at least ready to speak to her ex-husband.

'You've let yourself go to seed, Derek. You're at least two stones overweight. No, I don't want to see your brats. They'll be as ghastly as children always are. You ought to take yourself in hand though.'

'Well, Rosie, you haven't changed. You were for ever telling me what was good for me, even when you were just a kid yourself.'

'Don't get sentimental.' She gripped Dallas harder, as if he might take the opportunity offered by this reunion to slip away. 'You won't believe it,' she said to him, 'but this thing was beautiful once. An athlete with red-gold hair. What a laugh.' She snatched the photograph from Derek. 'That one,' she said, 'is going to look a bit like the way he did.'

'Aye aye,' Fraser said, 'he needs a woman, that's what it is.'

'Nobody need think it'll be me again.'

She broke free, through the crowd, out of the room. The men exchanged glances.

'Should I . . .' Dallas started.

Fraser grabbed his arm.

'Take a rest, he said. 'Now, Derek, now's the hour. Awa after her, loon.'

Derek, with a heavy nod, his eyes bemused, something unconvinced in his slow deliberation, obeyed. Perhaps he was one of those who would always obey.

'It'll no' harm you,' Fraser said, 'to be free of Rosie a wee while. I can see her claw marks on your shoulder. She's been eating you up, eh? She's a grand girl, whiles, but the whiles dinna come awfy affen. And do you ken the reason why? She

98

hates what she's doing, that's why. There's nae release in it for her. She doesna appreciate what freedom is. She's bound and blinkered in her wee bourgeois ghetto that offers nae mair glimpse o' the sky than a Glasgow close in a weet December.'

He steered Dallas to a sofa in the corner of the room. 'What way did you no' come to our meeting the other night? You should come, you're the sort of loon the party needs.' Dallas disclaimed interest; Fraser brushed his words aside. 'Oh aye, it's natural you should be a Tory. You hinna thought about it, that's all.' Class was a determinant of political affiliation, but only while you stayed passive, unreflective. You had to get beyond it, 'transcend it'—he actually used that expression. For it was, Dallas must see, all that class business that bound Scots to the framework of British politics. 'A class-based system demands class-based political parties.' That was obvious. 'But we've no call to be that way in Scotland. Our tradition is a democratic one. We'd an educational system that strove to cultivate the democratic intellect . . .' That being so, the politics of the imperial-British state were as unnatural and irrelevant as a strait-jacket. 'They really are a strait-jacket, you ken. They dinna serve our interests or satisfy our natures.'

He had, Dallas was surprised to realize, thought a bit for himself. A good deal of what he said was doubtless regurgitated. Well, we all spewed out our reading. But there was something of his own here too.

'Take Rosie again.' Fraser drummed his fingers on Dallas's knee. 'She's neurotic of course, you'll have found that out for yourself, eh loon, but she's no' just that. Do you ken what she is: she's a fucking paradigm of the imperial-British connection and what it engenders. Aye, that's what she is. Christ, she's a fornicating civil war. Her nature and instincts tug her one way, to freedom, self-expression, democracy, but a' her notions of "good form"'—he screwed up his mouth to pronounce the phrase with a prissy la-di-dah expression that conjured up a whole world of tea-rooms and ladies in monstrous hats—'fuck her up.'

Her case—didn't Dallas see?—supported his argument for a thorough-going Revolution. 'It's no' just a matter of adjusting the constitutional question. That would solve nothing. It wouldna necessarily release our energies. That's where I part company from mony in the Party. For you see, Dallas, a' the agencies o' traditional power in Scotland are part of the same con-game to deny the people of Scotland the opportunity to realize themselves. The Kirk, the Law, the Schools, they're a' as socially repressive as the British class system—they're part o' it indeed—and they a' lead to the alienation of the individual. You'll have thought of these things yourself maybe —that alienation's the great question o' our times—but you'll have thought they don't concern you. You're free of them a'. But are you really free? Is naebody pressing you, to tak ane instance, to mak a career for yourself? A respectable career. Mak you into a wee Edinburgh advocate for instance?'

But what, Dallas wondered, about Power? Where did that come into Fraser's scheme of things? Presumably he wasn't an Anarchist?

The piggy eyes gleamed. He was enjoying himself; the call to display mental energy was important to him. Energy and ingenuity; he revealed a powerful sinuous mind, untrained certainly, but you could over-value intellectual training. Dallas was caught up; for the moment anyway; he responded to the vitality—it was more than an expression of personality. Though the personality flourished, no doubt about that: the man was a Leader.

'Anarchism's attractive, oh aye, of course it is. But the trouble is everything it leaves out. It has no room for the drive to power, you've put your finger on it, laddie, and no room for the dark side o' our nature, the side that's attuned'—he took a long swallow of his whisky, flicked his tongue over his lips—'to the old pagan gods. And so it's no' enough, for we can't deny them without being false to our blood.' He swallowed again, pressed Dallas's knee. 'But listen, boyo, I dinna want you to think that I'm just into what they ca' permissiveness. No fear. By itself that's just another form of social repression. After a', that's what Rosie's caught up in. Na, na, *Playboy* by itself is just lined up to replace the Bible as the opium of the people. You have to dig deeper than that. It's a matter o' the synthesis o' the personality, the release o' the buried forces of nature.' He paused, repeated the phrase; the party swirled round then, dancing like Israelites about the Golden Calf. 'That's what we're crying out for. And to go back, the establishment o' a Scottish State free o' a' the worn-out claptrap o' the imperial-British anachronism's no' but the necessary first step. These are deep words for a party, Dallas. And dry ones. We'll hae a talk about it another time.'

He heaved himself off the arm of the sofa, running his hand through Dallas's hair; then inclined his mouth to the boy's ear.

'Did you see yon quine from the manse is here? Is that no' a triumph for me?'

He swaggered through the crowd, bestowing a word like a benison to subject-guests, a man radiating the idea that the world was going his way. Dallas had never met anyone so determined to take life by the throat and thrust it where he wished. In one sense of course this party was ordinary enough: a crowd of admittedly disparate men and women drinking too much, dancing a bit, doubtless upstairs in the bedrooms fucking a bit. He had attended similar affairs in London; it went a bit further than Cambridge, only to be expected. Yet, in another way . . . he felt a hand on his shoulder. He looked up into a thin yellow old face.

'I'm delighted to encounter you,' it said. A reptilian old man, whom Dallas had never seen, like the Sutherland portrait of Maugham, eased himself on to the sofa.

'The last time I saw you you were screaming at a minister —your christening of course—and now I see you in deep colloquy with our dangerous host, and you clearly know him and haven't the faintest notion who I am?'

Little black eyes twinkled. Dallas was at once the nice-mannered public schoolboy dealing with decrepit don routine: 'I'm sorry, sir, afraid not, sir, sure I should, sir . . .' and such-like inanities.

'You could call me Great-Uncle Ebenezer, but I'd much rather you didn't. But I see that suggestion conveys nothing to you either.'

'I'm sorry sir . . .'

'I was married to your great-aunt Annie, of whom you may have heard. She was killed in the London blitz, poor Annie, having determined from pure curiosity to see the effects of bombing at close quarters. Her sisters blamed me for not controlling her. They little knew their Annie. So they removed their business from my hands—I was a lawyer—and handed family affairs over to that stick Hugh Buchanan. A wretched piece of work, Hugh, as nutritious as yesterday's Melba toast.'

Dallas laughed, 'He's my guardian, too.'

'Of course he is . . . And they tell me you are actually living at Canaan?'

'For the summer anyway.'

'How charming. The parties your grandmother used to have there, how they used to astonish and infuriate the oafs of the county. And now there you are. A young man on the threshold of life. What a rare and Victorian position. If this were a Trollope novel we would all be scheming for you to marry well. Canaan needs a rich wife. But I shan't ask you about your intentions. Either you don't know, and the question would bore and irritate you. Or you do, and I'm afraid the answer would bore me. Instead, let me ask you what you make of all this?'

'Well . . .'

'You're right. Rum, very rum, isn't it. I've known Fraser a long time. His father was a client of mine. Not, you understand, one of my respectable ones. But I always had a weakness for the louche. It added to your great-aunt's distrust. Your uncle Hugh of course has no criminal practice. So I knew Fraser from when he was a boy. Such energy, even then. I helped keep him out of a Borstal, you know. Something about stripping lead from church roofs. And then I took him in hand, helped him form his first company. He's come a long way since then, wouldn't you say? He was a remarkable and refreshing young man, though. I don't know that you could call him refreshing now, could you? Wouldn't you say, dear boy, there was something just a bit gamey about it all?'

He floated long fingers as he talked. His manner had perhaps been adopted—oh, half a century ago, or more—as a means of warding off any assumption of intimacy; now it encouraged just that relationship. The fact was that exquisite manners of this sort now seemed theatrically confidential.

'But perhaps you know few people here? Let me be your Virgil and lead you by the hand through the Inferno that Fraser has called into being. Do you see that lean lady in purple, with teeth like a garden rake? That, dear boy, is the Countess of Aplin. Yes, the lady whose morals, according to Lord Kerr's judgement, were of a depravity that would have made the sisters of Gomorrah blench. You would think that might have sunk her. It would have done so when I was young. But now, not a bit of it. Only the other week I saw her opening a charity bazaar in Edinburgh, and the young man with whom she is dancing is an ornament of the Edinburgh financial establishment. Delightfully rum, eh? It's a little coup for Fraser to have such people here, or would be if he cared for that side of life.'

'Oh I should think he does care, in an oblique sort of way perhaps.'

'My dear boy, you are absolutely right. You must have some penetration. I wonder who on earth you get it from. It's not a quality I associate with any of your family, not even your dear grandmother, charming though she has always been.'

The old man—Dallas wondered just how old he was—fell silent, his promise to play Virgil forgotten. Dallas considered whether he could, with decency, move on. This was hardly the most exhilarating of company. Jimmy came round, in his Ganymede role. Ebenezer gave a small sniff of disdain as he held out his glass; his eye had caught Jimmy's glance and measured its meaning. Dallas watched Candy across the room talking to a slim girl, pale, with tired eyes, streaked hair and something of nervous refinement in her manner.

Ebenezer plucked at his sleeve. 'I feel myself a shade here, already taken passage with Charon. All the same, I still feel a disinterested social curiosity, and I find myself asking: is there anything new here? Well, is there, dear boy?'

'It's difficult for me to say.'

Candy had leant forward and, with very delicate precision, was extracting something from the pale girl's eye. A swell of sensuality filled him; he looked around to see if Rosemary had returned; saw instead her father enter, at the head of a troupe, conspicuous among whom was Mansie Niven, in flowered-silk waistcoat, deep-purple in background with Chinese motifs; and also—but why?—his cousin Grant, regularly attired in blazer and striped tie.

'Because you have no point of comparison, you mean?'

'I suppose so, yes.'

'And yet your reading must suggest some.'

'Probably misleading, wouldn't you say.'

'Because we are indeed in a situation, a society, where everything is permitted.'

'Up to a point.'

'Interesting.'

Dallas felt he wasn't doing very well. 'After all,' he floundered, 'in the Western world anyway, we've solved our economic problems. We've abolished famine and poverty. No one's ever done that before. And—which is rare enough for a whole society—we've dispensed with God. And we've exploded the after-life. All that, put together, must make a difference.'

'And progress? Do you believe in progress?'

'Progress, not necessarily, change yes.'

Dallas was surprised by the ping-pong of the conversation. But there was no reason why this aged lawyer shouldn't conduct it like a good don giving a supervision. And the family link was so feeble as to be quite uninhibitory.

Ebenezer said, 'Fantasies of freedom always involve wilful blindness and self-deception. Progress likewise. That doesn't change. We are about to be interrupted. I should like to talk to you again.'

The interruption was a large square-faced woman in a strikingly striped frock, but it was old Ebenezer she wanted to speak to, not Dallas; he had been deceived for the first moments because of the way she squinted. Soon the woman —what on earth was she doing at a party like this?—was launched on a long account of family matters, retailed in a monotoned whine. Dallas took the opportunity to slip away.

For a moment in the middle of the room he was detached from it all. Rosemary and Derek had not reappeared. Were they engaged in recrimination or reunion? Everyone around him seemed fully occupied. Voices were rising; the party's tide swooping up the beach. Dallas didn't belong; he was a piece of driftwood above the water mark. And he had suddenly lost all powers of observation. He didn't want to be there, but without a car there was no means of escape. He forced his way through the mob towards the window, but it was now almost dark outside. He could discern only the swaying shapes of trees. There were no lights to be seen except those reflected from the house.

His unbearably hollow sensation was not new. He remembered his first evening in Cambridge, how he had sat on a hard settee in a bare and cold attic room, dark grey in Fenland October gloom, reading College and University Regulations, and feeling that he should never have come there; the place was wholly alien to him, the world quite out of sympathy. It wasn't pain he experienced; it was as if everything was withdrawing from him. How had that evening ended?

He knew how he had killed the feeling next time he experienced it. That had been in Rome a year ago. He had gone there to meet Judy who had been doing a stint as au pair with an Italian family. Quite ignorant of the city, he asked Guy, his cosmopolitan mentor, where he should arrange to meet her. ' "Bricktops" in the Via Veneto,' Guy replied at once, though he hadn't actually been in Rome since he was a child. Well, 'Bricktops' no longer existed. Dallas even now wasn't sure if there had ever been a Rome branch of the famous Paris Bar. He had spent hours looking for it, then more hours trying to telephone Judy from the American Bar of the Excelsior Hotel. When, eventually, someone had answered, her Italian had been far too rapid for him to understand. He had walked disconsolately along Via Sistina, arriving at Trinita dei Monti just as the sun set, the black horses on the top of the Victor Emmanuel monument rampant and, in that unique moment, beautiful against the rose-pink and yellow of the sky; it was as if the pit of his stomach had been removed. He belonged nowhere, had no refuge. In a bar he bought a bottle of whisky and fled to his mean *pensione* and lay in bed drinking the whisky and reading Graham Greene's *The Ministry of Fear*.

Dallas was not sensitive to other people. It never occurred to him to ask whether this feeling was common. And would it have mattered if he had been assured that it is common to have moments when we feel strangers here, when we are afflicted by sudden glimpses of impermanence, of our fleeting passage, and are horrified to realize that the world which normally we perceive as arranged for our private enjoyment goes past, indifferent to what we feel, indifferent to our existence?

A girl's voice said, 'You look out of things.'

It was the pale girl Candy had been speaking to.

'I was for a moment.'

'You looked as if you were hearing footsteps on your grave, or whatever the expression is.'

As an opening gambit it wasn't bad, but it didn't lead naturally into the middle game. For a moment neither could find a follow-up.

'I noticed you speaking with Candy,' he said, 'I was surprised to see her here.'

'I asked her to come.'

'I didn't think it was her style of thing.'

'It's not mine either. That's why I asked her. I wouldn't have come otherwise, whatever my husband said, however much he insisted.'

Her voice was so quiet that Dallas had to reach close to her to catch what she said against the party chatter and the music.

'I only came to speak to you because Candy said you were nice and then I thought you looked as if you didn't belong. You don't belong, do you?'

This was flattery; Dallas smiled and said nothing.

'So I thought I'd come and say hello.'

'Hello. And you were quite right about the footsteps. You must be psychic.'

'No, I'm not. Not at all. I can't read the future at all. I've difficulty enough working out the present. Do you believe you can know what's going to happen?'

'It's well authenticated,' Dallas said. 'For myself, on the whole I prefer to take things as they come. *Carpe diem*, gather ye rosebuds, that sort of style. I don't even know your name.'

'It's Lorna Donnelly. I know yours.'

He was taken aback. He had looked for something downtrodden, a bit of a poor thing, for, ignorant as he was of marriage, he had only stereotypes to apply. Lorna Donnelly jolted him. He hadn't admittedly speculated much, but this pale girl with her air of distinction didn't square with his picture of how the wife of a man like Fraser Donnelly would present herself to a world that must eye her with pity or mockery; it didn't click with Jimmy's version of the wee girl from a back close in Aberdeen consoled for her husband's carrying-on by her fitted kitchen and charge accounts at the local stores. She must have done a lot of work on her voice.

'Candy's a nice girl, isn't she?

'I don't know what I'd do without her.'

Who at that moment joined them carrying two glasses of white wine, one of which she gave to Lorna.

'Your ears should be red, Candy, I've been telling Dallas I don't know what I'd do without you.'

'I was shocked to see you here,' Dallas said, 'but Lorna says you came to support her.'

'Someone has to,' Candy said, and blushed. Lorna slipped her arm round her shoulders.

'It's nice to have someone playing on my side,' she said. 'At last.'

That moment a sharper Dallas might have seen the shape of things through a gap in the curtain of time. But it is so often only in retrospect that we recognize what we have seen; and Dallas was then like a man walking down a meaningless street who half-observes a car stop and the driver wind down the window to speak to a little boy or girl. He thinks nothing of it. The exchange is friendly and natural. Even when the child gets into the car and it drives off he only thinks—if indeed he thinks of the incident at all—that the man is family, or friend of the family. More likely, he hardly notices what has happened. It doesn't impinge on his consciousness. He is occupied with his own affairs, with the girl he is going to meet, or his golf swing; or with nothing at all really. It is only later when there is news of a child missing that a faint memory stirs; he wonders if he should report it. But even then, probably, he has seen nothing. He couldn't describe the child, which might not even be the same one, or the man, and he doesn't even know if the car was a Ford or what.

So now, Dallas, seeing them stand like doubles partners

being photographed after winning a tennis tournament, thought only they were nice girls, a little dull maybe, fastidious in a way that separated them from the general tone of the party.

'Someone has to,' Candy said again, and smiled at Lorna. Even then, Dallas caught nothing of her *contra mundum* spirit.

Two hours later he was on the way to being drunk. He had danced once with Lorna and twice with Candy. Holding Lorna was like holding music in his arms. Candy danced with the stiff-legged deliberation of a girl sent under protest to a dancing class. Then, between the loo and the sideboard, Dallas lost them. He searched for a bit, concluded that Lorna must all at once have had enough, felt her obligations to Fraser sufficiently discharged. They might at least have said good-bye. It was then he started drinking faster.

Rosemary had not reappeared. He pictured her heading with the lout Derek in the sports car to a low hotel, sitting, inviting his advances, in a saloon bar, twisting those thin legs round his gross beefiness in the stale air of a hotel room smelling of dry-rot; he shuddered. He fell into conversation with three or four people he didn't know, and drifted off again, aware of a curiosity that once bordered on contempt. He watched Alick Duguid on a sofa with the Countess of Aplin. She was sitting bolt upright and talking hard while Alick lay back, his lips closed on a fat cigar, his expression yielding nothing. Once he leaned forward, tapped her very precisely on the leg just above the knee, shook his head, and expelled smoke. Then he resumed his former pose, the cigar wedged between fat lips, eyes narrowed almost shut. She went on talking, but was now pressing herself against his shoulder, fingers twisting themselves in his hair.

'This is a pretty odd business if you ask me.' An odd business? Dallas turned to find, nudging his elbow, his cousin Grant; well, any business save Business was odd for him. Still, this time his judgement couldn't be quite denied . . .

'Ah Grant, saw you come in. There's a complex message in that tableau. Orchardson would have painted it superbly.'

'Don't know what you mean. It's all a bit fishy, if you ask

me. I came because Colonel Mickle urged me to. Didn't want to offend him. All the same, there are limits. That chap on the sofa. He's a Red, you know. Someone said he was actually a Communist.'

'But don't you see, we must have Communists at our parties.' Mansie Niven's face, never entirely without simian resemblances, twisted with impure monkey glee. 'Dallas —heavenly to see you, dear boy—and I realize that, even if you don't. Face up to it, Grant, you're quite out of your element here. Your sort of party is one where everyone wears the same tie and the same dreary suit. Or blazer even. But, don't you know, the days of the bourgeois ghetto are numbered. They have been weighed in the balance and found wanting. Mind you, Dallas, it's easy to exaggerate the significance of that tableau. I do so agree by the way, pure Orchardson, quite my favourite painter these days. But that sort of scene isn't new—as indeed the fact that we recognize it as an Orchardson proves. We've always had women like dear Cynthia Aplin. And thank God for them. Read your Victorian novelists. Read Thackeray. Between the lines of course. It's all there. Nothing changes. That's why I'm a Tory. My convictions are rooted in the eternal recurrence of human types and human situations. There is nothing new under the sun.'

He took a big, perhaps celebratory or confirmatory, swig of whisky.

'It's a great social work, darlings, Cynthia's, every bit as invaluable a service as those offered by her commoner sisters who do it for cash. She is engaged on a great and beneficent work. The corruption of the barbarians. What to do with the class enemy? You, Grant, in your oafish Edinburgh way, would try to freeze them out. Can't be did, ducky, not now it can't. More subtle souls like our dear Cynthia and Dallas and myself know that the thing to do is'—he dropped his voice to the whisper of a villain in melodrama or a horror movie— 'to seduce them. Bread and circuses for the People, sex, brandy and cigars for their champions. That's what I understand by democracy. Careers open to all sorts of talents. Pliability's the name of the game. I'm sure this naughty boy understands that,' he stretched out an arm and caught Jimmy who was passing with a bottle of Johnny Walker Black Label, 'come on, ducky, you've been playing Ganymede long enough. Sit down beside us, with the whisky, natch, and join in the fun. You agree about pliability, don't you? What a pretty chain you're wearing.' He drew Jimmy on to the sofa. 'You have been working hard. You're sweating. Or do you merely glow?'

'Oh, I glow all right,' Jimmy said.

'I'm sure you do. Of course, children, I know the argument can be put into reverse. They always can, can't they? The notion is that you can destroy the Establishment by penetrating it, the Trojan Horse syndrome. Don't you believe it, angels. The Establishment is endlessly resilient. It sucks in fiery pieces like that red-head, and sucks them off.'

Mansie's eyes sought the ceiling. His hand lay, with the negligent authority of a hand in a Renaissance painting (Titian or Veronese) on Jimmy's leg.

'It's magic,' he said. 'We preserve by corruption. I'm serious, you know. Society—I mean civil society as understood by Hobbes or Burke or the great Oakeshott (whom God preserve)—is a serious business. Anarchy lurks round the corner; the beast may stumble but waits to be born. Now, a hundred years back, in the Victorian noonday, the notion, not put forward only for public consumption but really believed in, was that you had to defend society and the social order by setting standards. High moral standards capable of being justified by reason as well as the appeal to divine authority that had ordained the rich man in his castle, poor man at gate, road-show. It won't work that way now. No fear, my children. Post-Freud we all recognize the power of the irrational. Primitive instinct, attraction of violence and destruction. Post-the Christian order—and anyone who doesn't realize we're post that needs his tiny wits examined—the appeal of the Millennium transported to the here and now. So, I repeat the only way to keep the barbarians from storming the citadel, is to invite them in. If you can't beat them, invite them to join you. And that means corruption, lovely unprincipled foetid corruption.'

Grant said, 'You can't knock standards like that. There have got to be standards.'

Mansie extracted a tortoiseshell and amber snuff-box from his waistcoat, flicked it open with the forefinger of the left hand that held the box, dipped his right thumb and forefinger in the dust and thrust them up his nostril. He sniffed noisily.

The party swirled around Dallas; he had no idea what time it was. Leaning on a doorpost, looking through the smoke, listening beyond the babble, the scuffles of feet, the whole orchestra of party music, he picked up the words 'there is absolutely nothing worth doing'. Familiar refrain, so often to be repeated; the tune life's barrel-organ grinds out to Sunday streets. He was on a grey stretch of shingled beach, with a grey sea hardly lapping, and grey dawn dunes stretching around; no object defined, no landmark to serve as direction-post, no boats on the water.

Parties exist to give a jolt to life, to displace consciousness; and yet there was his cousin Grant, buttons undimmed on his college blazer, now talking to the little minister. And Grant, with his self-assurance, as dull and undistinguished as a timid neo-Georgian housing development, could never guess that, at parties, people were driven by exactly the same impulses that persuaded others up mountains, that they were putting their nerve to the test, their equilibrium at risk. You could ask of a party, as of a mountain, that it should tell you what sort of man you were.

He heard Grant say, 'Of course I'm a good Scot. Nobody's more patriotic than me. Nobody cheers louder at Murrayfield or even Hampden. But that's hardly the point. I'm British too, you see. The Union's part of our fabric. I can tell you that if you tried to separate our economy from the English, we'd be in the soup.'

Gavin Gregory said, 'That's completely unacceptable. The Scottish people have got nothing from the Union. Indeed it's impoverished the quality of our national life. As Fraser said in his speech the other night, we're in a colonial situation here. The bourgeoisie are the white settlers. So to the bourgeois fear of the working-class is joined a colonial elite's fear of a subject race. You Edinburgh lawyers and accountants are quislings. Nothing but quislings.'

Gavin Gregory's head-nodding brought him excitedly forward. The second 'quisling' was delivered with such an emphatic nod that Grant, driven to evasion, stepped backwards, toppling over the arm of a sofa, to land on top of a stout woman, who, to his evident embarrassment, began to kiss him. Someone raised a little cheer.

'Sterile arguments, wouldn't you say?'

A hand plucked at Dallas's sleeve. He was amazed to see old Ebenezer still on the go.

'You've got stamina,' he said.

'I'm an old man who sleeps little. And I've unearthed some tolerable claret. Come and discuss it with me. You know,' they settled themselves in a corner, 'that fool of a minister is not so wide of the mark. We are white settlers, but he forgets white settlers can put down roots. Look at the Anglo-Irish. Remember Yeats. Where he is wrong—as Yeats was wrong—is in thinking that anything can be done about it. Let Scotland be as independent as they wish, it will not alter the fact that there's little—outside those institutions he denigrates, one of which he disgraces also—to keep talent here. Of course a political framework would retain a few—but how many? Ireland is governed by grocers. The men of energy on whom the vitality of a society depends would still take wing; the world is for the big battalions. Small countries cannot withstand it, especially when they are not protected by the barrier of a different language. Their geographical fate determines their nature. You won't stay in Scotland, Dallas. For all the protestations of clowns like Mr Gregory and men of exuberant but ill-directed will like Fraser, Scotland will grow ever less Scottish and ever less stimulating; we live in a withered culture. Sounds of energy are the energy of the death-rattle. The Union may not have been the end of an auld sang, but it led us into the last verse. They talk of a new National Anthem. There is only one that fits us: "The Flowers of the Forest". Dismiss what I am saying as the wails of a dying old man; you'll find my words justified by events. I've seen the inexorable force history exerts on the living. In my youth,

Dallas, we were distinct. Now? That's gone. So, my dear boy, get out, go where there is life, let your ancestral barracks tumble. Canaan . . . what a choicely ironic name. The Promised Land is always a cheat and delusion. I'm an old man at the end of the fool's errand. I can't believe this land can be redeemed. Redemption and sacrifice, these are delusions too. You will know how we went to war in 1914. You will have read of the mood. It was all true. Now God be thanked who has matched us with this hour. I marched in that spirit myself, sang that tune. We had lived well, loved beauty given us without a struggle. And we would pay willingly. Well, that was the last of that. Since then, we have all held on to what we could. Resolutely, sometimes, that was the mood in 1940, but without joy. We would cling on. Nothing more . . .'

His voice stopped. In the middle of his message he drifted into sleep. The thin lips lost their ironic twist, hung open. The glass dropped from his hand, spilling claret like blood across the map of Europe. Peace, let him go. We that are left; but that was the claret romancing the old man. What had come across was in fact commonplace: a regret for time lost, a sense of life's desert. Who couldn't say the same. Was there anyone who could confidently and truthfully say, 'Life's been exactly the bowl of cherries it was sold to me as. . . ?'

A fiddler struck up a tune. All at once there was a bustle and a clamour, as people formed into sets for a reel. Dallas did not join in. He watched the hard-faced, too-blonde woman sitting on the lap of a gross red-faced man. Her fingers were working on his shirt buttons. He lay back, content. Her hand opened the top button of his trousers. He sighed deeply. Someone whispered to Dallas that he was a police sergeant.

The tempo quickened. The dancers heughed and skirled. The woman worked her hand down the policeman's trousers. A scream came from upstairs. The policeman shifted in silent pleasure. No one but Dallas seemed to hear a door slam. A near-naked girl appeared at the head of the stairs, hesitated a moment clutching a bundle of clothes, and sped whimpering through the middle of the dancing set.

'Stop that quine.'

Fraser boomed the words from the stairhead. Nobody

responded in time. The girl was gone. Fraser descended the stairs with heavy imperial authority. He wore a towel round his waist, nothing else. He advanced into the middle of the room, seized a bottle and glass, called out 'on with the dance, ye buggers' and flopped down on a sofa. His eye fell on Dallas. He beckoned to him.

He was panting with exertion and exuberance, in no way discomfited by his prey's escape. Garb the dancers differently, transport the scene, Dallas thought, and Titian or Giorgione could have made something of it. Or even Poussin. A Bacchanal. The Rape of the Sabine Women. Anything vaguely mythological. Fraser a devouring Zeus.

'Rosie was asking for you a while back. You're no' mad at me for taking her away?'

'Mad at you?'

'Aye. I was curious, you see. I couldna resist it. She gave him hell when they were nobbut weans. I wanted to see what would happen.'

'And what has?'

'He hasna killed her.'

'Where is she?'

'In the far room at the end of the landing. But bide a wee. She can aye wait, women can aye wait. I saw you talking to my wife and her friend, the wee quine from the manse. Were they enjoying themselves?'

'They were very nice and friendly.'

'Were they now. They've gone off thegither, I see. It's a grand coupling instrument, a party. What happened to our Tory candidate?'

'He seems to have drifted off too.'

'I dinna see Jimmy either. That boy'll go far. He just needs a wee bit mair sophistication. Maybe you can help gie him it. And what are your ain plans, Dallas? Are you going in for the lawyering?'

Like a change of television channels the satyr vanished from view. The mentor of youth filled the screen; inquisitive, confiding, shrewd. Dallas was aware of giving too much away. The man caressed him into spontaneity. In the end he clapped Dallas on the knee, announced that he was right to 'play it cool' and said, 'Tell you what. We're a' off to Crete next month. I've taken a house there. I do it every year. I was in Greece as a loon in the army at the end of the war, and I've aye liked the place. Maybe you should come along. We'll hae a party.'

His hand transferred itself to Dallas's shoulder, pressed it hard.

'Now, awa off to Rosie,' he said.

He himself swung to his feet, ambled through the crowd, bestowing a pat, a squeeze, a smacking kiss here and there, all with the authority of a Hereford bull in a herd of cows.

The door was half-open. A voice called his name. He hesitated, not knowing what he might find.

Rosie was lying face down on the bed.

'Shut the door.'

He obeyed.

'What is it?' he said. 'Are you all right? I wondered what . . .'

There was absolutely no point in words. They had long lost any merit they might have had. She screwed her face round but he couldn't see if it was marked by tears or perhaps bruises. What had they been doing these long hours? It was too obvious. Why had the man left?

She threw back the coverings.

'Come on,' she said.

Again he hesitated, unwilling to enter where another had just been.

'Come on,' she said, 'you came to me.'

'I thought, when I got the message, you might be in trouble.'

A silly meaningless thing to say. What was this appetite if it wasn't trouble, of a serious sort?

He said, 'Why don't you get up, come home? It would be different there.'

'No,' she said, 'now.'

She turned on her back, spreading her legs, fixing his gaze on her dark moss of hair.

He recoiled. It must have been visible, for she reared

up, shrieking to him to fuck off, that he was like the rest, a coward.

He fled.

It was months before it came to him that it was more than insatiable appetite, that she longed for what they so demurely described as correction, that she had set it all up so that he would do to her what she had already demanded in his dreams.

But if he had dreamed that was her nature, didn't it mean it was what he wanted too?

Despite this, which made his nerves twitch for days, he still thought for a bit that he might go to Crete. He couldn't account to himself for the excitement it occasioned in him; he knew his friends, his real friends, would consider the party ludicrous.

Then, the following week, while nights were still disturbed by thoughts of Rosemary, and waking hours by the apprehension, which didn't by any means exclude desire, with which he waited for the little yellow sports car to sweep round by the rhododendron bushes, he got a letter from his friend Guy, saying he was back in London, about to hit on a flat. Would Dallas like a room?

'It can't be good for you, ducky, in that northern solitude. Your vowels will be lengthening again. It reminds me of dear Ovid's sojourn in Tomi, but unlike him you have not merited banishment as a result of your carryings-on with any whore of an emperor's daughter. Talking of which by the bye. I met Judy yesterday. She has landed a job as a feature writer for of all things the *Sketch*. *Facilis descensus Averni*, you will say, but she still spoke of you with affection. And of course we all miss you. Come south and resume larks.'

He was consumed with the sense that nothing would be real till he was back in London. Everything that had happened here in Canaan was immaterial. The real train was back on the rails, the engine getting up steam. Meeting Candy in the village he said to her, 'I'm off to London in a day or two. Strange party that.'

'I thought it was hell.'

'You left before the end.'

'It couldn't have got better. Lorna had had more than enough.'

'Are you still at the manse? What's happened about Gavin's wife?'

'She's taken the children to her mother's. What else can she do? No, Lorna asked me to spend a few days with her. Then we're all off to Crete. I was told you were coming.'

'It was just an idea, a party idea. Not serious.'

'Oh.' Did the grey eyes mist over? 'I think Lorna needs me,' she said. 'She's got no one else.'

'Have a good time then, see you some time, good luck.'

'Good luck, see you, good luck.'

'Give my love to Lorna. I liked her.'

'She liked you. I'm sorry you're not coming. Good luck then.'

Good luck, good luck, luck, luck . . .

In a crisp autumn morning he walked round the dewy front of the house, gave Dod superfluous instructions. Things would go on here, creepingly. He didn't bother to write to Uncle Hugh. It could wait. He slung a couple of suitcases and a box of books in the back of the Citroen, and headed south; his heart sang agreement with Johnson's judgement: the fairest prospect a Scotchman sees . . .

In the nursery *Redgauntlet* remained open, face down on the chest by the leather armchair.

PART TWO

1

Dallas in London is closer to being me than Dallas in Scotland, partly because of geographical continuity—I have condemned myself to being a citizen of this sad, beautiful, corrupt sloven of a city, partly because I can see something of Gilesie in my memories of him. Yet there was an ineffectuality, a wayward-ness, that I don't recognize in Gilesie, whatever his problems. My sons' generation makes fewer unwarrantable assumptions about their position in the world; have perhaps also a better notion of what they want out of life.

Dallas arrived in London ignorant of precise intention. And, I remember, short of cash. He discovered that most of his friends were settling themselves with natural English com-promise into what looked suspiciously like careers. Disgust twinged him; was it he, not the absurd Grant, who was odd man out? Then, Guy's flat had (mysteriously) fallen through; Guy himself, by paternal edict, was whisked back to New York. Dallas was compelled to stay a few weeks in a flat belonging to two brothers, not among his closest chums. He felt odd when they set off to work in the morning. Then it was put to him that he might pay some rent.

Judy was hardly dying to see him either. She was friendly, little sunshine, a couple of times went to bed with him, then, one morning, a Sunday, zipping up jeans, 'You're beginning to smell of bad luck. Your boyish charm's looking as fresh as a British Rail sandwich . . .'

So he couldn't move in there either. The other girls in the flat—what were their distant names, one surely must have been a Caroline?—had anyway already made that clear. 'It's the rule we agreed on, Jude.' But he had hoped to wear down their mistrust.

Her words hurt. Yet the Judy who trotted off eagerly to the

Sketch office, flashing matchless, white-stockinged legs under a short skirt, wasn't his Cambridge girl. He couldn't respond to her bubbling enthusiasm over interviews with adenoidal twits called Pop Stars. He didn't like her antiseptic briskness. One night as they made love he had found himself thinking of Rosie.

It was a cold autumn. Railway-smoke thick, fog hung from the trees in Cornwall Gardens. Dallas drifted into a job teaching English in a crook school there and drifted into a bed-sitting room. In the evenings he wrote stories which died young. Sometimes he met his friend James in a pub. James, equally bored and lost, was working for something called the Central Office of Information. He couldn't explain what he did. He was planning to leave for the USA as soon as he could fix a visa. He urged Dallas to do the same.

'Europe's finished, there's still life over there. Come west, young man, come west.'

Dallas shook his head. He searched in his pockets for money to buy another round—no credit in London—failed to come up with enough. James managed a few pence. They shared a bottle of Brown Ale.

'You see,' James said.

But James had family problems which made emigration seem a solution.

Dallas said, 'I met a chap in Scotland who'd emigrated. He showed me photographs of what he called the kids.'

'That's absurd. New York is sharper than London. Has more style. They make the driest Martinis in the world. Drier than Heygate's even. Civilization can be judged by the quality of its Martinis. Look what we're reduced to here. Lukewarm beer, with the zing of horse-piss, watered down at that, my man.'

The cream of the Brown Ale smeared itself on the empty glass. They shrugged on overcoats and out into the indifferent night.

One week-end Dallas took a French girl from his language class down to Brighton. They walked to the end of the pier. Fog rolled up the Channel and lay on the sea. The girl pressed herself against Dallas: 'Take me back to the hotel'. The bed creaked in a room smelling of adultery, and hair-oil. They heard the lovers at work in the room next door. 'Sex,' Dallas said, 'will set you free. I don't think.' 'Whatzat you think, Dallas. It's cold.'

The next week she dropped out of the class. 'She has the bad cold,' another French girl, small, sturdy, black-moustached, almond-scented, said. Dallas added her to the autumn's list of failures. The almond girl asked him to tea and talked about her time as an au pair in Yeovil.

Yes, I find no difficult in identifying with the Dallas of that season.

He was on the sidelines. Awareness penetrated his egoism of the fact that his life was peripheral to all others, none of which would have been touched beyond modest regret if he had yielded to one of the many temptations of youth: the razor-blade for the wrists, the dark inviting pills on the bedside table, the purely imaginary revolver with its loaded promise of release.

So the story must move away from Dallas. Indeed, I can't help reflecting that if I was the 'lonely old artist man' I used to aspire to be, then I would have to confess that placing Dallas centre-stage has been an almighty blunder. Yet, trying to tell the truth, how else could I have done it? I only know the characters as they presented themselves to his callow interpretation. His perception is my necessary point of entry. And, since the story aims, in part at least, to tell how Dallas became me, this jaded *antiquaire*, that being its therapeutic intent, there is really no other route I could have taken.

But now, with Dallas in his mean London room—the wall-paper, a fantasy of vine-leaves, peels from the damp plaster—I find myself in the position of the Chorus in *Henry V* (Dallas saw the Olivier film again that autumn at the Academy) and must ask you to 'entertain conjecture', 'to mind true things by what their mockeries seem', 'to eke out my performance with your mind . . .'

No point asking for a Muse of Fire.

Nobody, I suppose, much heeded Dallas's departure from Scotland. Rosemary? I don't know. She drops from the story, where indeed she belonged rather for her moral and emblematic value than for any contribution to the plot. Her departure and Dallas's reduce our dramatis personae to a number not beyond the resources of a contemporary civic theatre.

There were six bound for Crete. I can't see the expedition as anything but a piece of theatre, directed by Fraser, cast as follows:

Fraser Donnelly : politician and liberationist.

Lorna Donnelly : his wife.

Jimmy Cullas : his secretary.

Rev. Gavin Gregory : his chaplain.

Kate Cullas : his whore.

Candida Sheen : confidante to Lorna.

Cast-lists always tell you less than you'd like to know, are often calculated to mislead. To call Jimmy 'Fraser's secretary' isn't an exact statement of his role. It's neutral enough though, less prejudicial than describing him as 'Fraser's catamite', even if that was a part also expected of him at times. It may seem absurd to label Gavin Gregory as chaplain. The conduct of religious services was no part of his business. Yet the designation has this value: it emphasizes that what Fraser had gathered about him constituted a Court as well as a supporting cast. And the fact that Gavin Gregory was in Holy Orders gave zest to his inclusion in the party. You do after all require a priest if you wish to celebrate the Black Mass. And what is that but an example of Alternative Theology? A Liberation Sacrament, wouldn't you say?

They spent a month in Crete. From the first it was clear that Fraser was offering—and hoping to receive—more than just sun, sea and retsina. It wasn't your standard Club Mediterranée romp. He said to Jimmy, 'Sometimes you have to go back in time to make the next leap.'

'Oh that sort of crap,' Dallas said. 'Very old, very Crowley.'

'It was an experiment for him, see', Jimmy said to Dallas, months later, providing for him the first pieces of the mosaic, which with the help of others supplied by Candy he was eventually to construct. 'He had us all in his power,' Jimmy said, 'like being in a laboratory. Subjects for experiment. Candy was the only one who had any money—apart from Fraser—and he paid her hotel bill too, you ken. Very generous, eh?'

'Oh very.'

'No' really. It was the way he liked things to be. As for what he meant by a' that going back in time, well, he'd been doing an awfy lot of reading—that surprises you, that Fraser's a great reader, it shouldna—about old religions, the Ancient Greek Mysteries, and he'd got haud of the notion that they offered the sort of transcendental experience you needed for real sexual liberation. You see, the mistake most people make about Fraser is thinking all his talk of a new Revolution is just blethers. A lot of it is blethers of course, but no' all. And he was looking for some sort of answer, some kind of breakthrough in Crete. It might be something specific, then whiles he had the notion that what he ca'ed the spirit of the Mysteries must linger on. It couldna just evaporate. That's why he insisted we must all go to this religious festival.'

It was some local saint's day. They wound up the mountain, scented with thyme and origano, in a big hired American Buick. Fraser had got it into his head that the origin of the ceremony had nothing to do with Christianity. The Church had annexed a pagan festival. He didn't seem to have decided whether it was the death of Adonis or the birth of the Great Mother or some primeval vegetable cult—so inexact was his knowledge that it couldn't have mattered to him which. His conviction was that any pagan ceremony must be intended to liberate the Life-Force. That was sufficient. He glowed at the thought.

He repeatedly turned to the young driver, Costas, for confirmation. The boy had only a few parrot or monkey phrases of English, but he nodded and bobbed in agreement; Fraser was as good as dollars. Candy wound down the window, inhaled great wafts of the thyme-scented sweetness of a nobler antiquity and gazed down the tumbling rocks and precipitous clefts to the dazzling sea.

'Up to then I thought he was just nasty. But I began to wonder. It sounded completely mad to me. Actually I wondered if he might be getting GPI. He sounded completely paranoid, and his lucidity frightened me. I'd read about GPI, and it all seemed to fit.'

They climbed and twisted, twisted and climbed. Darkness hovered at the sky's rim as they cruised down to a broad valley, a little plain, in the high mountains. Away to the west, red sun streaks gashed the evening like a child's painting. To the east, over Asia, a cloud gloom had swollen. In a clearing, on the flat ground below the saint's tenth-century little church, booths and stalls had been set up, selling spiced kebabs and flat loaves of bread and ranks of gleaming and oozing watermelons. There were great jars of wine and bottles of beer and lemonade and Coca-Cola, and a band played music with something gypsy in its ancient melancholy. Donkeys, tethered in the olive groves that twisted up the flanks of the hill, brayed to a big straw-coloured moon rising out of Africa. Children ran everywhere. Shawled and cowled grandmothers sat round trestle tables with deep baskets of food between their black skirts. They cut busily with small shiny-bladed knives at vegetables and fruit and the round flat loaves of greyish bread. Every now and then, through the velvet of the still early autumn evening, from up the mountain and down the valleys, the angry nervous bark of sheepdogs cut through the hum and babble of conversation, the children's laughter.

Costas, full of consequence, bustled them to a table. Room was respectfully made for the foreigners. Food was produced, and wine-flasks, some made of the goat-skin Odysseus would have known, or Jason have handed round Argo's deck, or Ariadne held against Theseus' fear-cracked lips as he emerged from the labyrinth below.

It was impossible not to feel that Fraser had given them something of profound reminiscent appeal; that the Buick had carried them like a chariot across the gulfs of history, back to the dawn, to a time when a bonding of flesh and spirit was natural to man, before sense was dulled by moral convention, to a time when the primal moving forces of the world acted directly on tingling nerves.

Even Candida said, 'Someone pointed to the mountains and said "birthplace of Zeus" and it wasn't just a piece of interesting mythological information.'

Then the dancing began. At first it was formal and stately. They were all encouraged to take part. Fraser danced with a respect for the motion. 'He moved as if he belonged there,' Jimmy said. 'As if he'd danced this way before. A bit hesitant, at first, as if the steps were coming back, from a deep remembering. But aye with respect. His face, I can't explain his face. It was all set and distant. So was Kate's. She was . . . rapt. I was feart to think she was my sister. It was uncanny.'

Jimmy shivered. The sun dipped out of sight. That accounted for the chill. Gavin Gregory had made off in the direction of the olive groves with Costas. Lorna and Candy had their heads together, their hair gleaming under a light cradled in the bowl of a chestnut tree. He shivered again. It was more than the chill.

'The fact that I couldna think of anything to be feart of made it worse. It sounds daft, doesn't it? D'you know what it was like? It was like walking along a road at night when you're sure you're being followed, even when you know there's nobody there. The more you tell yourself to take a grip, the more feart you are. In the end I couldna sit there any more. I felt hellish randy too.'

He followed a straggly procession of priests in their tall black hats and spade beards up to the church. It stank of incense and sweat. They were chanting something, a prayer, he supposed; it was like a call for redemption that no one could be sure of. Tallow candles, thick as a man's forearm, lit the altar; they were the only light in the little building.

Candy and Lorna, left alone, talked the nothings friends talk. Lorna was uneasy though. After a bit—she had (unusually for her) been drinking retsina fast—she said, 'Fraser's up to something. I can smell it. It's a sort of drug to him. He's come here looking for a fix.'

Then the music changed tempo. The gypsy note came through more clearly, mocking the liturgical murmur from the chapel. Steps quickened. The dancers grew younger. They reared back and lunged towards each other. It was none of the bucolic romping of a Scottish country dance; too urgent for that. The sweat stood out on Fraser's face; Kate arched herself in his arms. They held the pose for a break in the music, a tableau, models for a Baroque painting of Bacchanalian frenzy. Then they broke from each other, steps pounded as the music raced. The lights went out. All was silent, the blanket of the dark fell, to be pierced by a mountain piping, as of a lonely goat-herd.

'Whaur's the wee minister?' Fraser led a red-lipped Kate back to the table, now lit up again. 'Are a' the wee buggers canoodling?'

He grinned, threw himself down panting, 'What a night.' He stretched for the goat-skin flask and flung his head back and drank as if the wine came straight from the sky, so vertically had he tipped the skin. 'It'll be the makings of the minister,' he said. He seized two gobbets of kid from a kebab that a neighbour held out to him, thrust them into his mouth. 'What for are you quines no' dancing?' He chewed the kid with relish; a little oil trickled out of the side of his mouth.

Lorna and Candy, neither of them, found reply. They lowered their eyes. He uttered a humphing, body-shaking laugh, and thrust his hand hard between Kate's legs which closed and then crossed upon it.

'Wi' the minister it's a right case o' Greek love meets Greek, is it no'? Maybe a threesome reel eh?'

Kate bit her lip. Her eyes dilated. It seemed she couldn't trust herself to speak, had gone beyond words. The interpretation is of course fanciful, but then every time Candy recounted Crete to Dallas that was the point she made: 'fanciful interpretations were imperative. You couldn't help thinking that way.'

'But what for are you no' dancing? You'll dance wi' me next round, do you hear.'

Lorna still didn't look at him.

'Aye but you will,' he said.

She might have turned into a laurel, a flower or a nightingale; but metamorphosis requires the aid of a friendly goddess.

'Aye, but you will. You will that, my lizzie.'

And of course she did. But limply. Maiden not mænad.

Night closed thick and soft about them. Children drifted into unwilled sleep; grandmothers watched. Old men remembered, country legends, ancient echoes, mingling interchangeably with tales of the Resistance in the mountains. Jimmy, back from the church, found Fraser and the girls silent.

'All the time Fraser and Lorna danced, not long really,' Candy said, 'Kate said nothing to me. There was nothing much I ever had to say to her of course, but I made the odd conversational starter. Nothing. She was somewhere quite different in her mind.'

Fraser bullied and cajoled; the party died on him. Kate plucked his sleeve and whispered in his ear. He turned his head round against hers to bring his lips to her left ear. They held the pose.

Cocks crowed from valley farms.

Fraser stumbled to his feet. Kate glided erect. He grasped wine, grasped the girl and they disappeared up the hillside towards the olive groves, the goat-skin dangling.

Perhaps the girls slept. Time passed. If not asleep they had drifted into an airport state of mind, consciousness atrophied. The hours crumble; mind and senses blunt. Candida didn't notice when Lorna left. And then, seeing her not there, roused herself to assume she had gone perhaps to find a tent in use as a Ladies; bizarre conjunction, but there must be some such place, for, beneath the antique and mediaeval elements, or rather above and beyond them, the thing was organized; the Coca-Cola and the buses parked half a mile away proved that.

Or perhaps she had gone for a stroll. It was nothing to worry about.

Only, she didn't return. The moon re-emerged from the pall of cloud drifting down the valley to rain over the morning sea. Braziers made little dots of red among the olives. Music and dancing were stilled. Low murmuration crept down the slope from the church; feet still shuffled up the stony track.

She might have gone to the church. Candy set off in that direction.

So neither girl was there when Costas came to the table at a run, calling to Jimmy, to 'come quick'. There was going to be trouble, Jimmy made that much out. Costas's English was deserting him; his message was like scrambled radio.

Jimmy hurried after him, up the hill. And what he found wasn't, at first glance, too horrible, insufficient reason for such agitation. Fraser and Kate and Gavin Gregory were there in a little clearing. A number of dark-suited, much-moustachioed figures stood round them. But something had happened. They were the objects of pointed fingers and high jabber. And then a high voice of command. Kate was beside a flat rock. Her fingers gripped the belt or cord of her skirt. Fraser's chest heaved. He had nothing to say. Then someone whimpered, gave a little yelp of pain. Two of the elders had grasped Gavin Gregory, and begun to twist the little minister's arms behind his back. Every now and then one of them gave a little twist, as if to punctuate the speech he was making. It sounded angry.

Jimmy took that in.

Someone shouted from the edge of the crowd—there must have been twenty now. In any language it was a curse, an obscenity. Something whizzed through the air. Kate's head went back, her hand flew to her cheek, and came away with a glisten on it. Fraser bellowed—the first cry from him, a bellow as unreal as from a crowd scene in a mediaeval movie. He flung himself forward. Two men seized him, shouting. He struggled. They held him fast.

'Oxi,' shouted an old man, dancing in excitement, 'Oxi.'

Jimmy saw his sister's cheek was wet with blood.

Commands were yelled. Some sort of order was established. Jimmy's arms were seized too. A little procession was formed. They were frog-marched down a steep path towards the cars and buses. When Jimmy stumbled, he was pulled roughly up. He could hear Fraser struggling and swearing. The two men who gripped him stopped, halting the procession. They forced Fraser back against a rock. One produced a knife from his belt. He held it against Fraser's throat. The struggles stopped. Then with a great sweep the knife descended till its point rested in Fraser's groin. It was slowly, theatrically, withdrawn. The man stood back. He held his left hand out, straight out, at eye level, bunched as if round a tubular object, like a man holding out a torch to light a sacrifice. The knife slashed the empty air above the bunched fist. Jimmy felt a hot flow of piss. Fraser's tongue moved across his lips. He stopped straining. The man nodded twice. The procession resumed its descent. They were forced into the car. Doors were slammed.

Nobody spoke as Costas drove fast down the mountain.

'Then, 'Daft buggers, daft crazy buggers,' Fraser said.

The hot piss turned cold and feary. Fraser laughed once.

When they reached the plain Costas turned the radio on to a wail of enfolding music. He still drove very fast. Back in Heraklion he took money from Fraser. He didn't say good-bye.

Lorna wasn't at the church. Candy went in and found herself on her knees. She had nothing to say to a God she had long disowned, and she didn't know what kept her there. But she stayed a long time, maybe ten minutes, and at last found herself muttering what she knew to be the General Confession. And Lorna who had been wandering on the hillside and entered the church unthinking found her there, and knelt beside her.

Afterwards they sat outside the church and talked. They had been growing closer to each other, but the friendship had still been interrupted by a barrier reef of reserve. Lorna was too proud, too accustomed to repress her feelings, to indulge in confidences. There was nothing in her intellectual inheritance or in her upbringing to encourage her to talk things out. Was it about this time that the cant expression 'let it all hang out' became popular? That wasn't her style at all.

Even now, after a minute or two, she couldn't immediately talk about what was distressing her; but she broke down in tears, in vast heaving unexpected sobs; and Candy, shaken out of her own habitual coolness, held her in her arms and kissed her damp brow.

'And the thing is,' Lorna said, 'I know that when he wants me, he can do it any time. I hate myself for it.'

She had been walking in the olive-groves, half-hoping, half-fearing to come on Fraser and Kate. She wasn't, she said, jealous. Jealousy would have ended things long ago. But she was distressed and afraid of Kate, as she had never been afraid of any of Fraser's other girls.

'The thing is, Candy, she encourages his worst fantasies. She's ready to see herself the same mad way he wants to see her. It's hard to put in words. It's obscene. He calls her a priestess. Do you think he's mad? He must be mad.'

Candy must have given her that level grey-eyed look that told how hard she found it not to speak the truth.

'I've wondered. It's all new to me.'

'It's been getting worse. I don't know if he's really . . . it might just be drugs.'

'Drugs?'

'You've surely noticed he's always popping pills. I don't know what they are.'

That hadn't occurred to Candy. She was reluctant to accept the idea. For her, people weren't some sort of chemistry and nothing more, their natures capable of being transformed by some sort of chemical injection. She was, rather naively, an essentialist. People had natures for her. She even divided them simply into good and bad. Lorna was, as she had said to Dallas, a good person, Fraser a bad one. She never wavered from that view. What you did, couldn't by itself determine for Candy what you were. She went arrow-straight to a person's essence. Nature was more than the sum of one's actions, even though usually expressed through them.

Candy's simplicity consoled Lorna. In time she stopped crying. They sat still holding each other while night rumours buzzed around them. Then they descended the hill, slowly, hand in hand, nerving themselves to meet the others again, and were relieved to find them absent. When they concluded that they had left, momentary surprise gave way to a feeling of release. It was a remission from nightmare.

But people were looking at them. They felt curiosity like

insects on their skin. Even suspicion. In retrospect they recognized pity too.

A man detached himself from a group at a nearby table, a silver-haired man in the uniform dark suit, but bearing the air of not being a peasant in his Sunday best.

'There is a bus,' he said. 'You must get on it. I will guide you to it myself.'

His English wasn't at all bad. Candy told him they were with friends.

'Your friends have gone,' he said, 'that is why you must take the bus.'

'Did they ask you to tell us?'

'No,' he said, 'I am not their messenger. But you must go. It is necessary. The bus will leave in twenty minutes. I will guide you to it. Come.'

'I don't understand,' Lorna said.

'People here are old-fashioned, perhaps. I think that is so,' he said. 'I am different. I have lived out of Crete. New York, London, Birmingham. I understand there are different cultures, different ways of life. What is permitted in one place is not permitted in another. You understand, people here are old-fashioned, traditional, there are many things they do not like, do not permit. So your friends had to leave. And you must go too. My friends are angry. They are not easily disgusted, but they are disgusted now. I think it is better you persuade your friends to leave Crete also, but you must certainly take the bus. Come, we will walk down to it now. It will take us perhaps ten minutes.'

Neither Lorna nor Candy could bring herself to ask for details.

'We both knew it was something shameful, something that shouldn't be talked about. It was simpler, better, to do as he said. We couldn't not, actually. I have never felt so dirty. We were contaminated. You could read that in the way they looked at us. Nobody looked at us straight, but they never stopped flicking glances at us. And it was horrible. We were like people carrying the plague. The man wouldn't even hand us into the bus and you know how ready Greeks always are to do that for a girl.'

In the morning Fraser, though his face was shadowed by a mutinous cloud, shook himself like a water spaniel emerging from a pond. No one ventured to recall what had happened; all brooded on it. Gavin Gregory twittered his alarm to Jimmy, but the alarm was shot through with excitement. He babbled of the inadequacies of conventional religion, of the aridity of a merely social conception of man. But it was all babble. He had to put away a full half-litre of retsina before his hand stopped shaking; and, as he came all over Jimmy that siesta, he cried, 'I won't believe in the devil.'

'What do you mean?'

Gavin Gregory held the boy tight, shuddering.

'That's what he wanted. He called him the old gods. I won't believe . . .'

He gripped the boy closer still, and would say no more.

Jimmy's own nerves were sharp-edged when, months later, he told Dallas this, sitting twisting the sleeve of his jacket and not noticing what he was doing. It was the first time he confessed to sleeping with the little minister, and maybe he didn't notice that confession either. But he had plenty of reason for agitation.

'Crete made Fraser think he could do anything. That doesn't make sense after what happened. I know it doesn't. But it's how it was. I think before they were interrupted Fraser got a sensation he'd never had before, he saw through to what he was aiming at, and after the shock of being thrown out faded, it came back to him. A sense of power.'

And power, undoubtedly, is what he was after. Liberation is power, I suppose, or the sensation of power. (You will understand that such an observation from me is nothing but theory. I have never been interested in power. I don't know what it feels like, experience no attraction that way.) It occurs to me that, a hundred years back, Fraser would have been most terrifically God-fearing. A real Victorian heavy, a repressive prophet of a doom-laden morality. That would have satisfied him just as well. In one sense he was no rebel. He liked to pose a bit as *une âme maudite*, but he was too much of his time to be a rebel. He got a whiff of what was in the general air and it intoxicated him.

The last night in Crete he followed Candida on to a moon-white beach. She saw the heavy figure lumber over the rocks and regretted her decision to cheat insomnia by walking there. He moved towards her with heavy crunching stride. There was no avoiding him.

She smelled sweat, brandy and semen.

'What do you want here?'

'Can a man no' walk by the sea?'

She didn't reply to that. It was a remark pointless in itself, only intended as an opening to discourse. He could make his own running.

'You're a chilly wee bitch, aren't you?'

Mockery overlaid the insolence of the words. Again she didn't reply.

'Lorna was keen you should come,' he sat down on the rock beside her. 'And I was curious mysel'. I wanted to see if it would open you up, but, no, you're a right chilly wee bitch. And what's more, you're a wee bitch that presumes to criticize me.'

She made to get up at that. He grabbed her wrist and pulled her down.

'You'll bide and hear what I have to say.'

'I could scream,' she said. 'I could scream very loud. Someone would hear me. They don't think much of you here. If I screamed you would be in trouble.'

He made a clicking sound with his tongue. She could have slapped him for his complacency.

'They wouldna worry,' he said. 'Between foreigners, on a beach, they wouldna worry. They were a' hepped-up at that festival but they wouldna worry down here. Aye, Lorna wanted to bring you and I agreed, being curious. I wondered just why she wanted you, you see. I thought maybe she fancied you'd distract me from wee Kate. Maybe you hoped for that yoursel'.'

'You're obsessed,' she said. 'You really are mad. I wouldn't touch you if . . .'

'If I was the last man left on earth? Would you no'? We could see about that. Mind you, I ken better noo. I've seen the way you look at Lorna, you see, and I ken fine what you'd like, though you're ower much o' a prissy Presbyterian quine to reach out and take it. You're the epitome of Scotland you wee bitch, a feart wee bourgeois quine. And since you're feart to take what you'd like, you set up against me. In an intellectual alliance wi' my wife. You make me sick, do you ken that? You wi' your middle-class, lace-curtain mentality and morality. I wouldna gie a docken for it. It's deid, a' deid, like you and your class and your culture. And it winna work. Do you ken where I've come from? I've come from my wife's bed. And,' he leaned his face into hers and gave her his foetid breath, 'do you ken whit I've done there? I've had her in the arse.'

2

Candy didn't, even for a moment, disbelieve him.

With the authority and sense of timing of a talented film director, he cut straight from that line. She was seized with nausea as she watched him roll his way back to the hotel. And towards whose bed? What he had done to his wife was to her, watching the departing swagger of his back, the supreme macho act of contempt. It was an imposition of naked will that horrified and disgusted her. She pictured Lorna, stretched out, naked as his will, biting the pillow so as not to scream. But the thought that followed was more horrible still. Had Lorna permitted it, accepted what was being done to her, in an infatuated gesture of self-abasement that might recall her husband to her? For, if that was what he wanted to inflict on a woman, would Kate have permitted it? She might, so infected by what Candy imagined might have been done at the festival that any sexual act, no matter how filthy, seemed a proper submission to the god's will.

Nothing in Candy's life had prepared her for this. She had landed herself in a country whose rules she didn't know. She couldn't be sure there were any longer any rules; and her whole upbringing and education had been circumscribed by rules, rules in which it was impossible to disentangle moral requirements from a code of social behaviour. For Candida the done thing carried the weight of a moral command. That has to be understood.

Yet something besides the rules of the game we have been brought up to play operates upon us; and this is emotion. Harnessed by the rules, it is yet always likely to break free. And Candy was, from this moment, in the grip of the most potent of emotional drugs, the one which most certainly corrupts free action: pity. If she had acted on the advice that the voices of her education forced on her, she would simply, immediately on her return, have divorced herself from Fraser and all his set. It would not have been difficult. There was nothing now to hold her in the North-East. She had discharged her obligation to Maggie Gregory, who had anyway now cut herself loose. And indeed the whole logic of Candy's life—her implicit future—pointed her away. She should return to Edinburgh, find a job, embark on a career.

She knew this. Nobody would blame her. Indeed the reverse was true. It would be blameworthy, incomprehensible, open to all sorts of misrepresentation, to do anything else. But she couldn't. Pity gnawed at her resolution, imposed a burden she couldn't decline. Pity committed her.

It committed her from that moment on the beach, as she sat alone on the rock lapped by the Aegean. It surged over her even as a thin spew of disgust shook her body, as she retched over a rock pool. It clamped its rivets on her in the morning when, seeing Fraser established in open-shirted-mood with Kate and Jimmy at the café table, she took a cup of straw-coloured tea to Lorna.

She was just stirring from sleep, her face mazed with the morning; it was a troubled and abased loveliness that offered itself to Candida. The bedroom was large, cool-tiled, roses hung round the window, and the sun, sliding its rays through the Venetian blind, chequer-boarded the floor. Lorna gathered a wisp of négligé about her; memory streaked her face, darkened her eyes which couldn't fix themselves on Candy.

'I've brought you some tea.'

For some minutes they didn't talk. Lorna sipped the tea, wincing a little. Candy busied herself picking clothes up from the floor and hanging them over the backs of chairs, and then, when she could find nothing else of this sort to do, went and stood looking out over the sea. There was a little verandah and she drew the blind up enough to enable her to step out on to it. Behind her, she heard Lorna place the cup and saucer, with a little tinkle of teaspoon, on the table by the bed.

'Are they all down there?'

'Except for the minister.'

'Is there anything planned?'

Candy turned back into the room.

'The plane's at four o'clock. I haven't spoken to any of them this morning.'

'Oh.'

They waited, each fearful that the other would speak. Candy couldn't bring herself to go—she couldn't imagine how Lorna would feel, alone, awake, after—and she knew Lorna was willing her to stay. And, besides, where else was there to go? She hadn't enjoyed waking in her own room that morning. Then she heard sobs from the bed.

She put her arms round Lorna in comfort; it went no further than that. Despite later allegations, despite the confident gossip that was to pursue them, I don't believe it ever did. For a little Lorna sobbed, Candy held her, Lorna talked of missing the children, and said it was silly, they were sure to be having a fine time with their grandmother.

'Don't leave me,' she said.

'I wasn't going to.'

'I mean, when we get back. Come and stay. You will, won't you? You don't really need to find a job at once, not really, do you?'

'I don't know.'

'Say yes. I need someone there. I need you. If I don't have one friend, I don't think I can stand it.'

There was nothing in this appeal beyond the surface meaning of the words. The friend could not in any way divert Fraser from whatever he wanted to do. But Lorna thought she could bear it if she had one adult there who wasn't going to hurt her. She deceived herself; but it was natural enough.

'Fraser came to me on the beach last night.'

The words appalled Candy before she had finished the sentence. They were exactly what she had determined not to say. If Lorna wanted to make the reference, that was one thing. And yet here she was herself dropping the most resounding hint.

'He didn't try anything, did he?'

The possibility alarmed them both, for it now came to Candy that he might very well—in his mad mood of triumph —have attempted just that; while Lorna's words brought into the open a fear she had been hiding even from herself, that Fraser, seeing she had acquired a friend, would set himself to seduce her. She was already, notwithstanding the composure she presented to the world, living a nightmare in which she saw herself bound to a stake while Fraser stood contemplating the faggots with a lighted brand in his hand. She had ascribed his madness to drugs; when she found her fingernails digging into her palms, when she saw lurid colours dance before her eyes, she could offer no such cause for her own derangement. Nothing but terror could explain it to her. She read in all his actions a plot against her sanity, a war against whatever values she struggled to cling on to.

So there was fear in the voice which said, 'He didn't try anything, did he?'

'No,' Candy said, 'no.' She was once again the decisive schoolgirl, the resolute prefect in that negative. 'And if he did I'd soon tell him where to get off.'

The sanity reassured Lorna. For the second time Candy was horrified by what she heard herself saying. That was, after all, what Lorna had so patently failed to do. She was ashamed lest Lorna read criticism of her in them. Nothing could have been further from her intention. As she saw it, Lorna had had no such choice. What had been imposed on her was beyond her resisting. She had long ago in her marriage lost the privilege of free action.

And even as she blushed at hearing her own words, Candy knew that from now on any assumption of such privilege on her part would be delusory. Pity had seen to that.

That morning, over the cups of tea, over the coffee which in a little Candy ordered up from the bar, cemented their alliance. It was *contra mundum* henceforth. Yes, Candy would go back and stay with Lorna. They wouldn't consult Fraser, simply face him with it. But both knew, with a sick tremor, that he wouldn't oppose. He saw Candy as a challenge. He couldn't begin to resist such a test of his power.

Of what had happened the night before, nothing was said; and both felt that it was better that way.

3

Fraser's behaviour grew wilder with the autumn gales. He came to be talked about beyond his own set. Policemen who had been at his parties began to find reasons why they didn't know him. One of them—a sergeant Dallas had seen embracing big blonde Vera at the party he had attended—suddenly left the Force. The more respectable among Fraser's acquaintance in the county, the sort who had been accustomed to refer to him as 'an awful fellow of course, but what a man', or 'not one of us of course but an amazing chap', grew wary. Word got round that he was going it a bit; association with him wouldn't do anyone's reputation much good.

Colonel Mickle was one of the first to distance himself. I've presented him as a figure of fun, because that was how he seemed to the young Dallas as he fumbled pound notes with blotchy hands in the back bar of the Caledonian Hotel, fulminating against the young and the ingratitude and contrariness of women; seen that way, he was a comic character.

But Dallas was naive to see him only that way. He had not considered that the face presented in hours of relaxation is always itself a mask. It's a mistake to consider we are mostly ourselves when at play.

Alick Duguid knew this, even if Dallas didn't, and he found Dallas's inability to distinguish between Mickle the comedian, and Mickle the 'shrewd operator' more evidence of his blinkered view of things and, in Alick's language, incapacity to understand political realities.

'Mickle,' he said to Dallas, long after they had overcome their initial antipathy, 'was aye canny. And he saw where Fraser was heading. Mickle's a businessman and it's part of his business to keep a grip on local politics. It's his interest too, it's the kind of power he enjoys. He likes fixing things. Doesna matter what. That's power to him. No' the mystical windy nonsense Fraser was spouting when he came back from Crete. Mickle was one of the first to take up Fraser, you ken. They came across each other in business, and he liked Fraser's head for it. They were aye putting a bit in the other's way. And then he liked Fraser because he saw him as a chiel who could provide him with a bit of fun. But for Mickle, you see, fun's no' something can be allowed to run riot. It's a spare time activity. He's no objection to dissipation, no' even to what's a bit unorthodox, but it's confined to leisure hours, and it's got to leave you with a clear head for business in the morn.

'You've seen his house,' Alick said. 'Solid granite. You canna get mair solid nor that. Nor permanent. And it's full of big mahogany tables and chests of drawers and wardrobes. And where it's no' mahogany it's oak or walnut. Nae fucking chipboard. There's a grand show of roses in the garden; they win prizes, he's famous for his roses, just like the town itself. But they're no' allowed to wander. They keep their place, in flower beds. How could a man wi' that sort of taste take Fraser's nonsense seriously? You tell me.

'The trouble wi' you, Dallas, is ignorance, sheer fucking ignorance. You're a Romantic. You ken things from books, no' from life. And that means you really ken fuck all. Nothing of ony substance. You're fooled by the froth. Take Fraser and his daft politics. If you kent onything, you'd ken that the SNP are wee sma-toon bodies. As open to innovation as an oyster. You'd have seen straightaway that Fraser and them had nothing in common. Even the rhetoric parted company. You see, Scotland's a douce, canny, shy place. The mair it's a failure, and by God it's a failure, the mair loth it is to turn to anything new. Whether it's creative or Fraser's Californian bullshit. I ken this about Scotland, right through to my marrow. Theoretically and philosophically I'm a Marxist, and my theory and philosophy make me a determinist and tell me capitalism's in its death throes and the Revolution'll come. And when it does it'll be a real revolution arising out of the class structure of our economy, no' Fraser's Revolution o' fucking consciousness. I ken that intellectually. But when I look around me . . .'

Alick let the arm holding his tankard sweep over the hotel bar, taking in the handful of businessmen in dark suits and the striped ties of the local school, the group of students gingering themselves up for a college hop, the pinched rectitude of the two barmaids in their neat black dresses . . .

'. . . my philosophy withers. I see a douce wee managerial society with nae fire in its belly except it's put there by whisky. I dinna see a lamp-post waiting Councillor Mickle, not yet you, Dallas. But the one thing this comfortable wee society is sure of, is its enemies. So the minute Fraser moved from being a bit of a lad to something serious, they pulled their skirts away from him.'

'Serious? You can call him serious?'

'Oh he was serious right enough. He may have been demented, but he was serious in rejecting bourgeois morality.'

It wasn't obvious to Fraser that doors were shutting on him, if only because so many of the doors through which he was accustomed to pass belonged to public houses. He didn't even notice that his business associates were less eager to spend time with him because, infatuated by his vision, he spent less time on business. The one explicit rejection of the autumn, his failure to be adopted as prospective parliamentary candidate for the constituency, was easily surmounted; the choice of his old and despised rival, Provost Barclay, simply demonstrated the party's fogeyism.

He disappeared from home for days on end—to Lorna's relief and Candy's satisfaction. They didn't ask whether he was staying at the cottage up the glen or with Kate in her flat in Aberdeen or simply ranging the pubs and putting up at one-night hotels. It was enough that he wasn't there.

In the darkening afternoons and long evenings Candy urged Lorna to leave him. She pointed out how the children's nerves were suffering. She observed Lorna's deepening unhappiness and apprehension. She even said, 'He'll kill you one day. I'm really afraid he'll kill you.' One morning she brought her a letter, glowing with happiness, from Maggie Gregory; it spoke more eloquently than she could, with the authority of experience, of the relief escape afforded. Lorna read the letter with tears in her eyes, but said, 'Fraser's not Gavin Gregory.' Did that mean he still exercised fascination over her? Or that he wouldn't allow her to escape? Candy couldn't tell; Lorna saw herself as a gypsy bird in a cage, held fast with a rusted padlock.

The leaves fell in long moribund silence. November mists seeped through windows open in the morning. Candy wondered what good she was doing. She suggested leaving. Lorna wept again. Candy followed her to her room; she could hardly see the rose pattern of the wallpaper. Lorna was a grey shape crouched on the bed.

'I'll stay, of course I'll stay,' Candy said, 'but why won't you . . . ?'

'You don't know Fraser.' Her fingers twisted themselves like a search for truth. 'He'd never let me go. He'd never let the children go.'

Candy assured her there were courts that would protect her; she would be certain of custody. Her case was unanswerable.

'Courts? You think Fraser would care for the likes of courts?'

'You ought at least to see a lawyer,' Candy said. 'Let him explain.'

Oh yes, let him explain the facts of civilized existence to this poor, frightened, desperate girl whom Candy loved and yet found herself in this moment revolted by; nobody should submit to another's will as Lorna to Fraser's. It was a matter of principle as much as courage.

Lorna's fingers twisted as if she would wrench them from her hands. Candy couldn't catch her mutter. Lorna shook her head.

'He'd kill me sooner.'

She looked up, huge open eyes and face quite without expression, tears arrested.

'You don't believe me, but it's true. He would kill me sooner.'

Was it true? Candy had no means of knowing. She couldn't believe it but she also sensed that no outsider can ever be really certain of the relations between man and wife. And she couldn't doubt Lorna's conviction, or her fear. She saw too that she was trapped herself. Pity held her here in this farmhouse with its fake repro furniture that spoke of Lorna's hesitant good taste.

Frost came early in December and held them fast in blue, icy weather that brought the hills close. A couple of miles off, the police called on Gavin Gregory when the last stars were still pale in the sky, long before a sun had risen or the pale winter moon set. They beat on the manse door till the little minister dragged himself from the couch where he had collapsed. The hall was dark, electricity cut off, and they shone torches in his sick, frightened face. It was a matter of a complaint raised by the father of a boy in his Bible class. There was no respect in their questioning. They had no doubt of his guilt and his offence disgusted them. They were sure too that the complaint related to only one of a number of such acts. They hustled him down to the station. A sergeant and two constables stayed behind to wait for the light that would help them search the manse for any documentary, possibly photographic, evidence, that would incriminate the little man more completely.

The news came to the farmhouse in the late afternoon. Gavin Gregory had, after hours of questioning, rallied sufficiently to call for a lawyer, and it was he who, in cold distasteful tones, asked to speak to Fraser. Jimmy took the call. He had driven Fraser home the night before, and he tried to find out the nature of the business from the lawyer. The lawyer refused to say. He would speak to nobody but Fraser.

'Can I get him to call you back?' Jimmy said, for he knew that Fraser still lay reeking of stale brandy in Kate's arms in the spare bedroom. The lawyer assented. 'I'll be leaving my office in half an hour. It must be before then.'

'Can you not give me some notion of what it's about?' Jimmy said. 'Mr Donnelly'll want to know.'

'You can say I'm acting on behalf of the Reverend Gavin Gregory,' the lawyer said.

Jimmy felt the silence Lorna and Candy made around him as an accusation. They held him responsible for bringing Fraser and Kate there though they knew he had no real responsibility. And to their mute accusation was now added the quickening fear and guilt provoked by the telephone message. Logically, Gavin might have turned to his lawyer and thence to Fraser for some help through his maze of debt. Jimmy knew a deeper and more fearful logic. He could see a policeman's boot swinging towards him.

The news stimulated Fraser. He shook his hangover off like a dog coming out of a pond. He mocked the wretched minister, even while he inveighed against the law which threatened him. Of course he would stand bail for the poor chiel. Nobody need be short of a friend while Fraser Donnelly was about. He banged the receiver down and called on Lorna to provide him with breakfast. Bacon and eggs, three eggs.

'He canna be summarily bailed,' he said. 'The wee man'll have to stay in the gyle till he's brought before the sheriff in the morning. We'll hae to start early, Jimmy. I said I'd see Fiddes the lawyer before the court sits.'

Jimmy didn't dare to shake his head, but the expedition wasn't on. He wasn't going to get that close to the business. There was no knowing what the minister mightn't have said. He caught a whiff of the rank smell of the cells, and started like a thoroughbred filly. But he dared not hint to Fraser that he was going to run.

Instead he watched, fascinated, as Fraser tore the ring from a can of export; as he took a quick and greedy swig from a glass tankard; as he smacked his lips, ran a quick tongue round them to suck in the foam. Jimmy shrank from the man's delight in action. The farmhouse, it came home to him, had never been the place for him; now it was so less than ever. His stomach hollowed. His ears pricked for the police.

Lorna brought the bacon and eggs through. Fraser wolfed them. Kate drifted in wrapped in a white dressing-gown. She looked Lorna in the face. Jimmy flushed; it came to him that Lorna and Candy were right to accuse him.

Kate said, 'Get me coffee, Jimmy,' and he was glad to slip through to the kitchen.'

*   *   *

'So how did you get away?'

Dallas, at a corner table in a neutral Shepherd Market pub, was amazed by the story, amazed and envious too: it seemed he hadn't been living here in London, sunk in his ridiculous job and his equally futile attempts at writing; while, all the time, five hundred miles of wasteland from the metropolis, you found this technicoloured life.

'Well, in the end, they went to bed, and I slipped out and down to the main road and hitched a lift from a fish lorry. I can't tell you the relief. To be getting out. Then to be really out. You've no idea, Dallas, what it's been like there. It's a terrible thing to say, when I think of Gavin, but it took this to move me. To give me the impetus. I feel myself, and free, for the first time in God knows how long.'

I remember Dallas looking at him; the soft nervous face, framed in abundant dark, waving hair is a photograph I still carry with me, one that comes back when so many others have faded. It's my first real photograph of Jimmy, and my possession of it is the result of the shaft of sadism Dallas then experienced.

'But you're not out of it, are you? You're not free, not that I can see.'

'What do you mean?'

'If you'd reason to run, they've reason to chase. What makes you think they won't?'

Jimmy looked up at the mirror, as if scanning the pub behind for huntsmen, police dogs.

'You did have reason to run?'

The boy nodded.

'I don't mind telling you,' he said, and Dallas winced at the complicity in the stressed pronoun, winced but thrilled too. 'There was a sort of party at the manse. A half dozen boys. I was the only one over twenty-one. Not that they were wee boys. I wouldn't have anything to do wi' wee boys. But seventeen, eighteen, well, I'd be in trouble, wouldn't I? When Gavin talks. And he'll no' be able to keep silent.'

Dallas saw: the clumsy games of strip poker, the giggling scuffles on dusty sofas, the shame-faced bravado of departure. He felt: disgust.

'Why are you telling me this? We've had fun together, but I don't know that that gives you the right to involve me. How did you find me anyway?'

'I called that girl you mentioned who works on the *Sketch*. She gave me your number.'

Judy-Judas. He had been pleased to hear Jimmy's voice. He picked up the pint mugs, hearing again the shrill squealing of dirty boys. The barman, himself a pink-shirted boy with blubbery lips and a mop of black frizzy hair, looked him straight with insolent appraising eye as he handed over the change. Dallas blamed Jimmy for that too.

Jimmy said, 'The thing is, London's a big place. You can easy lose yourself here. They won't want me that much. I'm not important. They've got Gavin. They'll be satisfied with him.'

'What'll you do?' Please God, don't let him ask for my help.

'Och I'll find something. You can aye find work in London.' He gave a timid smile. 'You're not mad at me, are you?'

'Mad at you? No, why should I be?'

But of course he was. He resented the emotional demand Jimmy was making.

'I can't put you up,' he said. 'I've only a miserable room. And the hell of a landlady. It would be misunderstood if you stayed there even one night. Besides, someone might give the police my name. They might look for you through me.'

'But they won't know where you're living?'

'My bank does.'

147

It was ridiculous. Jimmy had no answer. His animation seeped into the shadows.

'How are you for money?' Dallas hoped the answer would be that he was short; giving cash is balm to a troubled conscience.

'I'm OK.'

'Well then . . .'

'You're not mad, though, are you? I was sure you would understand. And I had to tell someone . . .'

The evening deepened on them as the pub thinned; the men in striped suits and club ties were going home to their wives in the suburbs, making their way to the underground car parks where they had day long left their Jaguars, Rovers or Zephyrs, or catching the Tube at Hyde Park Corner to main-line stations; and they had not yet been replaced by chaps in sweaters waiting for girls in trousers. It was an interim half-hour. Dallas went through to the Gents. ('Leather Slave seeks Leather Master', 'Man's Long Agony to Lift Shaft'). When he came back Jimmy was at the bar talking to the frizzy-haired boy.

Dallas wanted out, but there were already a couple of pints lined up on the counter. He would have to drink his. He wanted, imperatively, to drink whisky, alone, in another pub. Months spread around him like the most rain-sodden of Midland landscapes; he lived his life in wide fields of beet.

'The boy there thinks he can fix me up.'

'Fix you up?'

'Aye, with a job and a bed.'

'You mean, you just asked him? Like that? Out of the blue?'

'Oh aye, why not?'

'Someone you don't know from Adam?'

Jimmy smiled.

'He's prettier than Adam,' he said.

4

I found three days ago I couldn't write any more. I had reached a point where the reconstruction of the past was posing too many questions about the present, a moment when cowardice came into the open. I remember Dallas waking with a sore head and a sag of nausea and the picture of Jimmy and the frizzy boy waking too in a bed-sitter like his, as dirty-distempered, as evil-smelling; but they would put on music and laugh at each other. Dallas turned over in bed seeing Gavin Gregory crouch in a police cell, watching him pluck up courage to flirt with his guards; and then he thought of Candy.

And of course it is Candy-Candida who has made it impossible for me to go on straight with my story, just as it was she who started me on it. It is because I am approaching the moment when I find it hard to present Dallas as a fictional character.

'What on earth are you writing up there?' Ann said.

'Memoirs of my dead life.'

She didn't pursue the matter; dead life having no attractions for my brisk wife. She's not the sort to be found hanging round desolate graveyards or sitting in dim-lit High Anglican churches. And she may have suspected mockery.

'We've had to scrap that chum of yours from the programme. She turned quite difficult. Wasn't any good really. Knowing when to cut your losses, that's what it's all about.'

She deftly extracted the stone from her avocado.

'I don't know what advice you gave Giles the other night because I don't know what his problem was. But from the way he was looking when he set off for school this morning, he's in trouble of some kind. I know that bright-eyed, light-footed shiftiness. You spoil the boy when you take any interest in him. You know, Dallas, it's a great mistake for you to ever get involved in the boys' emotional problems. You have absolutely no talent for emotional counselling at all. How could you? You've always run like hell from emotions. Maybe that's what was wrong with your chum. She's a clam that woman, a super-clam.'

'Oh yes?'

She left for the studio, or somewhere; and left me the day.

I sighed: I couldn't climb the stairs to re-enter that world that Dallas languished in, of saloon bars and bed-sitters behind peeling eighteen-forties stucco. Nor could I bring myself to accompany him on a winter's journey to the North-East, one reluctant purpose of which was to fetch a suitcase which Jimmy had left in Alick Duguid's flat. It contained the boy's passport, and Dallas hoped that by getting it he might free himself from obscure guilt.

And, if I couldn't do that, then I might try to re-assemble the past by confronting the restored present: which meant starting from Paddington.

Poplars trembled beside the misty line, vapours hung over the Thames. A yellow-grey sky caressed the suburban roof-tops. No factory chimneys thrust themselves above the light-industry sheds. Nothing happened in that limp salad landscape. It was a lie of course. The same loves, jealousies and hatreds must breed there as elsewhere. Only you couldn't believe it. I entered a taxi at the station and it brought me to a drab street of late Victorian artisans' cottages. The red brick of No. 14 needed pointing. There were a couple of ragged posters in a dusty window. I should have telephoned.

A black-bearded man, dressed in the careless uniform of the professional carer, asked how he could help. I told him I was looking for Miss Sheen. Small lips, under the beard, pouted; my reply was a judgement on him.

'It has to be Miss Sheen, I'm afraid.'

He gestured towards a hard-backed seat.

'She's out at present. You may have a long wait.'

He made a few telephone calls. I sat and smoked. He shot glances at me over a desk piled high with files.

'I can't say when she'll be back. Who sent you by the way?'

'Sent me?'

'Yes, how did you hear about us? I always like to know. It's one of our constant problems, getting the right sort of co-operative input.'

He patted the files. They assured him that he was of service. Eagerness overcame his initial resentment. I had declined his offer of help; that made me a challenge. I couldn't blame him for assuming I was a client.

'Yes,' he said, 'our work would be so much easier if people would only accept that we have no function except a supportive one. There's no need to be shy.'

I was saved from his attentions by Candy who that moment came in weighed down by carrier bags.

She bustled in with a smile and a remark about bloody buses; and then she saw me, and was wary.

'Oh,' Blackbeard said, 'you know him, he's not a client then?'

'A client, no.' She introduced us; his name was Ken.

'Oh,' he said again. 'Are you Ann Graham's husband? I see. Well, if you don't mind my saying so, she's behaved very badly to us in general and to Candy in particular. I don't say it came as a surprise because it didn't. I've seen these media slummers too often. Do you know why they dropped us? We do too good a job and we do it without nonsense. I'd be grateful if you'd tell her so from me.'

As he spoke he made vague fanning gestures that contradicted the strength, even belligerence, of his words.

'I'm afraid,' I said, 'I've no connection with my wife's professional life.'

But I sympathized with him. Theirs was hardly my world, but anyone critical of Ann's *Guardian* Women's Page manner towards other people's lives had my approval.

Candy had put the carrier bags down in the corner—the thickness of her rump as she did so brought a sad memory of her old figure—'So,' she said, 'what did you come for? It wasn't curiosity, I'll be bound.'

'Curiosity, no. I came to see if you'd have lunch with me.'

'You came all the way to Wiltshire to ask me to lunch, on the off-chance.'

'Why not?'

'But I can't take more than three-quarters of an hour,' she said; and we both laughed.

'Well at least you look less tragic,' she said. 'Ken won't be so ready to take you for a client.'

'Oh tragedy's beyond me. Always has been. And I'm not the client type. Though I remember a girlfriend of mine who became a probation officer, and overheard the magistrate say, "Yum, yum, wouldn't mind being put on probation myself if I could be assigned to Miss Greaves." I see what he meant. You will have lunch with me, and stretch that forty-five minutes, won't you?'

'Is that O K Ken?'

'Oh I can manage. You know I can manage.'

'You mustn't mind Ken,' she said, as we turned the corner into a street where the pavement ran under trees heavy with apples. 'He thinks he's not appreciated. But he's all right, for a queer. So why have you come?'

'Seemed like a good idea, that's all.'

'You haven't changed, have you? Still affected and evasive.'

'Thanks a cluster. Look at my grey hairs. I've slowed up. Nice to live here.'

There was an autumn zest to the air, an ordered trimness to the houses, much fresh white paint, unfamiliar pub signs, shops that were closing for lunch.

'I always like that.'

'What?'

'Shops closing for lunch. There's a decency about it. Of course my own shop often doesn't open till after lunch. But that's a different matter.'

'You always do bring things back to yourself, don't you, always did.'

'That's sharp. Have I travelled all the way to Wiltshire simply to be insulted?'

'You chose to come down. I'm still waiting to hear why. Besides I wouldn't call that an insult. Just the truth. There's a pub over there I often go to. That do? They do a good home-made pork pie.'

'Fine.'

It had no carpet, which pleased me, and an open fire ('first of the year, Miss Sheen') and a fluffy black cat sleeping beside it. The pie was very good. Candy drank bitter, I Coca-Cola.

'You were speaking the truth weren't you, about having nothing to do with your wife's programme?'

'I was.'

'Good. I don't think she treated us well, but I'm not complaining. I leave that sort of thing to Ken. And I told you I didn't take to her. It seems it was mutual. So what is it?'

'But I was speaking the truth there too. I really did have no particular reason. I just wanted to see you again. Would you like some more beer?'

She shook her head.

'I've been writing my memoirs,' I said, 'perhaps that prompted it.'

She froze on me. It was a silly thing to say, so soon anyway, one of those careless remarks that can lie like unexploded mines in the terrain a conversation makes its way through.

'You know they're all very polite to me here, very polite and very nice. I sometimes think the small-town English must be the nicest people in the world. They know about me of course, it's the sort of thing that always gets known, as I keep telling our clients, but they're quite happy to keep my past at a distance. It's no concern of theirs. I like it that way, Dallas. Memoirs don't interest me.'

She hadn't lost her brisk, schoolmarmish certainties, which his reading of *Redgauntlet* had prompted Dallas to describe as Quaker.

'Well,' I said, 'it's perhaps because you have a distinct past. Which I haven't. Or that you've got a present. I'm not sure I have that either.'

'That's self-pity. I live now. There's nothing to be gained by harking back.'

She might be right. A coal hissed in the grate. Car horns sounded from the street. The outer door slammed and I could hear steps going up the stair. That was what living in the present meant, a random accumulation of sense-impressions. Only that; and all round them, darkness without echo.

I said, 'I asked you to marry me once. Why did you say no?'

'Has that been troubling you all these years?'

'No, but it's been troubling me the last few days.'

'It didn't trouble you then. You were relieved actually.'

'Then isn't now. I was rather drunk too, as I recall.'

'No doubt that was one reason.'

She looked into the fire. 'No doubt that was one reason,' she said again. 'But it made no sense, when you asked, how and why. Don't let's talk about it.'

'All right.'

But, almost at once, she said, 'Even if I'd loved you, it would have felt like running away. I was too deep in, by then. Besides, I could see, it was Lorna you really fancied. Even though you hardly knew her. You couldn't keep your eyes off her.'

'Nor could you. When you said no I was sure of that. I was sure you were having an affair.'

'No,' she said, 'it was never like that. Whatever people thought. Never quite. I loved her of course, but not that way. Really. Though even my counsel . . . it was one reason, I've always thought, why he was so useless . . .'

Her counsel—a grim, limited man, Mac-something, Macleod, Macfadyen, Mackillop?—had been, surprisingly, a gossip. I remembered that. Months, maybe a couple of years, after the trial, Dallas, briefly in Edinburgh, had dined with Mansie Niven at the Aperitif, that restaurant so long vanished but still regretted. In a corner under the pastel aquarian wall paintings Mansie, drinking Montrachet, had talked with the lack of discretion that contributed so much to his reputation.

'Of course Angus was shocked,' he said—how odd that I can remember the Q C's Christian name but not his surname —'the poor girl couldn't have landed herself with a less suitable counsel, dearie. He's a Wee Free, Angus. From Lewis I think. Spiritually and morally he's never left that community. What was curious was that he believed she was innocent as charged, but he was so disgusted by what he took to be her sin, not that that kind of sin is a crime, my dear, not among the lassies, that his heart wasn't really in the defence. We had tea together in the train coming south, and he wrinkled his nose and said, "They were lovers, you know. I don't understand that sort of thing, but there's no doubt they were. It revolts me." Little did he know, did he?'

That casual gossip, the easy spiteful judgement of the unco guid, lightened Dallas's sense of guilt. Oh, for a long time. But he never really believed it.

'People did fall in love with Lorna of course,' Candy said. 'She did have that magnetism. Even Fraser was still held in a way . . .'

Her voice tailed off, losing that briskness which she wore like a carapace. What was I doing there? Exploring with probing inquisitive tongue another's toothache? But it was my toothache too. I saw Lorna drifting towards me, by firelight, in a dull yellow dress, in December, with flames licking spectral shapes. Vulnerability was the name of her game; it held knights and sadists alike.

'I never slept with her,' I said.

'Of course you didn't. There wasn't the opportunity. Anyway she wouldn't have. If Lorna had liked sex things might have been different.'

'We were hardly even alone together.'

'Lorna aroused feelings, resisted their expression.'

Was it that which drew Dallas to her? Previous and subsequent loves were different. Judy certainly; Ann also. I have always known I married Ann for inadequate reasons, but it was self-deception, only now revealed to me, to say I had married her for stability. Or that was only one reason. I thought she could give me sex without strings. Perhaps I haven't made clear how very sexy Ann is. Even now she finds no difficulty in acquiring lovers as and when she fancies; and one reason, I'm sure, is that she makes so few emotional demands. Life is in its way quite simple with Ann, if only because she speaks her mind: 'I want, I don't want.' She reduces life to those terms. Even when I first saw her, across a table in an Indian restaurant, the way she looked at me said very clearly, 'I want . . .' Lack of complication appeals to the emotionally insecure and indeterminate. She offered an end to self-questioning, to emotional evasion and deceit. It was delusory, but, while we loved, it was simple; it worked for some years, just as Judy had worked for months and Rosemary Mickle for a day or two. Not that Rosemary was simple, though her demands were at first.

'And now, how do you live now?'

Candy smiled. 'From day to day, alone.'

'Do you ever hear from Lorna?'

'There's nothing left between us.'

Despite what she had said, Candy's lunch hour lengthened. Despite the warning she may have heard also. It is the case that we are, no matter how we try to change things, in the grip of recurrent or enduring emotions. That applies even to someone like Candy whose life had been broken by her capacity for pity. You would think she would have taken heed, wouldn't you? In a sense she had. She had tried to externalize it by the work she had taken up; it was a means of keeping pity at a distance, impersonal and official. It was reserved for office hours and checked by administrative requirements. That was one way of trying to deal with it, but dangerous, like the pederast who becomes a schoolmaster in the hope that the perilous emotion (which in youth he may only dimly recognize or even hide from himself) can be dissipated by numbers or channelled into acceptable platonic and paedagogic currents. But now, as the afternoon lengthened and we walked through the autumn streets of the little town after Candy had ('never done this before,' she said) telephoned her office to ask Ken if he would mind the shop, and as we talked of this and that, but increasingly of my own state (and it was of course to find an audience for such talk, an audience that knew me and was yet distant, that I had come down there), her capacity for pity freshened. She felt again stirrings of emotional responsibility. At any rate she suggested we go back to her flat for tea.

A small two-roomed flat, with tiny kitchen and cramped bathroom, above a greengrocer's, in a yellow-brick Edwardian street of two-up, two-down houses. A flat that was neat and uncluttered but not impersonal: the row of bookshelves, rich in the works of lady novelists—Woolf, Bowen, Lehmann,

Taylor, Pym, Hansford Johnson, all predictable enough, a whole shelf of Colette decidedly less so—contradicted any suggestion of anonymity. Still, a flat with no flowers, except a pot of white chrysanthemums, with few ornaments except one or two pieces of good china, a couple of mounted Worcester saucers, a Chien-Lung cup, a Wemyss bowl with plums the colour of old bruises. She made tea while I looked out of the window. A thin grey cloud came down behind the roof-tops, spiked with television aerials. No cars moved in the street below. The traffic sound from the High Street two blocks away came only as a murmuring hum.

Later she said, 'I don't think I can help you, Dallas, but if you want to stay, that sofa turns into a bed.'

And then: 'I was always a dull person to be with. But now I'm even duller. Deliberately. When I said you could stay I wasn't making any offers. You do realize that? It was just that you look in need of a break.'

And much later: 'Are you going to leave your wife?'

At least I didn't ask her if she thought I should. Instead I talked of my boredom with the antique business, and told her about Amanda and Neville and her barrister.

'It's a parody,' I said, 'hard to take seriously. I think they enjoy it.'

But then I remembered Neville weeping as he sat in his mauve baseball boots, and wondered at the way I had dressed them up to play a comedy of my own devising for Candy's pleasure.

'Do you ever go back to Scotland?' I said, late, when the television had died on us.

'No,' she said, 'I funk it.' She lit a cigarette and paused. 'I went back once, eighteen months ago, for my sister's funeral —cancer—and that was only Fife. I felt sick as I got to King's Cross and spewed all the way to Darlington. After that I was worn out. It wasn't grief for my sister. It was physical repugnance, sheer physical repugnance. Even the thought of the place—that shakes me, it's a cancer in itself or it's being eaten up by cancer. Things would have been different, you know, if we hadn't been Scots. It gave us a guilt, made us take our situation too seriously. Even Fraser.' She paused again; it was only the second time she had mentioned him. 'He couldn't just turn his back on religion like an Englishman or an American. He had to make a religion of doing so. And Lorna's damnable timidity, her inability to choose, her damn fatalism; that was Scots. She was in love with defeat, with a Fate that had singled her out as a victim. It's in the air there. It chokes you. No I can't go back, I'd spew again. It's the one thing left I'm afraid of, turning north.

5

The Citroen ran into a snowdrift at a corner a couple of miles from Canaan. A single light shone in the hollow coming from the farm of Auchenquine. The headlights of the car had half-buried themselves in the drift. Dallas swore, struggled out of the car on the passenger's side, intending to make for the farm and found himself in three or four yards waist-deep in the snow. The farm was cut off. There would be no help from there tonight. It had been foolish to come by this road, for he remembered now that this corner had a reputation for being easily blocked. He should have gone round the other road by the manse. But he had been loth to do so.

He forced his way back into the car. Should he spend the night there, with what was left of the half-bottle of whisky he had bought in an Edinburgh pub to fortify himself for the journey? He hadn't the necessary philosophy; besides, even in the car, it would get cold. Again he struggled out, this time on the driver's side, contrived to lock the door, and, leaving his baggage in the car, but with the whisky safe in the deep pocket of his tweed overcoat, set off through the snow.

'Every man his own St Bernard.'

After some five yards he was out of the drift and the snow was now only ankle-deep. But it still took him well over the hour to reach Canaan. As he rounded the bend at the top of the drive, that bend round which he had seen Hugh's Mini skid only four months ago, the sky cleared, and moonlight picked out the crenellations of battlement over the dark empty house. He remembered too how he had come back from the village to find Rosemary's sports car waiting.

The bed would be cold and damp. He found a couple of big tartan rugs in a cupboard, and, without bothering to undress, rolled himself in these, fell on top of the bed, and passed out.

He woke to a blue and white morning, all sparkle and hope. There was no coffee in the house, but he found some tins in the nursery cupboard and he breakfasted on tunny fish and borlotti beans washed down with whisky and a bottle of soda, part of the summer's store. It had been a crazy impulse to set out from London in defiance of the weather forecast, without even telephoning Dod to ask him to turn on the water. Well, Dod wouldn't be in today, it was a Saturday, but he could melt snow for washing. He himself had no idea how to turn the water on.

He had no clear notion why he had come north either.

He tried to telephone the farm to see if they had a tractor that could pull the car out, but got no reply. Their line must be down. He called the local garage. They would do what they could, but no chance today.

The country was locked; movement impossible.

In the nursery *Redgauntlet* lay on an armchair; with a marker where he had finished reading.

' "The true cant of the day," said Herries in a tone of scorn. "The privilege of free action belongs to no mortal—we are tied down by the fetters of duty—our moral path is limited by the regulations of honour—our most indifferent actions are but meshes in the web of destiny by which we are all surrounded . . .

' "The liberty of which the Englishman boasts gives as little real freedom to its owner as the despotism of an Eastern Sultan permits to his slave. The usurper, William of Nassau, went forth to hunt, and thought, doubtless that it was by an act of his own royal pleasure that the horse of his murdered victim was prepared for his kingly sport. But Heaven had other views; and before the sun was high a stumble of that very animal over an obstacle so inconsiderable as a mole-hillock, cost the haughty rider his life and his usurped crown. Do you think an inclination of the rein could have avoided that trifling impediment? I tell you it crossed his way as inevitably as all the long chain of Caucasus could have done. Yes, young man, in doing and suffering, we play but the part allotted by Destiny, the manager of this strange drama—stand bound to act no more than is prescribed, to say no more than is set down for us; and yet we mouth about free-will, and freedom of thought and action, as if Richard must not die, or Richmond conquer, exactly where the Author has decreed it shall be so . . ."'

'The true cant of Calvinism?' Dallas said. 'Though why a Jacobite should spout Calvinism beats me. But fine stuff, of course, fine stuff, can't be denied.'

Dallas was a young man of no convictions. If anyone asked him what he stood for, how he identified himself, justified himself in the eyes of a sceptical world, all he would have been able to utter, with more bravado than belief, would have been those shop-soiled, pub-polluted words, 'I'm a writer'; and the last few months' faltering efforts in London had done nothing to give substance to an assertion that not many of his acquaintance were ready to credit. Indeed he was now in every way as short of credit as of conviction.

He spent two days alone, wandering through the cold, echoing house, living out of tins, sitting with a book, drinking never quite too much whisky, waiting for winter to unlock and make movement possible.

When that happened over-night and the country was awash with melting snow he drove in thin trout-coloured light to Fraser's farmhouse.

Lorna and Candy were alone, having tea among the reproduction antiques and cabbage-rose chintz.

'If you're hoping to find Fraser, I've no idea where he is. We don't see much of my husband these days.'

The firelight played on their faces, like nuns in choir-stalls. He felt gauche, an intruder. They were settled together, domestic. There were scones on the plates. He realized that, thanks to Jimmy's accounts of Crete, he knew them much better than they knew him. Indeed, he had met Lorna only once. But it didn't feel like that.

He talked rather wildly of London, told them about his adventure in the snowdrift, recounted with not much exaggeration and a wayward humour the condition of Canaan; watched himself doing all this, watched them not responding. They regarded him as an ally of Fraser's. He was outside their palisade. He was for them, using the word exactly, a barbarian.

'I heard about Gavin Gregory,' he said. 'Has his case come up yet?'

'It won't,' Candida said. 'Hadn't you heard that? He couldn't face it. He took an overdose.'

'They say he was afraid of what they'd do to him in prison,' Lorna said.

'How did you hear about him anyway?'

'Jimmy told me.'

'Oh.'

'Jimmy's well out of it,' Lorna said.

There was nothing he could do with them, no meeting. He was sorry he had come.

'I was surprised to hear from you,' Alick said.

'Well, I told you why. What are you for?'

'Oh aye. Pint. He's a wee fool, Jimmy.'

'He's in a state. Would they still want him now . . . ?'

'I wouldna think so. It'd be different if they'd charged him maybe. But now they'd forget about him. He's no' important. More sinned against than sinning. Mind you that's just my opinion of what they'll do. It's no' my opinion about the sinning, no' that I'd ca' it a sin. But Jimmy kent fine what he was doing. He's a wee fool and a wee bugger. And if he runs away wi' the passport that's in that case—I ken fine why he wants it—he'll just run into mair trouble. I'm no' sure he's worth bothering about.'

Dallas had come to the same conclusion; he didn't like hearing his own thoughts on Alick's lips.

'And how's my friend the councillor?'

'You don't mean your friend his daughter by any chance?'

'No,' Dallas said, though suddenly he saw Rosemary's thin legs, felt them twisting themselves about him, felt himself Laocoön in their grip, 'no, not Rosemary, the councillor.'

'A bit hot for you, was she? Her feyther's fine. He's aye steering the same canny course.'

It was then that he told Dallas of how Colonel Mickle had been disengaging himself from Fraser that autumn.

And he said, 'The councillor and me, we're on different sides of the fence, but we understand each other and we understand Scotland. Fraser's gone clean daft wi' his half-baked notions of California, which have as muckle application in Scotland as they'd hae in Mars. A' this liberation he blethers about, well, it pre-supposes the existence of an alienated individual. Now I'm a good Marxist and I ken fine about alienation—that's inevitable under capitalism. Nevertheless what we have here in Scotland, even in Glasgow, hell, no, especially in Glasgow, is a strong sense of the tribe. It's paramount. We a' belong and we ken we do. Except maybe the bourgeoisie, but wha cares a fuck for the Scots bourgeoisie, they're hardly even Scots—I'm no' talking about a' the Scots middle class because paradoxically they're no a' bourgeois except in their economic functions. Take the councillor himself. He looks bourgeois, he talks bourgeois, Christ he even smells bourgeois, but he's no' your actual bourgeois as you find them a' over England. He's still got vertical social attachments, he still belongs to the tribe. Na, na, the Scots bourgeoisie, the echt beast's confined to a few wee ghettoes, in Glasgow but maistly in Edinburgh, and they can fucking well rot there. But,' he downed the rest of his beer and held out the empty glass, 'Fraser's detached himself, gone off into his Californian clouds, and so he doesna count now, except maybe with a few other lost souls. You were impressed by him, I ken, for you're deracinated yourself. You want to stop frigging about wi' that Canaan of yours, boy, and either sell it or make something of it.'

Dallas, rising to fetch more beer, responded to what he found cogently attractive in the argument: to re-enter the tribe would be to accept others' reality. And it could be done; he had felt the stirrings and the possibility in the summer. Wasn't that part of what he found in the bar of the Royal?—a very inadequate discovery, he admitted. Wasn't it also what had drawn him to Fraser, that he had seen him as a tribal chief? And now it seemed he was wrong about that. Fraser was a deviant, an exile.

Coming back, he said, 'Do you know Mansie Niven?'

'Oh aye.'

'At that party in Fraser's cottage, he was saying something on the same lines. Different words and different emphasis, but same idea.'

'Aye, the emphasis would be different. I'd screw Mansie, politically speaking you understand, the morn's morn; he's got nae morals, political or any other kind, that wouldna disgrace the randiest alley tomcat, but he's got a heid. You ken he's been adopted as Tory candidate here? For the Labour seat. He hasna a hope in hell, but he'll be in Parliament afore long. As I say, I'd screw him, for free, but he's got a heid and he's no fucking liberal. There's aye a sense of social cohesion in him that acts as a restraining influence on his daft notions.'

He sat back. They were in a little bar of the same hotel where they had first met, a bar that had been a smart cocktail bar ten or fifteen years before when this hotel, which gave the impression of going downhill in most visible ways as well as in its increasingly seedy ambience, had been the principal hotel and rendezvous in the city. Despite the tattiness—scuffed leather, ashtrays left unemptied, a general need for a coat of paint, the imitation copper, which gave the bar its name, decidedly short of a polish—it was certainly smarter than the tartan-lined back bar. Jimmy, with them that first time, would have stood out a bit here, not so much because of his ever more obvious sexual orientation as because of a lack of assurance or poise. It was an insider's bar: he glanced at the three figures sitting on stools at the counter, an oldish man in a Glenurquhart check, perhaps a local laird, and a pink-faced chappie in a double-breasted dinner-jacket who was accompanied by a squawk-voiced scrawny woman in an unbecoming purple evening-gown; they would have lifted the eyebrow at Jimmy. But not, curiously, at Alick Duguid, who in the last few months had lost something farouche in his manner without apparently compromising his opinions. Dallas could see that Mansie might be right about Alick, though whether he was in fact on the way to being corrupted or had persuaded the Establishment to admit him through self-breached walls as a Trojan horse, was too early to say. Whatever the answer, it was clear that Mansie and Alick were quite likely to encounter at Westminster; and yet Alick was only a couple of years older than Dallas himself, with none of his advantages, no better a brain, no . . . Dallas felt his inadequacy. Could he really be said to exist for anyone but himself?

'Oh Goad,' Alick looked up, 'speak o' the bloody deil.'

The bar was suddenly full, and it was full of Fraser and a troop that followed him.

Seeing them, he clapped a hand to his brow in mock-agony:

'I thought you'd deserted us, loon,' he thrust his hand into Dallas's hair and ruffled it.

'Aye, Alick,' he brandished a clenched fist, 'up the Revolution.'

The purple woman said, 'It's that awful Fraser Donnelly, Johnny': she spoke in 'who cares if the servants hear?' tones.

'And that awfu' Fraser Donnelly'll have large drinks a' roon'.'

His voice filled the bar as if it was a public meeting. He planked himself down on the bench seat beside Dallas. His eyes glistened. He smacked Dallas on the knee.

'Sit you doon my babies, and . . . it had better be brandy for a'body.'

But the barman had disappeared. Fraser lumbered to his feet again, advanced to the bar, bellowed into the recesses, and turned round, leaning heavily on his right elbow and swinging his left foot; he fixed imperial eyes on the purple woman, daring her to speak. Instead, she finished her drink in one swallow, muttered to her husband and swept out. He glanced at his still sizeable drink, shrugged his shoulders to indicate that there was more where it came from, and tailed his wife, as he had done the past forty years. Fraser's laughter pursued him through the revolving doors.

Fraser turned on the lairdly chap:

'Did you ever see the like o' thon?'

'Couldn't say, old boy. Seem a bit huffy-puffy, eh? If you ask me, they don't care for you, eh?'

'They do not . . . Christ, is there no service in this fucking bar?'

Fraser's companions, entranced by the show perhaps, were silent. That was standard mid-season form for Kate of course. She had responded to Dallas's greeting with a curt nod; she suggested a more than usually intense sulkiness. It was occasioned by, certainly directed at, a slim, blonde girl in a pink sack that came only half-way down her thighs. She sat with her long legs crossed and her pink mouth a little open and her cornflower eyes fixed on Fraser; she had the divine silliness of a Botticelli angel, and she had thrown down what looked to Dallas like a real fur coat, cream-coloured and very expensive; she had dropped it with the casualness of a girl accustomed to property. And she was perhaps eighteen.

'Where the hell are you from?' Alick asked.

'Perthshire really, though Edinburgh too, just now . . . but our family house is in Perthshire.'

'She's with me,' the younger and shorter of the two men said; a red-head in jeans and a sports jacket; he had an Edinburgh public school voice and looked like a scrum-half.

'Is she now?' Alick said, letting his gaze wander over the boy's face. 'Is she now?'

'Where the fuck are those drinks?' the other man said. His hand shook as he took a cigarette from a packet. He was a big rangy fellow with crinkly fair hair and a big hooked nose veined with little red lines.

The scrum-half said, 'I'm Alastair and this is Caroline and this here is Roy. Oh, I'm sorry,' he turned to Kate, 'I don't know your name.'

'They ken it fine,' she said.

'And you're a' in tow?' Alick said.

'I'm sorry, I don't understand.'

The barman returned, spoke to Fraser in a whisper, was answered with a roar, and vanished again. Dallas caught a whiff of trouble. The blonde girl looked still at Fraser; her mouth continued to hang open.

'Isn't he the most amazing man?' she said. 'You know I've

never met anyone like him. Not remotely. You wouldn't believe the things we've done. We're on the way to his house for a party. I don't think we'll ever get there. This is the third or fourth bar we've stopped in, and there are miles and miles to go. It's simply amazing, absolutely out of this world.'

She was going to be eaten up. The scrum-half would be ditched somewhere, or, more likely paired off somehow. Perhaps with Kate, though Dallas didn't think she would welcome the transfer. And the brutish Roy? Perhaps he was Jimmy's successor. One thing was sure, as one after another they flickered their eyes at Fraser: they were all under the magician's spell. Ringmaster was maybe a better description. He cracked the whip, and, in brisk succession, Kate, Jimmy, Rosemary, Gavin Gregory, now this Caroline and Co., they went through the routine: 'One staff-officer jumps right over another staff officer's back.' But Dallas was immune. It was like having had mumps during an epidemic. Alick was immune too, with only this difference: he had never been in danger, while Dallas had felt the attraction, responded to the touch of the whip, very nearly signed on for the duration. He blushed. And he had to admit, even now, that if either of these girls turned their eyes on him, he wouldn't say no. But not, perhaps, if they did it at Fraser's direction; it would have to be spontaneous.

The barman came back again, this time accompanied by a man in a dark suit, with the Jacob manner of hotel managers. He leant over the counter and spoke to Fraser. He shook his head; it hurt him more than it hurt Fraser, but . . . The signs were familiar; Dallas recognized housemaster's hypocrisy. Fraser's neck swelled over his collar, rearing up like an angry swan. The lairdly chap made to contribute something, checked himself, not getting beyond, 'Steady-weady now, chaps . . .' The manager was firm, shook his head, pursed his lips. Fraser shot his hand across the bar, grabbed the manager by the tie. The bar froze.

'Ye canting wee futret,'—every syllable was given a big production—'I'll mind this. You needna look for my custom again. Or my friends'. And you'll regret it. You needna think I'll no' see you do that.' He swept across to the table; Lear quitting Goneril's house; Claverhouse defying the Lords o' Convention; Cagney rejecting the DA: 'We're no' stayin' here a minute more. We'll off to Hardie's. There'll be nae bloody nonsense there.'

The troop rose, obedient. Caroline picked up her fur starlet's coat.

'Are you wi' us?'

Alick indicated they had business to finish, might join them later. The bar was all at once all but empty.

'What was that about?'

'Och nothing new. Like I said, word's getting about that Fraser's trouble. He's no' exactly welcome where he used to be. That's a'. What a crew he's got, eh? That wee quine hasna a notion.'

'What sort of place is this Hardie's?'

'Oh it's just a wee hotel in Mannofield where they don't question who's in whose room, and interpret the licensing laws as if they're going out of fashion. Do you want to go there?'

Dallas could smell the place: the overhanging odour of cooking fat, stale beer, extinct tobacco; the dry rot in the bedrooms; the stuffy clamminess of hoovered carpets in the morning; the air long protected by closed and curtained windows.

'I think not. I'll sit this one out.'

'Well,' Alick said, 'you could be right. We'd better no' forget that wee bugger's case. He's well out of it too, I'll give him that.'

6

'Coffee, I don't like wine in the afternoon.'

Dallas resented Candy's primness. It sounded like reproof for the open bottle of claret by his chair. But when she looked round the nursery with the Beatrix Potter frieze he had known all his life, and said, 'What a nice room,' he was pleased she was there.

But her own discomfort was apparent; it was moral rather than social embarrassment.

'We weren't either of us very nice when you called the other day. Lorna was sorry and upset about it later. Me, too.'

'Oh nonsense. Here, take this.'

He handed her the coffee.

'No, it's not nonsense. Anyway that's why I've come. To say sorry.'

'That's all right.'

She took her coffee over to the bow window and stood looking out. The sun had gone and the bare trees and half-light gave the glen a pinched look.

'Don't you find it depressing, being here, on your own?'

'No, it's all right.'

'Yes, I suppose it might be. I gather you've seen Fraser.'

'Briefly.'

'He wasn't pleased, you know. That you didn't go on with him. He was still in a state about it this morning. He doesn't like being stood up. He doesn't like thinking he can't get people to fall in with his wishes.'

'Yes, I realize that.'

'That's why he doesn't care for me . . .'

Then, in an intimacy that took Dallas by delightful surprise, she began to talk about Crete, filling in the yawning gaps in the story Jimmy had given him. When she came to the conversation on the beach with Fraser, she hesitated and twisted a handkerchief in her hands, and looked down at the nursery table with its stained and torn oil-cloth cover; she put a finger in one of the holes and worked at it.

'When he said that last horrible thing, where or how he had had Lorna, I was so confused. I wanted never more to have anything to do with it, or any of them, and yet I knew I couldn't bring myself to leave Lorna till I could get her to leave him. I would be ashamed to. But she won't, I'm afraid she won't ever. She's afraid to, even though she knows it's never going to get better, and though I tell her that leaving will be frightful at first, awfully difficult and frightening I can see that, but that wouldn't last. The law would protect her, wouldn't it?'

'Yes, I would think so. I'm sure it would.'

'I don't know what to do.'

He didn't want to speak or listen. He wanted to take Candy in his arms, hold her head against his chest, nuzzle her hair; just stop like that a long time. But all the same he was curious, and flattered that she had come here and was telling him all this. People were not in the habit of making him a confidant.

She began to cry. He sat still in his chair, unable to do what he wanted to do which was—he saw this even as he didn't do it—the natural warm human sympathetic action. She stopped, and sniffed, and dabbed at her eyes, and then looked at him:

'I'm sorry to inflict this on you. I've been bottling it up so long.' She sniffed again. 'Can I have a cigarette?'

Well, that at least wasn't beyond him. He even lit it for her.

'It's awful cheek,' she said, 'after the way we behaved, but what I wondered was, could you come and tell Lorna the same thing? She might believe it from you. Yes, she might. She thinks quite a bit of you. You impressed her at that party. She liked you after. That's partly why she was so sorry about how we behaved when you came over. Besides,' she said, 'Lorna's the sort of girl who is more likely to take advice from a man. It's her upbringing, I suppose.'

'But I hardly know her . . .'

'And,' she said, 'you've seen through Fraser. You have, haven't you? I felt that when he was so angry with you this morning. You really have seen through him, he can't ever impress you again, can he?'

It was true. In the summer he would certainly have followed Fraser to Hardie's Hotel or anywhere, like a small boy after a brass band. But that was indeed over. It was partly because of what he had learned from Candy and Jimmy and Alick Duguid; but it was also because his autumn's otherwise futile wrestling with words had hardened him a fraction, opened his eyes a little, made him more suspicious of appearances. It had taken him some time to get here. He remembered with shame how the first time he met her Candy had been ahead of him, and clearly said, 'Fuck Fraser', in other words, of course.

'He is mad, you know. You know that, don't you? And I'm afraid. I'm afraid of what he might do to Lorna. He might even kill her.'

He caught a whiff of fear, like the approach of nailed boots in a concrete corridor.

*   *   *

I looked up from the omelette she had made me.

'Do you remember coming over to Canaan? It was like one of those moments when you hear footsteps in an empty house. You said you were afraid Fraser might kill her. Was that true, did you really believe it?'

'What's the point?'

Candy poured herself a glass of water. She held the glass up in hard-worked fingers, with cracked skin and bitten nails.

'What's the point of going over it all?'

'You asked me to urge her to give herself a chance, a last chance, but in the end it was you I gave the chance to, and you turned it down. It wasn't just because I was drunk.'

Candy brushed crumbs from her brown shapeless skirt. She took a packet of cigarettes from her desk and lit one—'All of us ex-cons smoke like anything . . .'

'I think some music. I think Brahms. The violin concerto.'

The room was filled with longing, aspiration, a waste of regret.

'I spent years going over things. Now I prefer Brahms. Aimez-vous Brahms? The great thing with music is you don't have to find words for feelings. It's personal, yet impersonal. I couldn't do without Brahms.'

'All the same, that night, did we both go in your car? Or did we take mine as well? Or did you come in mine?'

'Let it be, Dallas.'

'No, but you see, that's what I've done all these years, pushed it into the background, out of sight, pretended it never

170

happened or had nothing to do with me. I'm sorry, I can see it's different for you.'

'Different in a rather more serious way than you seem to remember. It does no good to pick at the past. I've seen too many of my clients relapse because they can't let it go . . .'

But picking at the past was what was now irresistible. It lay like a scab over my life; and the scab had reached that maturity when you can raise its edge with your fingernail, giving a little twinge of pain, the kind you can't let go of, just as your tongue will unfailingly seek out and tease that decaying tooth.

7

Dallas was aware of long fingers and dancing firelight and the softness of a high-necked, charcoal-grey cashmere. For a moment Lorna was in his arms as she had been, dancing in Fraser's cottage; she laid her cheek against his, apology for his last visit, gratitude for this.

'I called my mother and asked her to come and take the kids for a couple of nights. Was I right, Candy? Fraser won't like it, but I wanted them away for a bit.'

(Later, they asked Dallas if Lorna had given any reason for sending the children away. Her mother had said she was 'surprised' by the request; it had come 'right out of the blue'. And he hadn't been able to say anything that helped. 'There was a lot of tension', nonsense like that.)

Candy said, 'Look, let's sit down.'

But Lorna couldn't settle. She thanked Dallas more than once for coming, but couldn't bring herself to listen to what he had to say.

'Look,' Candy said, 'Lorna . . .'—and even then Dallas wondered at her inability to employ any term of endearment, at the chill Presbyterian rectitude that threw her back on the formality of the name—'I've told Dallas everything . . .'

That stopped her. Her head dropped like a dying flower, 'Oh, no.'

'Yes, even Crete.'

There was a long silence, chill with apprehension and memory. Dallas cleared his throat,

'I'm awfully sorry but . . .'

Awfully sorry; he felt the words' inadequacy.

Lorna took no note. She crossed the room, picked up a photograph and handed it to Dallas.

'That was our wedding.' Fraser jolly, laughing, kilted, his hair curly, his head thrown back to reveal bad teeth; a plumper, altogether cruder Lorna, with none of the poetic distinction she had acquired, that admittedly nebulous distinction, the nature of which was beyond Dallas to determine, but which had so persuasively appealed to him from that first glimpse in the cottage when he didn't know who she was.

'But, Crete . . . that was the only time he's really ill-treated me.'

Candy looked at Dallas in a shared complicity of class. He read his own scorn and impatience there. Did their feeling of responsibility stem, I wonder, from their understanding that Lorna came from a culture that was different in one important respect from theirs, and, by reason of that difference, could properly be described as deprived? A culture that taught that the only real ill-treatment was physical; that had so little respect for the emotions, so little time for them, that it would regard any plea of emotional oppression as self-indulgent; a culture that accepted that women simply had to bear these things.

Dallas put the picture on the table, face-down. It was time to say his piece. He could feel Candy willing him on. And he tried. He pointed out how she had certainly grounds for divorce—there was no question after all but that Fraser had committed adultery time and again—he couldn't imagine there would be any difficulty in proving it. Condonation might be a problem; not beyond a good lawyer. As for her fears, that Fraser would never let her get away with it, that he wouldn't leave her alone—Dallas didn't go further and specify these fears as Candy had spelled them out to him lest Lorna take fright at his knowledge. Well, there too, as he understood it, she should have no difficulty, no real difficulty, you understand. She could easily get an injunction or whatever it was called, restraining him from approaching her pending divorce proceedings, and if he broke that, then it would be a matter for the police . . .

So he talked, on and on, round and about, polysyllabic, quasi-official, assuming authority, all the time knowing it was like trying to float a paper-boat of a love-letter down a dull canal. The boat might get there, but the words could no longer be read.

Lorna shook her head, not meeting his eyes.

Candy reinforced the argument: how much longer did Lorna think she could go on like this? Did she really think things might get better? Was there any possible change she could envisage?

'We've been over that again and again,' Lorna said.

'And we know there isn't.'

'I did go to the doctor . . .'

'And he gave you tranquillizers. Great.'

Dallas took the cue. What about Fraser's state of mind? Wasn't it unbalanced? Shouldn't he, perhaps?

'You'll not get Fraser to see a doctor. He says he's on top of the world. He doesn't even have hangovers.'

'I wasn't meaning that.'

'What were you meaning then?'

'To be frank, we've wondered whether he isn't . . . well, mad, nuts, off his head. To the point of being actually certifiable.'

For a moment Lorna seemed to consider it.

'He's not right in the head. I've known that a long time. But you've hardly seen him, Dallas, except when he's fou or playing about. You've not seen him at business. He's sharp enough at business . . .'

They weren't ever going to be able to urge her to action. She was mesmerized. Yet they couldn't leave her, and Dallas returned to the charge more than once in the next two or three days. Fraser continued absent, and Dallas took to spending most of his waking hours over in the farmhouse, where the same arguments met the same inert response. Yet they both continued to feel protective.

As Dallas drove home one night (a little drunk, for the intimacy that was developing had encouraged him to sit and sip as he would do at home), he said aloud:

'It'll have to be the Young Lochinvar stunt.'

But of course the next morning he couldn't nerve himself to make the suggestion. (And Lochinvars don't of course suggest; they act.) Instead, he continued to play the friend of the family, the warm supporter, Rizzio not Bothwell—at best the young man come about the trouble. It got them nowhere, but Dallas heard the harmonious chords of the trio's chamber music. He felt also warm gushes of unsatisfiable desire; he was caught in the troubadour situation, on-going and unviable.

8

But, when the door slammed and the house burst with sound, as Dallas sat there with a tumbler of whisky, in what was mirk-dead night, the three were numbed, like conspirators discovered; the near idyll shattered, as if a stone had been thrown through that mirror in which, all through that long, soft evening, Dallas had seen his garden landscape of Romantic Love reflected.

'Oh, so you're here now, are you?' Fraser thrust a red sweaty face into his, giving off a breath that would not have surprised him if it had come from a long-dead Pharaoh. 'You've taken to hanging round my wife, have you? You needna bother, boy. I've other plans for her.'

He gestured towards the door where the blond, rangy Roy was entering, stumbling a bit under a case of bottles. The whole gang was still there, the party begun in Aberdeen staggering to the end of its first week. The scrum-half type had long lost his tie, and seemingly his razor; his hair was all drunken dishevelled, his eyes bloodshot. He marched to the gramophone with the clumsy gait of a Hammer Films monster, knocking over a nest of occasional tables on the way. He fumbled around, put on a Presley record. Then he lurched towards Candy, offering her his arms. She tried to turn away but he caught hold of her and forced her down on the sofa. He pushed his face towards hers and began talking while his left hand grabbed her knee. Dallas began in their direction, but his own arm was seized by the blonde girl, Caroline, who had left off swinging on Fraser's to transfer herself to him.

'You really should have come on Tuesday. You can't imagine what you missed. We've had such a time, really quite quite out of this world.'

Her huge silly eyes flapped at him.

'You can't believe it,' she said again, 'it was really incredible. The grooviest.'

Her attentions distracted him—does your mother know you're out?

She pulled him to her, and, when he looked across the room, Candy had extricated herself from the scrum-half and marched from the room.

'Aifter her, loon,' Fraser yelled. 'She's a wee icicle, but like a wee icicles, she's a wee hoor at hert.'

'But the thing is,' Caroline said, 'I didn't know who you were, or I would have insisted, jolly well insisted. You're a chum of my cousin Mansie, and you're Grant's cousin yourself. Isn't that right? Well, you see, don't you, how it would have added to the fun. Alastair's a chum of Grant's too. Not me actually. He took me to a hunt ball, you know, and slobbered awfully in the car park. Not groovy. But it means you're one of us. Isn't this all heaven, absolutely mad, mad heaven? I mean, have you ever met anyone like Fraser, isn't he absolute heaven?'

Dallas's retreat had been blocked by an armchair. He subsided into it. Caroline landed herself on his lap. She began to kiss him, a bit damply, but with enthusiasm. Her tongue sought his. He put his arm round her and kissed back. Their bodies strained together. For a moment the indecisions and perplexities of days, weeks, months, narrowed and hardened into sensation, into this pink, silly-pretty piece of flesh urging itself against him, into their wrestling tongues, the young ardent limbs, the smell of brandy, sweat and French scent, the light abundance of hair in which his hand was lost.

A sharp pain broke the idyll. His head was yanked off Caroline's face, his hair torn backwards. He looked into a red fury. The grip shifted to seek the short hairs above his neck. For an instant he was a prep school boy again: 'the square, Graham'—tug, jerk—'on the hypotenuse, Graham'—tug, jerk—but this was worse, a thousand times worse. Fraser, advancing round the chair, pulled him upright, sending Caroline scrambling to the fleecy rug.

'You bloody wee stoat. You canna keep away from my wife, and now we're nae sooner here than you're having it off wi' this lassie. But she's reserved, you wee bugger, she's mine.'

Caroline hopped to her feet. She hovered between them, eyes shining. Men fighting over her—quite, quite out of this world.

'You're a right fucking wee stoat. Aye, an' you were wi' that bastard Duguid, and the pair of you needna think I dinna ken what that bugger's up tae.' He transferred his hold to Dallas's lapels and shook him. 'He's keeping a file on me, isna he? A bleeding dossier. And you're helping him, that's why the pair of ye wouldna come on tae Hardie's. You're no' just a wee stoat, you're a fucking spy.'

His face had swollen to fill Dallas's vision . . . .

'Oh for Christ sake, Fraser, for Christ sake . . . you're talking, you're mad or drunk . . .'

(Did Dallas say any of that, or does my vanity supply memory with the words . . ?)

'Mad, is it? You ca' me mad in my ain hoose. Well, you're fucking well no' staying here. Open the door someone and we'll hae him oot.'

He lifted Dallas off the ground, and marched him, their faces inches from each other, through the door. Still keeping Dallas up, he forced him along the passage to where the back door led to the yard. A surge of cold air took the back of Dallas's neck. Fraser held him off at arm's length, then, keeping hold of Dallas's right shoulder with his left hand, smacked his right fist into Dallas's belly. He doubled up, whining for breath. Fraser shifted his grip to the hair.

'Your bloody looks.'

A swinging blow caught Dallas on the mouth. He could only yelp. He choked on the blood, was still held upright, didn't see the boot coming for his groin. He hardly felt the cobbles. His hands convulsed to the pain. Hands reached for him. He was being lifted again . . . please God, please God, no . . . something, somewhere, hit the cobbles again.

He heard the smack of hands, a girl's tinkle voice, laughter.

(It makes me shiver to write that passage after twenty years; but—horribly—excites me too. Hadn't it been what Dallas deep down was asking for; isn't it what I have always known I deserved?)

9

Memory supplies nothing of surfacing, or next to nothing. Multi-coloured pain, retching, wet slimy cobbles, a cold wind and fear. Then the door; not again, please God not again.

Hands lifted him, half-way up, soft hands wiped blood, angel hands, nurse hands, Candy. And her voice saying sorry.

'God . . .'

'Your poor face, what a brute . . .'

Pity and anger. Dallas clings, nurse turns into mother, turns into . . .

'You got away from the scrum-half . . .'

'The? Oh yes, creep.'

Her fingers on his face, 'Poor you . . .'

His hand clutching hers.

'Poorest you, poorest us, poorest Lorna.'

Long silent comfort. She gets him up, to the car, stumbling, but relief, softness, pain ebbing, long long silence. Out of the wind. But lights in farmhouse offer menace, no story-book comfort of light in darkness.

Dallas places stiff and bruising arm round Candy's shoulder, draws her close, her head against his, turns her face, pushes bruised, bloody lips against her cheek, seeks her mouth . . .

'No,' she says, 'no . . .'

'Please. Come away, come with me, to London, marry me . . .'

He knows it's absurd, more absurd than before.

She draws back.

'I have to go in. I wish I could get Lorna out. I don't dare try. She wouldn't anyway, even now. But I'm frightened, Dallas.'

'Stay with me.'

'I can't. Dallas, will you fetch the police . . . ?'

That was the point he had to cling to and insist on, that Candy had asked him to fetch the police because she was so frightened. That was it. And with reason. Didn't his own condition suggest she had reason?

It was harder to drive than he had expected. He found his vision wavering. The road was slimy. Corners surprised him. And he probably drove too fast. He was after all running away, even if he was also running for help.

'There's a telephone a couple of miles down the road, at the Peterkirk cross-roads,' Candy had said. 'Call from there. That'll be quickest.'

It wasn't working. He lifted the receiver and got no sound at all. He wasted minutes agitating it. Failure tightened panic's grip. He drove faster, more dangerously.

There was a blue light behind him, the cry of a siren. Police car swept by, flashed him into the ditch. He felt relief, gratitude.

But they were interested in his driving, his condition, not in his story—'You're no' fit to be in a car, you'd better come to the station.' In the police car he tried again. 'There's going to be murder done. I was coming to you anyway.' He had pitched it too high, they weren't interested. 'It's Fraser Donnelly,' he said. They just laughed. 'Fraser is it? Och we ken Fraser fine.'

'You'll hae to see a doctor at the station, but we'll just charge you with dangerous driving in any case. You can aye tell this story of yours to the sergeant. I suspicion he'll no be interested.'

Later, of course, they denied all this. They said Dallas had been incoherent. 'Just making no sense at all.'

What about the doctor? Well, the doctor made him do sums: 'Let's just establish your condition first.' And this was the terrible thing: Dallas could make no sense of the figures. He couldn't write his name either.

He changed tack. 'Look, I've been beaten up. I want to lay a charge. Against Fraser Donnelly. He beat me up.'

They looked at the doctor, who was ready to sign a statement that Dallas was drunk.

'No,' he said, 'he's fallen over a few times. The condition he's in . . .'

'Aye, aye,' the sergeant said. 'Thank you doctor. Just as I thought.'

'Take him doon, Ian,' he said. 'Mind the wee bastard's footing on the stair.'

'You shouldna have said that aboot Fraser,' the constable Ian said. 'He's a respected man. It's no' right spreading stories o' that sort.'

'It's the truth for Christ sake.'

He didn't feel the boot. But the concrete floor surged up at him.

'Dinna try it again, son.'

They threw him on a bunk. The door slammed. It was dark. The footsteps died into silence.

He woke to grey light and pain, stiffness and fear. It was cold. He pulled the thin blanket round him and listened: to nothing. His face looked at a tiled wall. He waited.

A long while later there were voices. The door opened. A policeman stood there with a mug of tea and a hunk of bread. Dallas hadn't seen him before.

'You were in a fine state I hear. Making no sense at all. I wish to God you had been. They want to speak to you now. Here, put these shoes on.'

'Who are they?'

'CID.'

'What am I charged with?'

'Och, we'll see about that.'

I still dream about the cell, and, when I do, I try to escape from it by a tunnel that keeps closing on my shoulders. I've never talked to Ann about that night; indeed she hardly knows about the case except in the vaguest terms. Curiously, a couple of years back, when I was gyrating in one of my lower circles and sitting in the back room of the shop with a bottle of gin, I told the whole story to Amanda; and, do you know, she thought it was fantasy. She said it was unhealthy to try to induce guilt. She said, 'Neville's always doing that, that's how I know. He told me once he had raped his sister. Well, I was so worried I even asked her. Delicately, you understand. She was shocked. She said Neville had hardly ever even kissed her. It was all in his mind. You're drinking too much gin, you know.'

'Don't you understand,' I said, 'if I'd stayed sober, coherent, none of it would have happened. I'm an accessory before the fact. Do you wonder I've never been able to do anything since . . .' and more, and more, in the same vein.

'You'd better have some coffee,' she said. 'Ann telephoned to remind you you have people coming for dinner. You'd better sober up. I told her you were engaged on a deal. As I said to Neville, this sort of brooding on crimes you imagine you've committed is just a sort of alibi, it's an escape-mechanism.'

10

Fraser stretched, shook his hands above his head in a boxer's salute, kicked his legs out, threw himself into the sofa. His ejection of Dallas had banished ill humour, allayed testiness. As ever, action elated him. Moreover, Dallas had irritated him for days, as someone who had set his will against Fraser's, and witnessed his humiliation in the Caledonian Hotel, but not the subsequent effortless triumph at Hardie's. And the girl Caroline's obvious recognition that she shared something with Dallas, beside which her view of Fraser could only be as of a splendid exotic, had, as it were, touched the trigger of his anger, done the trick, lit the torch: there is a cornucopia of cliché to choose from in order to render what was a cliché in itself.

But now she too was excited by Fraser's violence. He felt her quiver.

He commanded everyone into the lounge, commanded all glasses to be re-charged. Even Lorna and Candy were compelled to assent. His will hummed. His good humour flourished. The deep sofa became a throne. Yet things had changed. A few months before the evening would have passed in anecdote, bawdry, songs, jokes, and, if the right spark had been struck, political or even, using the word loosely, philosophical, argument, which in this company, for there was no one to match him, would have turned into monologue. But not now. It wasn't anything immediate which caused the sun to withdraw, not even any awareness he may have had of Candy's hatred, touched with contempt, and Lorna's apprehension. The latter indeed had come to act on him as a stimulant. No, but all through the autumn he had grown to sense the isolation into which he was plunging, an isolation one has to call spiritual. Liquor, too, fretted his nerves. It was noted that it only elevated him momentarily now. Kate, who in her curious self-regarding way, probably came closer than anyone else to retaining a sort of love for him, observed that: 'Drink was taking him away.' Big blonde Vera gave an interview to one of the tabloids in which she was quoted as saying: 'It had come to a point where you could be frightened just to be with him. He felt they had rejected him and he wanted to hurt in revenge. I had to stop seeing him. It wasn't safe to be with him. I wasn't surprised by what happened.'

So it wasn't long before he started niggling. All the time he was fondling the girl Caroline, he was taunting Lorna. It was all self-contradictory, what he said. One minute she was frigid; 'as cold as a white bean-pole'; next, adulterous: 'I ken fine why that wee bugger was here. She likes the gentry, you see. Is that no' the case, hinny? You wouldna think I'd brought her oot o' a back-street close in Torry.' He squeezed Caroline, perhaps forgetting the girl's own origins, in his accusation of Lorna's presumed tastes; certainly blind to the irony linking his words and actions. Then came self-pity, mixed with anger when he spoke of how she had sent the children away from him.

'They're just with their granny for a couple of days,' she said; these were the only words she raised in her defence all evening.

'What on earth did Caroline think was happening?' Dallas asked Mansie Niven.

'Well by your own account, ducky, she was a bit plastered. And she'd been popping pills. It was some kind of game for her. And she liked being the prize. She's a very silly girl, without much grip on any objective reality.'

'All the same . . .'

'And, you ken, I'm good to her, that good to her.'

Fraser waved his hand round the room, proving his generosity by furniture and curtains, 'That good to her.' The gesture halted on the man Roy.

'Do you fancy my wife, Royboy? Dinna think I'll mind. Feel free. A'body has the right to feel free, and act accordingly. You could put roses in that whey face, eh boy?'

Roy's grin switched from Fraser to Lorna.

'Your man was telling me you were quite something. He said . . .'

Lorna gets up. From now on it is all a movie. She is pale, shaking, hardly beautiful at all. She says she is going to make some coffee. The words get her out of the room. Candy follows her to the kitchen. For a moment they hold each other, pressing against the big warm Aga. It is eleven o'clock; a cheap Smith's alarm ticks over the otherwise dead mid-winter silence.

Lorna says: 'Poor Dallas, is he all right?'

'Yes,' Candy opens her mouth again to mention the police. Surely she is going to promise their arrival. But the door opens and the red-headed scrum-half lurches in.

'I'm most awfully sorry,' he says.

'Get her away,' Candy says, 'just get that half-witted girl of yours away.'

'I'm most awfully sorry,' he repeats, 'I've just been sick in your loo. Could you let me have a glass of water?'

He takes a sip. Liquor and nausea have sucked out his bounce. His head slumps forwards, hits the table. He sprawls, passed out.

'That,' Candy says, 'was meant for me. Do you realize that? Look, Lorna, you must see, this evening settles it. It can't go on. You must see that now. There's Fraser with that half-wit deb, and that blond brute meant for you and this thing for me. It's no good. It's all quite impossible.'

'Oh yes,' Lorna says, 'I see that. In the morning.'

In the morning.

Yes, in the morning.

The house passes into darkness. Leaving the scrum-half Lorna and Candy slink upstairs. Separate beds and separate rooms. Locked doors. Candy throws open her window. Sister Annes for the police. A north-westerly scuds clouds across the moon. The great bare copper beech casts its shadow over the garden. Except for the wind, there is silence. The police aren't coming, Dallas has let her down. It matters less now. Tomorrow somehow it will be over. And indeed if the police arrive now, what will they find? A sleeping house, evidence of drinking, of immorality, nothing that's their business. The evening has been less terrible than she feared. Awful enough, but less terrible.

She gets into bed, wonders about the girl Caroline, how it is possible to be such a little fool.

Footsteps clumber in the room below. Silence resumes.

Candy is exhausted. Her nerves have gone beyond jangling to utter fatigue.

The noise below is the man Roy left in an armchair with a brandy bottle. He must have lurched to his feet, then toppled. Later he is found lying on the rug in front of the fire. There is a small cut on his head. The rug shows spots of blood.

Though Lorna had come to depend so greatly on Candy she had never been frank with her. She concealed one general truth about herself and three particular facts.

The general truth was something she could hardly bring herself to confess even in her own mind, for it was shaming. She had, in an old-fashioned way, been brought up impeccably honest. That was her mother's doing. The wife of a jobbing carpenter, Lorna's mother was possessed of exemplary rectitude. She considered she had lowered herself by her marriage, for her own mother had been a farmer's daughter who, early widowed, had been compelled by circumstance to take a job in a shop. This inheritance encouraged Lorna's mother to develop the strictest standards; her self-respect demanded that she arrest this slide in fortune. She could not do so socially; she could mount no economic ladder; her superiority had to be moral. Respectability became her goddess, but respectability with a firmly moral basis. She had to be better than her neighbours; she despised them for their dishonesty, shiftiness, moral disorganization. Lorna was educated in the narrowest and most self-regarding of creeds; and it didn't suit her temperament. Its rigour bruised her sensibilities. In consequence, childhood made her into an habitual liar. Later, recognizing this fact and disliking it (for it offended both what she had been taught and her own instinctive nature), she converted her habit of untruthfulness into an absolute reticence. Circumstances made it impossible for her to be honest; very well then, she would conceal both what she believed and what she felt. Such concealment led inevitably to self-deception. Even before her marriage she reached a point when she could not tell the truth about her feelings because she could not discover it for herself, or certainly admit to herself what she really felt about anything. She even came to wonder if emotional truth existed.

So when, mulishly, she refused to listen to Candy's arguments and leave Fraser, she was unable to say why. She substituted her children, then put forward her fear of what Fraser would do, the argument that he would never let her go. And she couldn't for a moment grant any cogency to Candy's counter-argument; or to Dallas's when Candy brought him in as reinforcement. Yet she was ashamed to examine her own mind for a reason for her obduracy. Dallas was left to wonder if she wasn't perhaps a masochist, half in love with Fraser's cruelty. Indeed that possibility occurred to her too. In an unguarded and tearful moment she once said to Candy: 'What he did in Crete would drive me away if I was normal.'

But—this is the first fact she concealed—what kept her there, what she couldn't bring herself to leave, was simply the house. I can only come to an intellectual understanding of the hold it exercised. I can't feel it. I suppose one of the temperamental divisions between people is the line that separates nomads from home-makers. Myself, I feel—always have felt—as much at home in a mean hotel room as anywhere. It gives an ironical shade to my occupation of the last twenty years. The fact that my own house reflects my taste, not Ann's, presents itself to me now as evidence of the effort of will I once applied to the cheating of my nature. Lorna however, brought up meanly in an ugly terraced tenement flat, had found in the furnishing and decoration of the farm-house the fullest expression of her nature. And she couldn't cut herself off from it. She knew Candy wouldn't understand this. She didn't understand it herself. Naturally introspective, she puzzled over it. But then, how often do we really understand the emotions that determine action? We can only make sense of feeling in retrospect—'I loved her because of the way she walked . . . because she carried with her the memory of hyacinths . . .'—that sort of thing. It is all rationalization, structuring experience in an attempt to persuade ourselves that life makes sense.

Well, Lorna's reluctance to leave the house makes that sort of rationalized sense to me. She could have conceived of a new life with a new husband or without one; but to abandon her sitting-room was to deny the thing in which she had invested all her values. You could call it her soul's expression. No doubt it was commonplace, as a thing in itself, even a bit vulgar—there is something common about the timidity that buys repro bureaux and puts them beside Chesterfield suites covered with flowered chintz. You would have said there was nothing there chosen because she had to have it; that the criterion of selection had been her tepid notion of good taste. But that would be the superficial view. The sitting-room was the necessary confirmation that she had escaped the tenement life into which she had been born.

The second fact she concealed from Candy—it was pride made her conceal it—was that, ever since Crete, she had locked her bedroom door against her husband.

And the third was that she kept, by her bed, a shotgun; which she loaded every night. In the morning she removed the cartridges and hid the gun on the top shelf of the wardrobe under piles of pullovers she no longer wore.

* * *

She said later she was half-asleep when she heard the screaming start, and then, she said, 'Something snapped.'

After that, we know almost nothing of what she later thought she thought then.

* * *

She gets up and puts on a dressing-gown and goes into the passage. Screams ring round the stair-well; mad screams of nightmare. And laughter cuts through them. It is when she hears the laughter she goes back for the gun. She has no intention of using it, she says later; it is just that she needs it.

The door of the room where Fraser has been sleeping on those infrequent nights at home—a room which in the first years of their marriage was occupied by his mother—is at the end of the landing. The handle turns. The door gives on screaming now subsided to sobs and moans. A wall-light over the mirror is still on. Fraser and the girl are in the bed. There is no surprise about that. Fraser is on top, the girl's struggles diminish. For a moment Lorna stands and watches. Then Fraser looks over his shoulder, sees his wife, and smiles.

The smile does it. He doesn't notice the gun. Perhaps it is in shadow. The smile stays as he turns away, resumes concentration on the act of rape. Lorna advances on the bed, lifts the gun, points it at Fraser's head, and fires. She fires both barrels.

She has never heard such a noise, seen such a mess. The girl Caroline struggles out from under, wide-eyed, white, quivering; her hands fly to cup her breasts. There is blood on her too. Neither can speak. Lorna lets the gun fall on the bed. The silence is complete. It is finished.

Feet run. Candy. Takes in the situation, takes charge, takes Caroline naked and quivering out, along to her room, sits her on the bed, throws a blanket round her, back for Lorna, out, shutting the slaughterhouse door behind. Behind.

For no idea how long the three girls sit.

'She screamed,' Lorna says, 'she kept on screaming. Like Crete, Candy.'

'Like Crete. She's in shock now.'

Caroline rocks, mouth open, eyes wide and empty of anything.

'No one else,' Candy says. Her brain, the only one functioning, is moving out of the icy grip of the present moment.

*   *   *

She looks at me. 'I was entirely mad. You must understand that. Normality was suspended, and I had least reason . . .'

*

'Will you be all right a moment?' she says, and goes, with inspired common sense, to make tea. The scrum-half Alastair still sleeps at the table, cheek flat among crumbs. The sight convinces her; it can be done. She can get Lorna off.

She takes mugs upstairs, forces Lorna to drink, goes to her own room for a T-shirt, sweater and jeans for Caroline.

'She's out . . .'

'Shock, drink.' Still Candy dresses her, with awkward angry determination, slaps her face, holds the mug to her lips. Then, 'You've got to dress, Lorna. We've things to do. And not much time. We must get the house cleared.'

'I can't go back there. I simply can't. You can't ask . . .'

'All right.'

Candy picks up the telephone, tries to ring Dallas— something I have clung to in my most self-despising moments, even though reason tells me it was not choice but necessity, there was simply no one else from whom she might hope for help. When she gets no answer, she goes back to what the newspapers will call the fatal bedroom. She is already quite clear what their only possible course is.

She wraps sheets and covers round the thing in the bed. Not even desperation though can give her the strength to lift it on her own. Lorna would have to return. Even so, they need a man. She must have cursed Dallas.

There is only one thing possible. Down to the kitchen, shakes the scrum-half . . .

—*She told me that Fraser had tried to rape Caroline, that they had struggled for a shot-gun and it had gone off. Fraser was dead and Caroline in shock. She said they needed my help.*

—*And did you believe her?*

—*I was drunk, my mind wasn't functioning, I didn't know what to think. Nothing like this had ever happened to me before.*

How long did it take? How much pleading? To bring him to the point of co-operation?

Somehow she manages. Somehow they get the wrapped object, the parcel, bumpity-bump, down the stairs, along the passage to the back door. (It was madness of course, they couldn't avoid a trail of bloodstains.) Candy fetches Fraser's soft-top Land-Rover. It is still grey-black outside, not even cock-crow yet.

—*Did she tell you what she planned?*
—*No, she seemed to just expect that I would fall in with whatever she intended, do as she asked.*
—*And you did?*
—*At the time, yes.*
—*Why was that, would you say?*
—*I was all confused, completely mixed up. My mind was all sort of muzzy.*
—*You didn't think of calling the police?*
—*I did, yes, I remember that, but then, you see, I believed the story she had told me about Caroline. I thought it was Caroline I was really helping.*
—*That story didn't strike you as a bit improbable?*
—*Only later, not at the time.*
—*But later?*
—*Well, then, yes, that's when I thought I'd better tell the police everything.*

They get the parcel, the wrapped thing, into the Land-Rover, letting it lie on the floor at the back.

Candy says, 'You'll have to follow in your car. Or mine, it doesn't matter.'

She leaves him there a moment, in the shivering cold, with snowflakes falling.

'*It was a risk, he might have run, done anything, but I had to see Lorna was all right. I got her and Caroline to bed. Yes, in the same bed. It seemed safer, I couldn't say why.*'

Outside the boy is still leaning against the Land-Rover. He has lit a cigarette. Snow isn't going to come to anything. There is no wind now. Sound would carry, but the country is hard stony silent.

'Come on then,' she says. 'It's about ten miles.'

People reluctant to believe how quickly the mind can work

in crisis were to read that remark, Candy's direct certainty, as evidence of premeditation: 'If she knew where she was going so soon after the crime, it must have been in her head already.'

She drives cautiously—'*I was more worried about the boy behind crashing. I mean, if anyone had stopped us, it would have been curtains, you see.*' Eventually, she turns off the road, down a bumpy, tractor-rutted track, stops, signals to Alastair to get out.

—*What did you think she was going to do?*
—*I was past thinking.*
—*Very well, then, what did she say next?*
—*She told me we had to get the . . . get Fraser . . . the body into the driving seat. I was nearly sick at the thought.*
—*And how did she seem?*
—*She was quite calm about it.*
(*Dallas glanced across: Quaker-calm.*)
—*So we heaved him out and up and in. It was gruesome. And then she leant across and let off the handbrake and the car lurched away down the slope, there's a huge cliff there, and it went straight over. The noise was terrible.*
—*And what did she say then?*
—*She wiped her hands on her jeans and said, 'Well, at least that gives us a chance.'*

Of course that was nonsense. They had no chance at all. However quickly Candy had thought, the notion that Fraser had driven there in order to charge into the sea would hardly . . . hold water. And the idea of an accident there wasn't on either. Besides, assuming the body was recovered—which was probable—forensic tests would have no difficulty in determining the cause of death. Of course, Candy's only hope was that the body mightn't be found. But that was the longest of long shots. Yet what else could she do? You can't fake suicide when a man has been shot in the back of the head.

Even so, there were simply too many people involved, and two of them, Caroline and Alastair, weren't going to be reticent. Caroline's condition would take some explaining too.

No, it was never on. A horse that wouldn't run.

11

Someone had picked up a scent. Someone had recalled that, at a higher level of officialdom, Fraser Donnelly wasn't exactly well thought of; that a missive had requested to be kept informed of his movements. This someone had made a telephone call. The CID had responded with an eagerness which must have not only disturbed, but, equally, disarmed, the hitherto unsuspecting station sergeant. (Actually he was off duty; he was to be faced with a *fait accompli*.)

So, after a mug of tea and a hunk of bread, and a long worried silence, broken only by boots in the corridor, and the coming and going of cars in the yard, Dallas was brought back before a plain clothes detective, flanked by a couple of constables, and the whole mood had changed. He was invited to sit down, another cup of tea was placed before him, he was offered a cigarette.

'There seems,' the detective said, in a soft voice (Inverness?) 'to have been a bit of a mix-up. A right mess. Of course you've been charged. That may have to stand, may not. It'll be up to the Procurator-Fiscal, not to me. But I might be making a report that'll cover that matter as well as others.'

He pushed a box of matches across the table. Dallas, still cold, shivery, aching, but just beginning to relax, lit the cigarette. He was ashamed of the fear he had felt. During the night all sorts of bangs and voices had invaded his mind. He had overheard plans to beat him up. They hadn't seemed like imaginings.

'I have a note that you claim you were coming to us anyway.'

Dallas, his mouth full of smoke, nodded.

Words came to him with a rush. Confidence seeped back. In the night he had been unaccommodated man; now ancestral voices spoke through him. He recalled Canaan, Rugby, Cambridge. He wasn't just anybody. (And that is blatant truth; he momentarily overcame the fear and guilt which authority naturally occasioned in him; his voice took on a brief arrogance of caste.)

The detective listened; he was a man for listening, didn't even shuffle the papers in front of him or play with his fingers, sat stock-still and listened. The constables were equally immobile.

Dallas said, 'So Candy, Miss Sheen that is, asked me to fetch the police. As you know I didn't exactly succeed. And God knows what has happened.'

'And what do you think might have happened?'

'Anything. I thought she was quite right. Fraser was in the mood for anything, violence of any kind. He could even have killed someone. I thought he was mad last night. I told him so.'

The detective—Dallas supposed he was an inspector—cleared his throat; it was a habit he had.

'What's someone like you doing getting himself involved with this sort of people?' he asked.

But he didn't wait for an answer, which anyway Dallas couldn't have given.

'It's what they call a mare's nest, isn't it? I've had a couple of boys out there this morning. And do you know, there's nobody there, except the two girls, Mrs Donnelly and Miss Sheen that is. They're clearing up. It looks as if you were wrong, doesn't it? Nothing's happened. But, do you know, I've an interest in Mr Donnelly, and I'm obliged to you. You say he beat you up, eh? Maybe you'd like to prefer a charge . . .'

Dallas had forgotten the possibility, and now it embarrassed him. Lorna wouldn't like it, would she? And it would make him look a fool. Nobody can fancy standing in the witness-box to recount his own humiliation. On the other hand . . .

'Tell you what,' he heard, 'it might influence your own case, you see. So this is what we'll do. You just make a statement now and then we'll drive out to the farmhouse and talk over the matter. There are things going on there that I don't like. It would be as well to get to the bottom of them. That party seems to have broken up very sudden-like from the account you've given me of it, surprisingly sudden I can't help thinking.'

The morning was dull and grey as a leading article. The sky had a pinned-down look to it. Dallas sat in the police Wolseley. Clouds hung below the hilltops. Nothing moved in the fields.

When they got to the farmhouse, they found the girls gone too.

'My, my,' said the inspector, 'that's strange now, too. They didn't say they were going out. I think we'll just take a look round, to be on the safe side, make sure nothing untoward has happened. Perhaps you'll be kind enough to accompany us. That way you'll be able to assure your friends we've done nothing amiss.'

That was how Dallas came to be with them when they found the bloodstains.

*

There was silence outside. The gramophone had run down a while back. Cigarette stubs overflowed the ashtray beside Candy.

'I suppose it's therapy of a sort for you,' she said, 'but for me you know it's another life. At the time it didn't seem like real life at all. It's a bit hackneyed, but it was nightmare.'

'Did you, I've always wanted to know, ever think you could get away with it?'

'You don't understand,' she said, 'there was no calculation. You could say we acted instinctively. I don't know. Everything was just a response to what went before. I mean, when I found Lorna with the gun in her hand, what could I do?'

'If I hadn't blundered about . . .'

'You indulge yourself with your guilt, like licking a sore place till you like the taste of blood and pus. You use your guilt to excuse yourself from action, to make it impossible. And yet you've no reason for guilt. You did what seemed best, what you could. We're not free agents. I've never felt any guilt at all. Anger at what I wasted, but anger at fate, not at myself. How could I have acted otherwise?'

I've seen faces like Candy's on Gothic windows. As she looked through the haze of cigarette smoke she took on the implacability of the saints.

*

The body was discovered that same day. The search was launched for the girls. They were arrested the following morning at a small hotel in the Highlands. Dallas was summoned to the police station to go over some points in his statement. He was questioned for hours. The same ground was covered and re-covered and he was not allowed to rest. He was taken over the whole course of his relations with Fraser. Even Gavin Gregory's case was revived.

Everything was in the passive voice. An application to see Candy was refused. Lorna was rumoured to be in a state of collapse. Dallas was told by two people that she was 'psychotic'; by a third that her condition was 'catatonic'. It was said she could never be brought to trial.

He telephoned Alick Duguid, but Alick soon tired of his vague and hopeless questions.

'If I was you,' Alick said, 'I'd get the hell out of it.'

'Are you going to be covering the trial?'

'I'm no' that sort of journalist.'

All the same, Dallas was aware of a suppressed simmering excitement in his voice, an excitement that hummed round the country.

PART THREE

1

'I warned you,' Hugh Buchanan said. His long pale fingers patted the desk, admonitory, advertising his scrupulously controlled impatience.

The study was as chill and mahogany-furnished as an undertaker's parlour. Lives were buried in the bookshelves. Ancestral portraits or portraits of long-dead legal eminences threw gloom on the living. Dallas had endured a family dinner of dry sole in a shroud of white sauce and Bakewell tart. Conversation had turned into an inquest on his life and condition. Now he sat in a straight-backed leather chair, placed obliquely to his uncle's desk. Only one bulb of an ornate electrolier was lit; that and a small desk lamp gave the room all its light. Thick, velvet curtains drawn across a shuttered window excluded all traffic noise; not that there was much life in the street. Hugh had recently masterminded a residents' protest which had prevented a private hotel in the crescent from obtaining a liquor licence.

'I urged a career on you. You came smelling of gin and you left laughing at me. And now, it seems likely you are fortunate not to be in the dock. It seems that's where your sympathies lie. I find it revolting, the whole affair utterly unseemly. To involve yourself in this way with people who have no notion how to behave.'

The case, still some months short of coming to trial, had seized the imagination of the country. All sorts of rumours about licence and perversion were current; there had been nothing like it in memory. Here was a murder that didn't involve only Glasgow hooligans. Wasn't it said that members of the peerage, county types, top policemen, MPs, advocates, who knew who else, had attended that man's parties? Now he was dead, who knew what might come out?

Dallas, coming to Edinburgh, having suddenly applied for, and being given, a job as an editorial assistant in an old-established firm of publishers, had been first staggered, then gratified by, then found himself resenting, the interest that his connection with the case aroused. The whole thing was prurient; he constituted himself the girls' champion.

'But,' he said, 'there could be nothing more serious or respectable than my position at Bannerman's.'

Actually the firm was moribund. He had soon found that out. Did Hugh know, he wondered? Old Bannerman lived in a claret-comforted retreat behind a rampart of old bindings.

They were months of waiting, of pretence life. Real life was held fast in that women's prison in the North-East. Shame kept him away from there. Shame kept him in the airless antiquity of the firm's office. Shame had brought him to Hugh's table tonight.

'I have discussed your proposal with the other trustees,' Hugh said. 'We can't, we feel, do just as you wish, but we see no reason now why we should not invite offers for Canaan.'

'What do you mean, not just as I wish?'

'Simply this. That even if the sale is effected—and we can't feel certain that it will be, the market is poor for such houses—we would not feel able to release the sum realized until you have reached the age specified in the will. Frankly, you haven't given any evidence of the sort of stability that would justify us in advancing the money to you.'

He leant forward to sniff the hothouse flower on his desk—the growing of such flowers, Dallas couldn't identify this one, was his sole expression of romanticism. The other trustees were ciphers. Hugh proposed. Hugh disposed. Or didn't.

'Furthermore, you have given no adequate reason . . .'

'I told you, now that I'm working at Bannerman's I thought I should like to buy a flat here. Apart from anything else, it would be an investment.'

'Ah yes, the trustees might consider doing that—in the Trust's name of course. But we should like to see how things develop before committing ourselves. Evidence of stability —we should have to have that. Meanwhile of course you are always welcome to stay here . . .'

Dallas knew he had run his skiff against the rock of respectability. It would take years to live down his connection with the case. He was marked. Aberdeen granite would not be more unyielding than Hugh, the Castle Rock as easily shifted. As for himself, he must move through the city like one wearing yellow star or pink triangle.

'You don't understand,' he said, 'you simply don't understand . . .'

The way the world is going. The phrase that he hadn't completed sang in his mind as he swayed a couple of hours later through the streets. At dinner Hugh had talked with intensity about a round of golf; that was the limit of the man's capacity for passion. It was the limit of the country's. Dallas, swinging round a railinged corner, experienced, for the first time in months, a shaft of sympathy for Fraser; he had after all known what he was up against.

2

The mood stayed with Dallas. Spring came late. Grey, heavy winds scudded up town from the port of Leith. In evening ramblings, searching adventure or oblivion, he hit on pubs in the Old Town where a rougher, more edgy life was to be found. But not one lived with conviction. He was always aware of the atmosphere of the undertaker's parlour that he had breathed in his uncle's study; it hung over the city as surely as the haar came in from the Firth.

He took to telephoning people he had known long ago, who had been boys at prep school with him, suggesting they should meet for a beer. To most of them he had to re-introduce himself. Even as he bought the first pints, he realized the futility of what he was doing. Yet he couldn't leave the city. He couldn't return to the North-East. And, even putting aside the possibility that he might be required as a witness, couldn't contemplate leaving Scotland till after the trial.

Judy, on a whim, having sacked one boyfriend—did she, he wondered, think of them as 'lovers' now?—flew up for a week-end. 'It's sick,' she said, when Dallas, in the darkness, after coition, exposed his mind to her; 'you're in danger of turning grotesque.'

'But life is grotesque,' he said, 'utterly grotesque. Don't you see that? Look,' he said, 'we read history, right. We can recognize the pattern. Look at the French Revolution. Who do you blame for the Terror of '93? Robespierre and the Jacobins? Absurd. They had no choice, they were caught in a trap they hadn't constructed. Stifled by the Ancien Régime, chained by the absolute logic of their own rational Enlightenment. Well, in the same way, all these people I've been telling you about, Fraser Donnelly, and Lorna, and Candy, were victims of this life-denying society.'

'Christ,' Judy snapped on a light, 'you really are bad news these days. You ought to snap out of it. If our time's about anything it's about our freedom to choose. Those girls of yours, they were just too jolly wet to step out and be free. Don't think I'm not sorry for them, or not on their side, but the fact is, Dallas, nobody but nobody has to be into bondage.'

Dallas listened but could not assent. Judy knew nothing of the determinist forces of Scottish life; she was quite ignorant in her mini-skirted Chelsea smartness, in her shiny Courrèges boots, which, even now, lay by the bedside, of the delusory nature of the choice she so brashly flaunted. A choice that Fraser too had claimed to make.

He groaned, 'Empirical, pig-ignorant English, blind to the inexorability of logic, no wonder Europe won't admit you. The English are the Americans of the old world. De Gaulle is right. All my life I have had a certain idea of Scotland, and it's no' a bonny one . . .'

He said none of this, but mused, as Judy hopped out of bed, and took her little-girl body through to the bathroom.

On her return she said again, 'You're growing bad news. This is really the last time. Make the most of it.'

*

Night arched above me and I could not sleep, any more than Dallas had managed it that night as Judy lay warmly breathing beside him, her hand out of trusting and generous habit between his legs. The bowl of night held suspended from its arc a pair of compasses or dividers, one point pricking Dallas then, the other me now. I could watch that Dallas like a figure on a cinema screen, but I could no longer inhabit him. To what extent then did that Dallas contain me? There must be some continuity of personality. Memory at least binds me to him; but could he have prevented or altered how I have turned out?

When the Dutch usurper, William of Nassau (or Orange) lay in bed in Hampton Court after his horse's fall over the molehill, did he perceive any pattern of consequence? Or was Judy right? Is each moment autonomous? Each act of judgement or decision free if we will it so?

I supposed Candy slept beyond the wall. Where did she travel in her night-mind? Through throats where many rivers meet, the curlew sings . . . Sings? Sounds? Calls?

For years I made lists to cheat sleeplessness or divert it: lists of battles, of cabinet-makers, of Roman Emperors, Derby winners, Napoleon's marshals, Foreign Secretaries, lists of cricketers beginning with each letter of the alphabet, of the best county teams of my time, of all the Scottish fly-halves, full backs, scrum-halves . . .

That boy whom we christened the scrum-half wasn't one of them. He may not even have been a scrum-half. I can still see the angle of his head in the witness-box, his house-prefect's chirpiness, his eagerness to abase himself before authority and yet remain cocky. He wore a blazer, didn't he, no badge, but lettered brass buttons; and surely an old school tie to let the judge see that his association with such riff-raff had been a mere temporary provisional aberration, now regretted; he was back on an even keel.

*

The Edinburgh months dragged out. The trial should have come on in June, but was postponed. Dallas couldn't understand why. It was surely from the Crown's angle an easy enough case. Rumour insisted again that Lorna's collapse was so complete she wouldn't be fit to plead. Dallas was sceptical. But, if true, could they proceed against Candy? Poor Candy, was there a window in her cell through which she had seen the trees put on their green?

('I read,' she said, 'I read Gibbon, but he couldn't hold my attention. I found the certainty repellent. I read Proust, all of Proust. Combray made me think of family holidays in Tweeddale. And Dickens, *Little Dorrit* of course. And William Faulkner, I've never been able to read Faulkner since I came out of prison.')

Dallas was a little mad that year. He felt he should be in prison too. He was certainly an accessory before the fact and an accessory in sympathy. If he had actually been accessory in deed, he wouldn't have turned Queen's Evidence like Alastair. It looked as if Alastair's evidence would ditch them. It was said he would provide evidence of premeditation.

But Dallas knew that wasn't the case. They had sent him for the police. He must be able to give that story in court. He went in his perturbation (for which there was no rational cause, since he would certainly—but he couldn't believe it—be able to tell that story) to see his Great-Uncle Ebenezer.

A tall, blond man answered his ring at the doorbell of the drawing-room flat in Moray Place. He looked at Dallas with the insolence of possession.

'Oh,' he said, 'we're some sort of cousins.'

Dallas explained that he was sorry, he hadn't known, he was very ignorant of family, indeed he had only met Ebenezer himself once, but they had talked fully; now he had suddenly thought about him, and wanted to consult him.

'You thought too late. The old boy's in hospital. He's just about had it, I'm afraid. But come in if you like. I'm just putting a few things in order. My name's Simon Fergusson by the way. What did you want to see Eben about?'

Dallas followed him into the library. A tortoiseshell cat stalked across the desk-top and rubbed herself against his outstretched arm. The walls were covered with paintings, seascapes, pastoral landscapes, ploughing matches, harvest scenes, cottar gardens.

'The Glasgow School and the Scottish Colourists, and a couple of Dyce. He was quite a collector, old Eben. Worth a bit.'

'Must be.'

'This Orchardson was his favourite, it's a companion piece to the one in the National Gallery.'

He indicated a yellowy-green picture, with girls in long white dresses and straw hats. They were carrying tennis-racquets and were grouped round a wrought-iron table.

'He used to say it was beautifully mellow.'

Dallas sat in a deep leather armchair. The room had an undisturbed airless quality. The same afternoon light that Orchardson had caught—invented?—seeped through the long windows.

'Authentic 1914,' Dallas said. 'When I met him he talked about what we had lost since then. I suppose these paintings kept it fresh for him. What struck me was that he wasn't querulous or nostalgic, just accepted what had gone as a fact. I found him attractive, I don't usually like old men.'

'He was a wicked old boy though. There's a couple of shelves there of really juicy erotica. More to the immediate point there's some remarkably good sherry. Manzanilla, Solera 1907, if I remember.'

They drank the wine in a silence that held acknowledgement, of a life completed, of a room that was about to be consumed, transformed; the air held for a few moments essence of 1910. But of course in that year Eben would have been only a dozen years older than Dallas was now. When had he decided that was his period?

'You say we're cousins? I suppose if we were his generation I would know all about you. We'd have had maiden aunts to keep us informed. As it is, I'm surprised you've heard of me.'

Simon Fergusson gave him a blond, assured smile.

'Eben talked about you. He was an insatiable old gossip.

And then you're a man of interest at the moment. Besides my little sister had been babbling of you too.'

'Your sister?'

'My sister Caroline.'

He didn't elaborate but watched, with the same blond smile, Dallas's mood shiver. Of course, admittedly, Dallas had come there to talk about the case. He had come hoping that Eben would talk about Fraser; show him, in the light of what Dallas had thought of in those early hours when Judy had snapped out of bed saying he was bad news, just how Fraser had made that journey from the exuberant young man of the wedding photograph to being the bloated monster who so often disturbed Dallas's sleep; instead he was brought up against these blond bland words: my sister Caroline.

They were, as the speaker knew, a small bomb. Dallas reddened: he felt the girl, like an eager Spaniel puppy, in his arms. The hair bristled on his neck.

'Not that she's making much sense, poor Caro.'

'What do you mean?'

Simon Fergusson sipped sherry, crossed his ankle over on to his left knee, held his glass poised above the well made by the angle of his legs.

'She babbles.'

'I'm sorry, I don't understand.'

'Just that. Babbles. She's off her rocker, poor girl. Done her nut.'

'Do you mean . . . ?'

'Yes, that's right, that's where she is. In the bin, poor girl. Making no sense, absolutely no sense at all.'

He paused to let Dallas pluck the horror of his words from the dusty air.

''Swhy they can't bring the trial on, you know. Key witness crazy. Stark crazy, poor girl.'

Television screens and newspapers had recently been full of reports of an oil-tanker that had run aground, somewhere off Cornwall, spreading an oil-slick over the ocean; there had been pictures of seabirds, beautiful, fragile, free creatures, unable to fly, their wings smeared, pinioned by the corrupting oil. It seemed to Dallas that Fraser had released his own slick; here was another girl victim.

'Last week,' Fergusson said again, 'she babbled of you. I'd been meaning to get in touch. Now you've done it for me. She babbles a lot of course, and most of it's contradictory. But hoped you might help.'

He made it sound like an order.

'That fellow she was with, Alastair Drure. His first version was that Donnelly had tried to rape her, that they'd struggled for the shotgun and it'd gone off accidental. That was why he'd agreed to help in the salvage biznai. Lot of cock of course. Just the gospel according to the Sheen bird. How the hell would a shotgun be to hand in a bedroom for one thing? Didn't hold any water that story, leaky as hell. All the same something happened, something pretty unpleasant, and involving Caro. As I say, the girl's bonkers. Always was a bird-brain but you don't go bonkers for nothing.'

The harsh, jokey tone sharpened the horror; no doubt why it was adopted.

'Want to get her out of the madhouse. Thought you might help.'

'Me?'

'After all, you were there.'

'Not when it happened. Not when whatever happened happened.'

'Granted. But . . . you know the set-up, know the gang, can hazard a bet that Messrs Ladbrokes would put odds-on.'

'She was hot,' Dallas said; it felt like treachery. But he went on.

'She was hot for it. She was plastered of course, maybe drugged too, I wouldn't know, and she was really asking for something. I've never known a girl as hot for it, sorry to say so to you. Rape? I don't know. She could easily have got frightened and tried to back off. She struck me as inexperienced, for all that she was so keen. It was as if she was all wound up. It could have snapped when she realized what she was up against. She was a mess that night, you know. All the same, she was really hot.'

He aimed the words like darts at Fergusson's self-possession, his ineffable superiority. He hadn't liked that reference to 'the Sheen bird', detecting in it (correctly) an equation of social and moral judgement, that allowed Caroline, being of a different class, greater latitude, a more generous standard. He looked back at the Orchardson summer afternoon; how yellowy-gold the light was.

'What sort of place is she in?'

'Oh very tolerant, very understanding, very liberal, very *Guardian*ish even. But grim. Stinks of good intentions and high thinking. Look,' he rose from his chair to refill Dallas's glass, 'I detect distrust. And yet, you know, we should be on the same side. And our interest isn't served if you set out to brand my wee sister a whore. From your own point of view, since I gather you fancy one of the girls, if not both, you ought to stick at flirt. That's their only hope. Because if Caro wasn't being raped, if she was fucking her happy little arse off, then the wife shot out of plain jealousy, and she's sunk. Hook, line and very heavy sinker. So if you'd just open your tiny eyes, you'd see we are on the same bloody side. Must say I'd have thought you'd have the brains to see that. And now, the poor girl's in danger of being destroyed permanently. She may never come out of it. In the jargon, she's traumatized.'

But would the truth, whatever it might be, help her? Wasn't she destroyed by her apprehension of where her dancing steps had led her? It was what she had learned of her own nature had driven her nuts; like Ophelia. But now, he didn't know how anything he might say might be used against Lorna and Candy. He wasn't inclined to trust this smooth blond prefect who sat there and said 'we're on the same side'.

'I'm sorry,' he said, 'about Caroline. It's hellish. But I don't see that I can help. I wasn't there when he was killed. I was in a police cell. He was very much alive the last I saw of him . . .'

And your little sister was laughing in pleasure at the beating-up he was handing out to me, he might have added.

'No,' he said, and got up and left the flat.

Yet outside in a sunshine that had unexpectedly brought on a real summer evening summoning people in shirt-sleeves, assembling groups of beer-drinkers at the doors of pubs, setting old ladies on unaccustomed walks with fat terriers, his spirits lifted. Perhaps with Caroline, poor silly girl, confined babbling, the trial could never come on. How could Candy be charged with being an accessory after the fact of murder, if the murder could not be proved as a fact? Things were better than they had seemed. He had been right not to talk to Fergusson about Crete; it was the Cretan jigsaw he had put together that gave him even then a notion of what might have happened.

I find it hard to blame Dallas for his unwillingness to face things as they were, for the dream construction he concocted as he walked through the summer-scented rectitude of the New Town, forming a picture which allowed the girls out of gaol, the past to be abolished, Candy to come to him gratefully: to forget his grandmother's favourite saw, 'if wishes were horses, beggars would ride'. Walking under the laburnum trees, his cuff brushed by fragrant azalea, he saw a whole cohort of equestrian beggars.

And I've learned no greater wisdom since. A sense of reality has hardly been a feature of my life.

*   *   *

Candy rose early, as she had warned me. I found it impossible to sleep on the couch against the background of her brisk morning. It had changed to rain in the night, a dense silent rain, with clouds at roof-top level.

'I have to go. There's a lot of work I have to do.'

'That's all right.'

'Will you be OK?'

'Of course.'

'Have you any plans?'

The concern in her voice riled me more than indifference or impatience would have, the more so since I had no answer.

'Would you like me to go?'

'It's up to you. The couch is here if you want. I'll leave a spare set of keys by the door. They're hanging up there in fact. You'll have no difficulty in the kitchen.'

'Fine.'

'See you then.'

'See you, and thanks.'

3

I stayed a couple of days. We slipped into a pattern. It was like operating a machine with which you were long ago familiar. And that undemanding south-country town, round which I would stroll while she was at work, helped calm me. I telephoned Amanda in the shop and was able to listen with detachment and affection to her account of the latest episodes in her emotional life. She had had 'a terrible scene' with her Tory MP, which had ended in her threatening to launch a feminist campaign against him next Election; she had decided to go to Antibes with Charlotte. Why Antibes? 'It's a lot less jazzy than St Trop. I don't think Charlotte's the St Trop type. And Neville? Well, poor old Nev's not making much sense about it. But I see where I've gone wrong. I've been mothering the poor slob. I can't go on being a surrogate mum, can I?' 'Can't you?' 'No, I can't. Which reminds me, Ann telephoned to see if I knew where you were. Don't worry, I covered up.' 'But you don't know, do you?' 'No, but she sounded snappy like.'

And so on.

I looked at my watch. She would be at the studio. She wouldn't thank me to ring her there.

That night I said, 'Are you due any holidays?'

'Yes, as a matter of fact I am.'

'Would you like to come to France for a week or two?'

'France? I'd have to think about that. I don't like sudden invitations. It doesn't mean more than it seems to, does it?'

I was tempted to reply with the truth, then, fearful, shrugged.

'I feel the need of France. I don't want to go alone. I'd just sit round drinking pastis all day.'

'Well, I'll think about it.'

'Good. There's a Garbo film on the box. Do you want to watch it?'

'No,' she said, 'I can't stand Garbo. All that mute suffering.'

Ann used to be irritated by my bouts of insomnia, regarding them as a sort of affectation. Later she saw them, or pretended to see them, as symptoms of whatever she had decided was wrong with me; yet another reason why I should submit to a psycho-analyst. Her old reaction had merely irritated me; the new one disturbed. But it has always seemed strange that one whose response to life is so tepid and lacking in enthusiasm should be loth to sleep.

Rum.

Introspective, in thrall to the ego, unable ever to make the effort of the imagination that is necessary to enter another's life: of all this Ann has accused me, and pronounced me guilty. And the damnable thing is I can see no grounds for appeal.

*

Even when Dallas eventually yielded to Simon Fergusson's importunity, the request being repeated several times over the telephone, what memory plays back to me is a film in which the camera never leaves Dallas.

Dallas sitting in the passenger seat of Simon's white Jaguar sports car as they drove out of Edinburgh to a country house in the folds of the Pentlands that had been converted into a very expensive private nut-house; Dallas wrinkling his nostrils at the school smell of disinfectant in the corridors; Dallas twinge-ing as the nurse's uniform rustled past him; Dallas recoiling from the cream, distempered walls; Dallas listening through the antiseptic silence for the cries of anguish and lunacy that his imagination demanded.

They put them in a waiting-room with copies of *Punch* and *Country Life*. Simon crossed long Donegal-tweeded legs.

'Grimmish.'

'Very.'

'M'dad used to come here. Drying-out seshes in the first instance. Then th' old boy started hearin' voices rather more often than a sober chappie should. They bring Caro down to us. If it wasn't rainin' we could go out in the garden. As it is we're stuck in this godawful lounge.'

When she came in, dressed in white, a white dress coming down to just below her knees, and a white sash and a white cashmere cardigan draped round her shoulders, Dallas couldn't help thinking of Victorian novels: this was palpable Hollywood lunacy.

She said to Simon, 'Did you bring the roses?'

'What roses?'

'The ones I wanted.'

'I'm sorry, I didn't know. I'll bring some next time. You remember Dallas?'

She looked at him with soup-plate, unseeing eyes.

'Give her a jolt,' Simon had said; but he couldn't.

She began talking. But it was all a jumble, of ponies and patients. He couldn't be sure though that she wasn't consciously evading what she didn't want to speak about.

'It's no good, ducky,' Simon said, 'you've got to face up to it.'

'I'm the only member of the family who has a chance to get through to her. My mother's hopeless,' he had said in the car. 'But the kid used to see me as some sort of hero.' Even in the distress he may have felt, he glowed at the memory.

Now, with a tenderness Dallas hadn't expected, he tried to lure her on the treacherous marshes of memory, hoping he could pick out the tussocks of firm ground that would permit them to hop, like experienced naturalists, over the mire that threatened to suck her under.

They were a couple of bungling amateurs. Why on earth had the doctors sanctioned the meeting? That question didn't concern Dallas at the time; he was only anxious to get away. Now, I can only suppose that Simon Fergusson overbore their doubts, exercising an inborn conviction of his superiority over experts.

Of course they got nowhere. She talked with an engaging candour, with the light and seductive lucidity of lunacy, about childhood and the trivia of daily life; but she shied away from anything approaching the case.

And Dallas was grateful even though he had come there in the end because he had been convinced by Simon's argument that Caroline's testimony was needed if Lorna and Candy were to have any chance at all.

'If you forgot the roses you might at least have brought buns.'

'Buns?'

'Yes, you take buns to the zoo don't you, for the bears and such like. Well, I'm a zoo creature, aren't I? You even bring people along to look at me. Why are you sitting there? Doing nothing. Get me out of here. Do you think I'm enjoying myself shut up with mad people? I want to go to the beach. You just come here and sit, like a sack of potatoes. Am I going to spend the rest of my life here? What are you doing to get me out? There's nothing wrong with me, is there? Not really?'

She started crying. Simon put his arm round her.

'You've had a sort of breakdown, Caro, but you'll be all right. In time. Of course you will.'

'Why have you brought that man here? He was there. I know he was. In that awful place. I can't talk about it. None of it, it wasn't nice. That's what Mummy always said, it's not nice, and I thought she was wrong and laughed at her, but she was quite right. There was this great purple thing and I was frightened because it wasn't nice, and then there was a big bang and it was over. Only it's not over because you've brought it back because he was there, make him go away and get me out . . .'

They never did. She wasn't of course fit to give evidence. The lawyers found a way round her absence. She retreated further and further into the recesses of her being. A few years ago I had a letter from one of my Edinburgh cousins.

'You remember poor Caro Fergusson who was a second cousin of ours. She killed herself last month. She'd tried two or three times before, saving up pills and so on. But they always managed to stop her. This time she got a torn towel and contrived to hang or strangle herself. Horrible. What a wrecked and wasted life . . .'

Part of the wreckage Fraser strewed in his wake. I never spoke to Simon Fergusson again, though I saw him once (I think) in the Members' Bar at Newbury. I quickly turned to the wall, lowering my head.

Candy said, 'Look, it does no good to talk on and on about these things. And it's no good feeling a victim or seeing others as victims. When I said I didn't want to see that Garbo film I was thinking of Lorna. We weren't allowed to speak to each other during the trial, but it was the trial that broke what was between us. I could see she was getting herself framed for a victim role . . .'

'But wasn't that her only possible defence?'

We were sitting by the river, in October sunshine, one of those English rivers which have no perceptible movement. Further up the bank sat a fisherman dangling his hook, baited with bread, in the deep stillness of the water.

'Oh yes, legally there was nothing else she could try for. Naturally. My counsel took the same line. That wasn't the trouble. But Lorna had come to believe it, as if it was all fated, as if she had had no choice. That's how I annoyed your wife by the way. She wanted to take the line that all our clients were victims of circumstance, victims of society. I wasn't having it . . .'

The fisherman hitched his rod under his elbow and began, with tiny delicate movements, to roll himself a cigarette.

'Lorna believed,' she said, 'no, I'm starting this the wrong way round. The mistake lies in thinking there's a clear cleavage between free will and—what's the opposite? Determinism, predestination, fate? It's not like that.' She nestled a Woodbine between her thin, nicotined fingers. 'You can easily go along with the course of events. Without volition. Just as if I dropped a piece of bread in this river, it would be carried downstream. And somewhere down there there's a weir. And if you've just gone with the stream then you may get swept over. If you do nothing to save yourself there comes a moment when you're quite powerless. At that moment you really have no choice. But earlier you could have got out, couldn't you?'

She looked into the brown, muddy water, at the poplars on the other bank just touched with autumn mist; there was a suggestion of dank chill in the air. A long way off we could hear a tractor ploughing, the only sound in the soft English landscape.

'Of course,' she said, 'you can suffer a nervous collapse of the will. That doesn't mean you don't have a will. And fatalism can take another form, a sort of weak optimism. Did you ever see that play, *Danton's Death*? Büchner, isn't it, Kleist, one of these people? Near the end there's a scene where Danton is on the run. Robespierre's agents are after him. He spends the night hiding out on a moor. In the morning he's cold and hungry, so, though he knows the danger, he goes home. Why? There's a line that says, "Whatever Reason tells us, deep down in us there's a small voice that says tomorrow will be like yesterday." I think he says "a small, smiling voice" actually. But the smile's not the point. The point is that we got through yesterday, so it's easy to fool ourselves about today. That's why people put up with things. Because they survived yesterday. It can result in a passive heroism. It was that spirit that led the Jews into the Death Camps. Heroic in a way, but acquiescent and weakly optimistic. It's a small step from there to abandoning your right to choose, and then to denying that a choice even exists. So you start seeing yourself as a victim. The thread that attaches you to the future snaps. You have no responsibility for what's going to happen. And that was Lorna's position, but she could have got out, she could have got out.'

4

But at last it came on.

Dallas drove north on a royal-blue autumn day with the wind in the east and the hills as sharp as the lines of a swan on a black loch. He turned aside from the road that ran along the curve of the foothills and cut across the red earth of the howe to the sea. There again he left the main road to follow a little track that led him to the cliffs, to the point where Candy had released the brake on Fraser's Land-Rover.

There was no movement but gulls. Far out to sea the speck of a fishing boat was caught as in one of the paintings on old Eben Murdoch's wall. The sharp sweet scent of a field of turnips mingled with the sea salt.

He stood on the cliff's edge. The waves rolled themselves in a spray of foam against the rocks. Dallas was indifferent to memory or imagination. The scene should say something —he hadn't known what—but there was nothing there but rocks, water, spray and hard sunlight. He strove to summon up that night turning to morning when Candy and Alastair Drure had stood listening to the sea swallow up Fraser in his funeral car; but nothing came, no emanations, only the hard facts of sea and rock.

He sat in a little ante-room. His hands were cold, his calf scorched by a single-bar electric fire. Candida's counsel perched on his chair across the table, a junior to his left. Counsel had thin grey hair, streaked-back, and long, narrow-nostrilled nose.

'I've been going over your deposition again, Mr Graham.'

Dallas waited, a lump of phlegm in his throat.

'Where was the telephone in the farmhouse?'

'I'm not sure. I think there was more than one.'

'You see why I'm asking. Couldn't she have telephoned for the police herself? Why was it necessary to send you?'

'You must have asked her that. She's your client, after all.'

'Oh yes . . .'

Counsel cracked the knuckles of his long pale fingers and placed hands palms down on the table.

'I'd been thrown out, remember. I was going off. It was natural Candy should ask me to fetch the police. She might have been frightened of telephoning. How can I tell? It seems natural enough to me.'

'Natural behaviour has a way of sounding bizarre in a court of law . . .'

That at least was true enough. The newspaper account of the Crown's evidence taught Dallas that. He learned the transforming power of the recorded word. Nothing he found there fitted with his memory of how it had been. Even the accounts of Fraser's cottage parties, seized on so zestfully by the tabloids, more fully but with an equal unreality by the quality papers, were less real than what he read in novels. The Countess of Aplin, called for no reason he immediately understood, spoke of someone he couldn't recognize; her Fraser was 'a man of extraordinary vitality and vision . . .' she had been 'amazed and horrified' to hear of his death . . . 'I couldn't imagine he could be wiped out like that. A man of such enormous natural force. It is a loss to the country,' she said.

'The Crown was in a real fix about Fraser,' Alick Duguid told Dallas. 'They couldn't paint him too black, or it might look like the girls were justified. You canna let the jury sympathize ower much with the accused. But conversely they had to establish motive, and that meant they couldna whitewash him either. So one minute he had to be a monster of depravity—that's what the Glasgow press fastened on wi' their captions of "Kinky Cottage"—the next it was the man of vision cut off in his prime. There were logical difficulties, none of the easy type-casting they like in trials. They brought it off just the same. Recruiting Cynthia Aplin was a master-stroke. No' just the title; it helped that she's got a reputation herself. It gave just the right touch of up-market raffishness, William Hickey stuff. And then Cynthia wouldna gie a docken for any logical difficulty. It was your pal Mansie's notion to hire her. And, would you believe it, he didna even have to twist her arm. Cynth'll do anything for publicity, she'd crawl knicker-naked through mud to get her picture in the papers.'

So the Crown had a problem—Alick was right—but Dallas couldn't see any defence strategy at all. There were of course two separate defences, but they were hardly differentiated and they went nowhere. Counsels' only interventions seemed intended to cast doubt on tiny points in the Crown case, points that couldn't affect its substance. There was no heart there.

They were afraid to attack Fraser's character. And yet to plead justification was surely the only hope?

So, Dallas, repeating the oath after the clerk, promised he would come out with it; he would make it clear how intolerable their situation had been.

Candy's counsel took him briskly through his account of how he had known Fraser, what their relations had been. His answers dropped like pebbles in the attentive room. He was caught in these questions, these programmed answers. His will ebbed.

—Did Miss Sheen seem anxious you should fetch the police?

—Yes, she insisted.

—It was her idea?

—Yes, I agreed with it. But it was her idea in the first place.

—Tell us what she said.

—She was afraid of Fraser's violence. He had already attacked me. She didn't think Lorna and she were safe.

—In what way? What was she afraid of?

—She thought he could easily kill them. She said that.

—And that was why she wanted you to fetch the police, to protect them?

—Yes.

—There was no other reason?

—No.

Shouldn't that have been enough?

Counsel sat down. Lorna's indicated that he had no questions for this witness, this witness who was so eager (suddenly) to explain how it had happened, but who found they weren't interested, that everything had in reality been decided, that he was caught in a web of collusion . . . as now, when Crown counsel rose, spreading his gown out behind him, running fingers over appraising chin, and looked with quizzing kindness . . .

—You're very young, aren't you?

—I'm twenty-two.

—And your experience of the world is limited to school and university?

216

—If you like . . .

—When you first met Mr Donnelly, how would you describe your state of mind?

—Normal enough.

—Weren't you rather confused and unsettled?

—Not particularly.

—Not particularly? But you had finished university and had not decided on a career. Isn't that right?

—I suppose so.

—And the society he represented was altogether strange to you?

—A bit . . .

The ring twitched Dallas's nose. He was being led into admissions of incompetence, inability to judge . . . he had to follow. Where else could he go? So that, when counsel, with a deep sniff, changed tack and said . . .

—Now this so-called attempt to summon the police, that wasn't successful now, was it?

He could only nod, dumbly.

—Will you tell the Court why?

—They didn't believe me. They weren't interested in what I had to say.

—I see. Why did you suppose that was?

—They just didn't seem interested.

—Not even when you . . . alleged . . . you had been beaten up yourself?

—No.

Counsel paused, to let wonder at the police indifference sweep the court.

—They didn't believe you had been coming to them?

—It seemed as if they didn't.

—Would you tell the Court why that was?

—I couldn't say . . .

—Let me help you. Was it because you were drunk, because they were about to charge you with being drunk in charge of a motor car?

—It may have been.

—Did they so charge you?

—Yes.

—So it was hardly surprising that they should not have
regarded you as a reliable witness . . .

What could he say? That the opposite, at any time of life,
would have astonished him more?

—You were drunk, and you had been beaten up. Would
you consider that a condition in which anyone's memory is
likely to be reliable?

—Not necessarily, but then again I don't see why not. I
often remember the most remarkable things after I've been
drunk.

—The most remarkable things? Quite so. Tell me, Mr
Graham, would you describe yourself as a chivalrous man?

Dallas hesitated. The pit lurked. Who could use such a
phrase, today, of himself, or indeed anyone else. And yet . .

—Not particularly.

—But you would regard it as your duty to protect a woman
who was in danger, wouldn't you?

He was being led into absurdity.

—Not only a woman. I hope I'd try to help anyone in that
position.

—Quite so. Did you resent Fraser Donnelly?

—Not especially. Why should I?

—Not especially? Why should you? You tell us he had given
you a beating, thrown you out of his house, and then ask us to
believe you didn't resent it. Are you of an unusually forgiving
nature?

—I didn't like it, obviously, but I hadn't time to resent it.
There were other worries, other fears.

Counsel held his eyes, waiting for Dallas to give way. Then—

—I put it to you that you were resentful. Nobody could
blame you for being so. And that in your mood of resentment
you wanted to make trouble for Fraser Donnelly. It is after all
perfectly proper to lay a charge—you did try to lay a charge,
didn't you?—to lay a charge of assault, when you have been
assaulted. And that it was only afterwards, in retrospect, with
the advantage of hindsight, that it occurred to you to claim
that the defendant had urged you to call the police. I put it to
you that the original idea to summon them was yours, and
yours alone; a perfectly proper intention, but solely yours . .

Dallas sensed movement among the jury, a satisfied shifting of buttocks as if, with one accord, they were saying, 'That's it, we can relax, relinquish concentration . . .'

—You must answer, you know.

It was the judge speaking, polite, even deferential, but adamant.

—It's not true, it wasn't my idea. Candy, Miss Sheen, the defendant, asked me to fetch them. That's the truth . . .

The words hung in the stale air, slowly, almost visibly, evaporating. His evidence was without substance, immaterial . . .

—Are you in love with the defendant? Or with both of them?

There was no record of these questions. No newspapers reported them. They were almost certainly never asked. And yet Dallas felt that this was exactly the matter on which he had been interrogated, and found wanting. It was in one sense love, using the word loosely to describe all warm and responsible emotion, that stood attacked; as, in a different way, love, as something going beyond sex, had been attacked by Fraser Donnelly. Who had proclaimed he stood for Liberation, as the Court for Justice; both were ideas. Love by contrast was something real, love was there, you could feel it, it was a fact of experience, and impermissible.

Counsel hadn't done with him yet. A tongue snaked over thin lips. The beast was enjoying his work.

—You had been to a good many of Fraser Donnelly's evenings, hadn't you?

—A few.

—Would you please tell us how they usually ended?

—What do you mean?

—I'm sorry. Let me put it another way. Did they usually end in murder?

—Of course not.

—Or did they end in people pairing off, going to bed together?

—Sometimes.

—We've heard evidence that suggests that that was intended on this evening too. Isn't it the case that Fraser Donnelly, in his role as sexual impresario, had arranged pairings? And that you were the odd man out?

—He may have had some such plans. That doesn't mean that other people were necessarily going to fall in with them.

—Quite so. (Dallas was rewarded with a smile.) Would you mind telling us again just why Fraser Donnelly attacked you?

Dallas looked round, as if for help; but it seemed everyone was as eager as counsel to hear his answer, as indifferent to his embarrassment. He recounted, without fluency, what had led up to it. There could be no doubt he held his audience, no doubt they found this part of his testimony convincing.

—And you repeat that you felt no resentment?

—It wasn't resentment made me go for the police.

—Let me remind you that the police apprehended you. We have only your word for it that you were going to them. That's the case, isn't it?

—Yes, but . . .

—Thank you, no more questions . . .

Dallas replayed that evidence for many nights. It ran like one of those tapes that will flick back to the beginning to play through again. He was certain he had missed some opportunity to establish what was the real truth, never able to find the chink that would have allowed it in. Instead each replay made him more certain that truth was muffled in the blanket of justice. The Court was like Procrustes' bed. What had happened was lopped off or stretched to get it the right length for the bed. It was like the cinema. However you set out to do it each movie genre had its own demanding logic to which all action inevitably came to conform.

He left the court at a run, down wooden stairs that held the sound of his footsteps.

5

Dallas couldn't help laughing. It was partly nerves, but still. There was this letter, you see, signed by all sorts of respectable folk, protesting at the slanderous portrait that had been drawn of their old chum and business associate, Fraser Donnelly, in the course of the recent trial at which his wife and another woman had been found guilty of murdering him.

The words sprang from the correspondence page of Dallas's *Scotsman*. They told of Fraser's good fellowship, of his keen business brain, of his selfless political work, 'with which not all of the signatories agreed, but which all of us admired for its characteristic energy and integrity'. It spoke of the sore loss that business and public life in Scotland had sustained, and deplored that a criminal trial should have become the occasion of tarnishing the name of a dead man. 'But his friends survive to protect his reputation.'

'De mortuis nil nisi chivalrous bunkum.'

Dallas couldn't stay in Edinburgh. He couldn't stay in Scotland. He had given his notice to Bannerman's. The country was stained—talk of tarnishing—by that scene outside the courthouse, by the righteous prurience, the mean anger, the witch-hunting zeal. It frightened him to think of it.

He had seen Candy's solicitor by his own request.

'Isn't there going to be an appeal?'

'We can't see any grounds.'

'But it wasn't murder.'

'I'm afraid it was. A few years ago, you know, they could have hanged.'

'My God, that would have pleased these women.'

He was nauseated by the delight that simmered round him. The whole country had given itself over to masturbatory frenzy. It was as if the stories told in stale tabloid prose had released dreams denied for centuries; the air of Edinburgh was cut with the crowing of cocks.

A boy with tight, red curls seized Dallas in a pub, not knowing who he was, and said, 'It was a fucking frame-up . . .'

Dallas warmed to him, but he had got it wrong. The boy wasn't concerned to defend Lorna and Candida.

'They smeared him,' he said, 'and do you know why? Because we're on the way up. They had to smear the party. And this was the way. Christ, it was the bloody prosecution smeared him worst, the fucking English Crown.'

He sat on the bar-stool in donkey jacket and skin-tight jeans, enclosed in the anger he held round him.

'If Scotland wasna dead from the waist down and the neck up, they'd have recognized they had a leader in him. But the way they went for his reputation was fucking terrible. And those wankers that head the party just looked on, didna say a word for him, no bloody fear . . .'

Dallas couldn't see Fraser as the lost leader. All the same this was an apt reminder of the distance that can be found to exist between private and public life. It did something to fix in him a distrust of the latter.

The boy withdrew his anger, as a snake might its fangs.

'Do you ever get tired of waiting for women?'

'Often.'

'You start wondering if it's worth it, eh?'

'You do indeed.'

'You're fucking English yourself then.'

'Not so.'

'You're no' Scots then.'

'Oh yes I am.'

'You dinna sound it.'

'Nevertheless.'

'Where do you come from then?'

'The North-East.'

'You could have fooled me.'

'Story of my life. In England friends mock my Scots accent. Here I'm shoved into the gutter as a bloody Englishman. You don't know how lucky you are.'

'Lucky, am I? Do you know what Scotland is? It's the greatest country in the world. And the greatest non-country, the greatest nothing, both at the same time. Do you wonder we're a' fucking neurotics?'

'Would you say that?'

'I would an' a'. Where the hell have you been?'

The remark was addressed over Dallas's shoulder. He turned round, and, as in one of those moments when you realize you've already seen the movie which you have actually been watching for the last twenty minutes or so without recognizing that fact, found Alick Duguid and Jimmy's sister Kate behind him. He acknowledged Alick with more confidence than Kate.

The girl said, speaking to the red-haired boy, 'I've been where I choose. Dinna speak that way to me.'

She gave Dallas a nod that had all the curt sullenness he had come to associate with her, which he still found attractive. They took their drinks away from the bar to a table in the corner.

Alick said to Dallas, 'You're aye aboot then?'

The red-haired boy and Kate settled into a bicker that sounded like an excerpt from a long-running serial.

'I thought you'd have run,' Alick said.

'Don't worry. I'm going to. But I had a job here. It's just finishing.'

'Jimmy's been on at me. Did you never get the boy his passport?'

''Fraid not. It's been on my mind. Not very often, of course, but it's been there. Do you have an address for him now in London?'

'Somewhere. Back in the flat. Did you know I'd moved to Edinburgh? I'm propping up the local branch of the capitalist press the now. Started last month.'

Dallas listened to the sing-song of voices, the clatter of glasses, the jukebox hammering out machine-made rock. The bar had filled up, mostly with business types, accountants and building society reps, in suits and striped ties. They came in with dripping umbrellas or heavy mackintoshes, and stood round the bar exchanging whatever mood they had brought from their offices for happier alternative selves. Some remained detached from the little groups that formed and reformed, and gazed into their pint mugs, like lovers or philosophers. But even they shared in the dream world of the pub which, like most dreams, offered a sharper image of reality than waking life could offer.

In a little the red-haired boy went off. He made no excuse. Perhaps his solitary and self-regarding anger couldn't thole the changed atmosphere of the full pub; he was a boy for the empty bar, the lonely perch in the corner, the steady silent pulling at pints.

Alick proposed lunch.

'Not here, not pub food for me,' Kate said.

Outside, rain was coming up from the Forth on a swirling wind, filling the street with a movement against which people walked fast, head lowered. There was a Chinese restaurant across the street. They headed for it.

Alick talked about his new paper, mostly against it. The others hardly listened. Waiting for their order, Kate repaired her face. She narrowed her eyes, looking into the little mirror which she held up in her left hand. She picked at mascara that had freed itself from her eyes and stood in little specks on her high cheek bone.

'Who was that boy then?' Alick said.

'Red? Och, he's a Romantic.'

'And you aren't?' Dallas said.

'Me? How the hell would I be that?'

Fraser's shadow fell across the table, creating a no-man's-land between Dallas and the girl.

'No' another,' Alick said, 'it's the curse of Scotland.'

'He's certainly got a Romantic notion of Scotland,' Dallas said.

'Everyone who's got any notion of Scotland has got that. It's our people's curse. They a' try to fix an image on the nation. But the word nation's itself evidence of misguided thinking. I'll tell you something, boy, if they ca'd it the SPP, no' the SNP, the Scottish People's Party, there would be some hope for them. It's this national bit that's as false and full of lees as a tourist brochure . . .''

He went on, and on. Kate finished attending to her face. She hadn't managed to expunge what experience had put there though. She began to eat the prawns and rice the waiter had placed before her. She used chopsticks.

'It's funny,' she said, 'I can't eat anything but Chinese. And I'm no' pregnant, Alick Duguid.'

Alick looked at his watch, swore, announced he was going to be late for a press conference, threw a couple of pound notes on the table, and said, 'That'll cover my share.'

Dallas and Kate were left alone. There was no one else in the restaurant except a family party, notably lacking in hilarity, even animation, at the far end of the narrow room.

'So you're no' a poof like Jimmy then. I thought you were.'

'Not at all,' Dallas said.

For the first time they looked directly at each other. What she'd gone through—and he couldn't do more than guess at what the case had meant to her—had done something curious to her face. It had refined it, and coarsened it at the same time. Which didn't make sense, yet was how he saw it.

'Do you think they have any brandy?' he said, 'Would you like some?'

She nodded.

'Thank God Alick's gone,' she said. 'I couldn't have taken more of that political nonsense of his. I've gone right off that sort of stuff.'

'Jimmy said you were red-hot. It won't be good brandy. We'd better have soda with it.'

'Ginger ale for me. Red-hot? What would wee Jimmy ken? I've had my bellyful any roads.'

He wanted to run his finger along the line of her lips, across her cheek, down the fine bone of her jaw.

'Why did you think I was queer?'

She didn't hesitate and she didn't smile.

'You looked a poof, and you talked pan-loafy, and the first time I saw you were wi' that wee bugger Gavin Gregory, and then Jimmy and you seemed to click. You went off together and he was crazy about you. You should have heard him talk.'

'I never fancied Jimmy. But I thought you belonged to Fraser.'

He wondered if he had gone too far; if the name, suddenly brought out into the open, would shatter the mood he had felt growing. For a long time she didn't speak. Chinese waiters flicked here and there, adjusting cutlery on neighbouring tables, chattering in staccato voices in the kitchen.

'Well, that's over and done with,' she said. 'Which of the girls did you really fancy?'

A waiter brought them their brandies and the bill at the same time. Dallas fumbled for money to add to what Alick left.

'Not that it would have done you much good, would it? They didn't have eyes for a boy, either of them.'

'Oh I don't know,' Dallas said.

'Or are you one of those boys that likes to fix on what he can't get? Some poofs do, as a cover-up.'

'No,' Dallas said, 'it wasn't like that at all.'

ENVOI

I stepped out of the austerity of early Romanesque where you could already sense approaching winter, enjoy one of those mental snapshots of the dank fogs which would then rise from the river curling round the rock on which the little mediæval town crouched, or taste the west wind that blew in from the Atlantic a hundred miles off, or imagine on your lips the keener wind which would sweep down the valley from the north-east, stripping the chestnut trees that lined the river and gave the surrounding country its wonderfully solid French prosperity, its air of unchanging centuries of good eating and drinking—unchanging at least since the Religious Wars which, as a monument in the little *place* testified, had certainly seen slaughter, mayhem and what have you where now was for me holiday. I paused at a bar to drink a *café crème*, to imbibe what was always more important and rewarding than the liquid, that aroma of France that is compounded of coffee, Gauloise tobacco, a touch of aniseed, stale fumes of the local white wine, and, from the kitchen beyond, the enticement of the day's *plat du jour*, something with onions, certainly, and probably lamb. I sat for a little reading the local paper, with its close-set dirty type, the unbroken solidity of its information about a shopkeeper who had been *fusillé*, a farmer guilty of incest over three decades (long ones for the girls, one shouldn't wonder), and small municipal scandals about blocked fountains and building permits that should never have been issued. I listened to French conversation playing its rhythm section riffs across the zinc bar counter. I was happy.

Outside in the little market set up in the *place*, I bought a beaded shawl for Candy and a walking-stick made of walnut for myself, some purple figs almost escaping their skins, a jar of marrons and another of plums in armagnac, making the

purchases as much for the pleasure of the exchanges with th
stall-keepers (all old women, dressed in the uniform black), a
for any desire for the objects I was buying. And I stopped at th
tabac to buy Gitanes in *papier maïs* solely for the pleasure o
letting the yellow paper differentiate them from those I wa
accustomed to smoke.

I made my way through narrow, cobbled, quite deserte
streets to the hotel, L'Auberge du Marquis, set back in its littl
courtyard, shaded by chestnut trees and one gnarled walnut
planted long before the Revolution has allowed Paris t
impose its will on this old France of the provinces, where w
had been staying for the past ten days. That France, sti
contained in these old towns, where life could still be lived i
the conventual seclusion of courtyards, where the long past c
Mediævalism and Renaissance refused quite to expire but sti
jostled and corrected the present on every corner, offered
harmony, at least to the visitor, hard to find elsewhere.
might admittedly be hard to sense it if you belonged there; tha
scarcely mattered to my mood.

Candy was sitting at a table under the walnut tree readin
Colette. It was just warm enough to sit in the filtered sunligh
She was wearing a thick jersey that caressed her neck, mad
her neat head seem smaller, more than usually distinct.

She looked up.

'I went to the church again,' I said, 'and the market. Look

'Nice, oh lovely, you shouldn't, but thanks. Curious yo
find that church so sympathetic. You don't think you'
getting religion, do you?'

'No, it's something different this place gives off. The churc
is only part of it. You could say Colette is too. How woul
you feel about living here?'

'Here particularly or here in France?'

'Here, in this part of France, for good.'

'It would be different if you lived here.'

'Different yes, not necessarily worse.'

'I have a job to do, to get back to.'

'It's that important?'

'Oh yes, it's me. This is merely an interlude. Time out.'

She lit a cigarette from the stub of the last one.

228

'Does your wife like France?'

'She likes it, she doesn't feel it. Anyway, as you know, she's got a job too. She might also say it was her. Certainly the way things are, she'd have difficulty recognizing herself without it.'

She said, 'I don't know why I'm delaying. There was a telephone call for you. Your son Giles. He sounded upset. He wants you to ring back. He's at your shop, he said.'

I sat down. The metal of the chair, which the sun had not yet reached, was cold from the night's frost.

'You see,' Candy said.

She left it there. Whatever the content of the telephone call, however urgent or not urgent the demand might be, her two breathed syllables, followed by long, significant, cloud-over-sun silence, made their point, brought me up, bang, against the limits of selfish imagination.

'It would be easier,' I said, 'if you had asked him to ring me again. Telephoning from France is a bore.'

'There is,' she said, 'you know, nowadays, a direct dialling system.'

'Oh God, oh Montreal.'

'Hey Dad, good of you to ring back.'

The voice was light, trustworthy as Puck; I warmed to him.

'I called from the shop to get out of Mum's way. She's going spare. Hope you're not going to.'

'Should I? Am I likely to?'

'Who can tell? No logical reason of course. But responses triggered by warps in the parental psyche are hard to calculate.'

'All right then.'

The little booth was stuffy, full of long-guarded air, with the sweet cloying smell of old age.

'The thing is, Dad, how'd you feel about being a grand-dad?'

'What?'

'Come on, Dad, you know what a grand-dad is.'

'You'd better tell me.'

'Well that girl I told you about. Angie, she's going to have my kid.'

'I see.'

'Well, look, the thing is, Mum's mad keen on an abortion. Says we'll fuck our lives up otherwise. So does Angie's mum, dirty-minded old bag called Brenda who writes for the posh papers and sits on commissions et cetera. But we say no. But, look, Dad, the pressure's intense. We want your help . . . Angie's dad was laid off in the dark ages.'

They looked like children. I had stifled the question, 'How old are you, Angie, fifteen?' But they still looked like children. Standing at the ticket barrier at Victoria, both, for all their teenage chic, seemed mere waifs, social-work fodder.

I said, 'What were you planning to do, Angie, before this?'

'Oh,' she said, 'I've a place at Somerville for next year.' She had a small neat blondeness, and, such nervousness as she showed being almost certainly superficial and transient, carried about her the air of a cream-eating cat. She was herself a girl to gobble up. I could see that, could see that Gilesie could hardly keep his hands off her. She was so demure. And indeed, as I said, '. . . and Gilesie has one at King's,' he took her right hand in his left.

'It sounds a difficult start to marriage,' I said. 'I take it you do intend to get married?'

'Sure.'

'It's so boring otherwise.'

'Seventies stuff, no style.'

'Quite,' I said, 'I used to be chums with Owen Carnody, your prospective tutor, as you know, Gilesie.'

'What you told me was he used to fancy you something rotten.'

'Well, that's all in the past, and I don't think that even for old times' sake he would consent to turning part of the Gibbs building into a matrimonial suite. Not on, I should say.'

Angie was too clever and determined to laugh at my frivolity; she wasn't going to let the conversation escape that way; all she accorded me was a brief tolerant smile.

'I've written to Somerville to give up my place,' she said. 'I've got the letter here. It only waits to be posted.'

'And I've done the same.'

'But I say he shouldn't. We should take a flat in Cambridge. Something small, a couple of rooms.'

'I'd rather get a job.'

'But that's silly, isn't it? The baby will be born before he goes up. And I've a little money. With his grant we'll be OK. That's one reason my mother's against it, you know, that I'll be spending this little bit of money. And of course she's career-mad. She regards her generation as the one that breached the walls—we've got to occupy the city. But I don't want to. Well, I'm not that keen, not sacrificial-keen.'

'Thing is,' Gilesie said, 'both our mas, they belong to that awful gabby generation of women. They fought for the right to have an abortion and they've conditioned themselves to think it's not just a right, but a duty.'

I don't suppose that really he put his finger on any spot at all. But it felt like one.

The day before, after the telephone call, we had had lunch in a little riverside restaurant a few hundred yards from the hotel. We ate perch, caught, we were told, 'just outside the window'. On the next table, occupied by a family of five or six, stood grouped three bottles of the local white wine, crisp as *pommes frites* as I remembered, dry with hardly a hint of sharpness, cellar-cool, the bottles showing a faint greenish glisten of moisture. The family drank and ate perch also and joked, and Candy and I sat almost silent beside them. Later the woman who ran the restaurant brought them a big creamy cake, chestnuts like vermicelli topped with great Alps of cream, and a bottle of the wine from the other side of the mountain, yellowish, with a remembered fragrance like elderflowers.

Candy said, 'If you don't mind, I'll stop off in Paris. There's a woman I've corresponded with, who does the same sort of work. It seems a good time to meet and exchange notes.'

'Will she be there?'

'Oh yes, I rang her and fixed it after I took your son's call.'

'I see.'

'Well, it was obvious really.'

The father at the next table called for some marc and framboise with their coffee.

I sat smoking in the buffet of the Gare du Nord. Outside, in the still half-light of morning, filled with that Seine valley fog that Monet loved to paint, may even be said to have invented, shops were just opening. The gutters, after overnight rain, ran with that murky yellow peculiar to Paris. There was an air of damp and melancholy urban bustle, matutinal acceptance of the state of things. A tall young Englishman with blond public school voice called out for 'café avec cognac, doo-bil cognac,' he insisted. He saw me, alone, watching him. 'It's a great city,' he said, 'if you don't weaken. I've spent the night in Fred Payne's English Bar, and I've almost weakened. But, once more into the breach, I say. Doo-bil cognac encore, s'il vous plait.'

I made no reply, lit another cigarette.

All my life I have wanted to cut and run; but from the Gare du Nord the trains all go in the wrong direction.

In the dining-car, as small anonymous towns twinkled into light, Candy had said, 'You see, you're still married.'

She held up a little mirror and drew lipstick across her mouth like a line drawn under an account that's settled.

*　　*　　*

Gilesie and Angie had stopped talking, and looked at me as if they expected a reply. But I hadn't noticed they had asked a question. They took my support for granted, oddly.

'Well, you're of age,' was all I could find to say.

'Whose life is it anyway?' Gilesie said.

'Oh yes, quite, I can't though promise to make things right with your mothers. It's not a talent of mine, making things right.'

'You have no idea of anything, have you,' my wife said. 'You live in your head. That was all that was needed, for you to come back and encourage them and fuck everything up. Brenda and I had it in hand, we were bringing them round to see sense. To saddle themselves with a child at their age, and with each other, it's insane. Well, I might have known that if there was one thing you could be relied on to do, it was to encourage insanity.'

That was just a sample. I let her talk. There was nothing else to do. She strode round the kitchen and banged dishes, like a woman in a television play, and talked, uninterrupted, unanswered. No doubt she was right; in her own way; I could see her point of view; since she wouldn't level at mine, dialogue was, fashionably, out.

There is something very inartistic in just telling the truth. But the trouble is, that's all I remember from this scene. She was angry at what she saw simply as waste; and I couldn't agree. She was trapped in the part she had written for herself, and I seemed to look at it from a powerless distance. I felt sorry for Ann certainly, as she spoke her speech from which no inclination of the rein could have diverted her; she was a plaything of the manager of our strange drama.

And yet, there was another reason for pity. Her future was fixed, limited as surely as if by that long chain of the Caucasus. Soon her career, which charged her life now, gave her speeches to speak, a comforting view of things, would wither. She would be thrown back into being what we all end up as, a family person, caught in that last reality of the purely human life which is constraining, irritating, wearisome; but outside which lies the wasteland.

So, in the end, all I said was, 'I'm going to take Gilesie to Scotland for a few days. Get him out of the hothouse. Give him a chance to make sure of what he is going to do.'

She clutched at the straw; she may even have been grateful.

It's hard to imagine,' he said, 'there was once a house here.'

Certainly the wilderness had conquered. Canaan, the promised land of my youth, was one with Nineveh. Brambles, rhododendrons and dead, wispy willow-herb, all tangled

together where the family had lived, loved, argued, eaten,
danced. Only, when you stood on the terrace, where the iron
railing was still not altogether lost under encroaching vegetation, and looked up the glen with your back to what had
once been the house, could any illusion from the past be
sustained.

'It doesn't stir ancestral throbbing?' I said.

' 'Fraid not.'

He turned and leant on the rail—'I'm not sure that that's
safe,' I said.

'Why did you let it go?'

'Money, lack of it, a combination of circumstances, disillusion. There's very seldom an identifiable reason for action, is
there?'

'Isn't there?' The question didn't interest him. 'I could have
fancied myself as the young laird.'

'I was hardly that. There was no land, just the house.'

'Why did you bring me here, really? It wasn't just to feel my
roots.'

'I couldn't face coming alone.'

'Come off it, Dad. You wanted to wallow. You really are a
sucker for nostalgia. And self-pity. And I bet you've been
hoping I would suddenly start feeling the prickings of my
Scottish blood.'

'And you don't?'

'Not a prick. Doesn't mean a thing to me. Which isn't to say
I'm not having fun. But all that sort of stuff, it's weird,
out-of-date. Schmuck stuff.'

And then, sitting on that ruined terrace, I told him; gave him
the whole story of that ruining summer that ran into a winter
as careless of lives as the bulldozer that had demolished Canaan
behind us of all the aspirations and vanities that had gone to the
building of the house and then inhabited it. I tried, in the
utterly still mellow gold of dying autumn, to bring Fraser
Donnelly to life. And shall these bones live, to show the power
of the wilful will? No wind breathed about us; smoke from my
long chain of cigarettes rose slowly straight to die blue in the
deepening gold that, as the afternoon passed and the narrative

234

hardened, shaded to grey. The importance of ruined lives stood out clamant-clear to me, not because of what they were in themselves—'what is man that thou art mindful of him?' —but for their emblematic value. I tried to pluck meaning from the air and impart it to him. I failed of course. You probably can't ever satisfactorily put into words these moments of the apprehension of some significant reality that are so very intense, yet, because also inherently evanescent, so confoundedly vague. Poets can, but I am no poet. And even then, even when you hear words that make the hair rise slow and stiff on the back of your neck, such as 'ah but to die, and go we know not where, to lie in cold obstruction and to rot', for instance, even then, the rightest words are but shadows of the real thing. There is always something that fails.

I could no more bring those months alive for Gilesie than they could die for me. You are always brought up against the otherness of other people. Imparted experience is not lived experience; the most that even magical words can offer is vicarious; and different.

A hawk hovered in the sky over the meadows far below, then dropped sheer out of sight.

I said to Gilesie, 'Does any of this tell you why I'm on your side now? Come on, I'll buy you a beer in the pub, then we'll drive to Aberdeen and find a hotel.'

At dinner, a sad fatigued hotel dinner in that old hotel, but we had been too tired to seek out anything better, he said, 'And the girl Lorna's still alive, you say, in this town?'

'So I'm told.'

'Would you recognize her?'

'Might do, might not.'

'She could even be one of those women at that table'—he gestured towards a long table on the other side of the dining-room where a group of a dozen women, representatives perhaps of a club or the whole of an office staff, or a sorority of deserted wives, were dining, with much sweet-wined hilarity.

'I think not,' I said, 'but I see what you mean.'

'Wouldn't you be curious to see her again?'

'No,' I said, 'I thought I would, but no, it's over.'

It would have embarrassed him if I had added that he had helped end it.

Later, as we sat in the almost empty lounge and Gilesie drank beer, he said, with the restlessness of a puppy offered its first bone, 'And the girl Kate? You shacked up with her that afternoon, didn't you? Did it last long?'

'No,' I said, 'just the once. Somehow it helped us both to let go. God knows what happened to her.'

'And these politicians,' he said. 'Jesus, I've seen them both on the box. What creeps life makes of people. All the same, Dad, I'd no idea. Murder, rape and whatnot, you've really lived, Dad.'

'It didn't feel like it,' I said.

We drove south, devouring miles in a thin rain. Dropping through the grey-black wet of Dundee to the bridge across the river, fog shrouded us; the coast of Fife could not be seen. Miles later, at the next firth, we hung suspended, motionless in jammed traffic, over a river that could not be known to exist. I felt life thrown in reverse. In youth, it had been the journey north that oppressed me, represented duty. Now, as I left Scotland, cutting through rainswept Border hills, my gaze fixed south through the windscreen wipers that etched their demanding rhythm on the day, I felt I was leaving my Past, a Past that had only recently seemed heavy and imposing but which now took on, as I drew the car up in a hillside lay-by to look back over the misty and rolling hills, the sensation of being a thing of fancy, a construction of the imagination. What lay behind me was all the pleasure of nostalgia and self indulgence, a means of cheating the Now.

It was tempting, oh only fleetingly tempting, a temptation with the lifespan of a butterfly, to turn back again, to proclaim that was where I belonged, even—God help me—take up a cause, even politics, throw myself into any of those self evading illusions . . .

'Are you and Mum splitting up?'

He had been silent a long time; I wondered how Angela would tolerate the long silences which were as much a part of

Gilesie's nature as the sudden and often prolonged birdsong of chatter.

'Would it matter to you if we did?'

'Not much. I'm out of it now. It's your life.'

'What about Francis?'

'That's different. He's Mum's boy. With all that implies. He'd hate it if she shacked up permanent-like with some other guy. You're no competition, if you don't mind me saying so.'

'No,' I said, 'I quite see that.'

'It's up to you, Dad.'

All the same I came close to asking him for advice. But refrained. There are decencies which should be preserved. So all I said was, 'It's probably up to your mother, in fact.'

'It's your life,' he said, 'you shouldn't leave her to take all the big decisions. You should make up your own mind.'

'Oh,' I said, pulling the car back on to the road, looking in the mirror for a last long view before the hills dipped out of sight, 'I've already done that.'

But events have their own irony. A couple of weeks later, after the wedding reception reluctantly held in Brenda's neat cream and gold box in Highgate, with a creamy cake and creamy champagne (Vichy thoughtfully provided for me, perhaps on Ann's instructions), after a brittle afternoon, and Brenda's peck on Gilesie's cheek (which as a kiss spoke with a coldness that Joan Crawford would have been proud to have achieved); after the departure when even Gilesie seemed momentarily lowered by the prevailing climate of east-wind emotion; we drove home, with Francis sullen, as he had been all afternoon, and my wife silent.

Then Francis said he was going out to a club and departed half an hour later in a sort of page-boy outfit (which certainly became him) and a big overcoat with a fur collar he had picked up on a stall.

And Ann and I were left alone, very completely alone.

Should we watch television? Cook something together? Play scrabble? Go out to a movie? Or a restaurant?

'What would you like to do? Seems a bit flat.'

She rattled the ice in her campari-soda.

'That's it,' she said. 'You've ruined his life. I don't think I'll ever forgive you.'

Those were the actual words. She really spoke them, melodramatic and movie-worn as they look springing from my typewriter.

They were not words easy to reply to. So I said nothing.

'They'll hate the child when they realize what it's cheated them of. That's normal. All studies show it's normal. I don't suppose you can understand that.'

'I can see it could happen. There's no reason why it should.'

'At the moment they're up in the clouds. But they'll wake up. They would have done so, but for you, with your own half-baked romanticism. So I can't take it any more. This is it, Dallas. I want out. Or rather I want you out.'

I can't help seeing it all, you see, as an exercise in irony. For of course, in one sense, Ann was quite right. My intervention could be ascribed to half-baked romanticism. What I was clear about was that they should take the consequences of their action. And that really is, in its arrogant division of life, Romantic. Because whatever happens you don't escape consequences—Fraser's fate, and Candy's and Lorna's, not to mention mine, all go to prove that, if you'll forgive the pun, there is ultimately no such thing as coming off scot-free. And, for Gilesie and his girl, abortion would have had its own consequences, subtler and harder to identify than those of marriage, yet possibly every bit as dire as my sub-Calvinist temper could wish.

Not of course that I hope they will be anything but happy.

Neville came into the shop today. He sat in the chair by my desk and crossed his legs and swung a mauve baseball boot in my face.

'How's things, man?' he said.

'Things is slow, not quite stationary.'

'Guess we're both in the same boat, eh. Up that old shit creek. Matter of fact, Dall, we ain't so much in a boat as boat ourselves. Frail barques washed up on the wide shore of life, as Tennyson put it. You missin' Ann, man?'

'Curiously, yes.'

'Me too, I ache, I ache for Amanda. What you been doing there?' He stabbed his finger at the wodge of typescript. 'Been writing your memoirs? You should see mine. Hot, man, they don't come jubier. But, you know, it's all kidding. No kidding, it's kidding. When you play the blues, you get the feel of truth coming through. But words just stays words. Ain't no good, just no fuckin' good. Still we could publish together. Two guys fucked up by frails. Juby title, eh? Grab the public?'

'I think not.'

'Yeah, would be a lie too, I guess. We're not fucked up by the birds. The whole goddam thing's a fuck-up. Life, what they sold us as existence.'

'Camel ride to the tomb,' I said.

'Yeah, man, camels. Guess the frails is fucked up themselves.'

It might do as an epigraph, I thought.

'Well, one thing,' I said, 'I miss Amanda here. She could deal with the customers. I don't mind the trade, Neville. But the ordinary chap or woman who comes in from the street, your actual punter, anathema; ah well, impenetrability, that's what I say.'

'Not so,' he said. 'Take heart, man. I'm not just here to pass the time of day. Have a proposition to make. Meet your new assistant. It's official what I said last time. Amanda's ditched Charlotte. Ivor's flight to Rome has had repercussions. Young Lochinvar is come out of the West, Amanda'll be lady of the manor.'

'I had a card myself. So you want to take her place. Well, why not? Why not, indeed?'

We talked terms a bit, crossed the road to Finch's where I bought a Guinness for Neville, a Coca-Cola for myself. We sat then in silence, Neville gazing in the best style into the peaty depths of the Guinness. It could work out.

'By the way,' I said, 'when you're next in communication with Amanda, tell her I've shifted the non-Burges Golden Jubilee sideboard. Actually to one of Ivor's colleagues, an old chum of mine called Mansie Niven. He drifted in the other day, his baroque eye fell on the object and he announced it was just the thing he wanted for a wedding present. My God, you don't suppose, do you?'

He did. We were bang right too. Laughter clinched the deal.

I said, 'Well, revenge is rich, and sometimes light-footed.'

Neville said, 'There is no escape, man. She really hated that sideboard. You said a mouthful 'bout revenge. There is no escape from Nemesis in the three-thirty.'

'Too true. Talking of which, how do you feel about the races? We might shut the shop, catch the train to Esher, take in Sandown, yes?'

Yes. Byron thought gamblers were the happiest of men, being always involved in the moment, with the future no more than five minutes away. As usual he had a point. And Nemesis won, at 2–1 against, ridiculous odds for a horse of that colour.

'In any book I made, Neville, that horse would always start odds-on.'

'Too right, man.'

We made our way through the scattering of betting-slips, once the hope of less fatalistic punters, to collect our winnings.